THE
SEVENTH SISTER

THE
SEVENTH SISTER

Paula Tanner Girard

Five Star • Waterville, Maine

Five Star Romance Series.

Published in 2001 in conjunction with Zebra Books, an imprint of Kensington Publishing Corp.

The text of this edition is unabridged.

Set in 11 pt. Plantin.

Printed in the United States on permanent paper.

Library of Congress Cataloging-in-Publication Data

Girard, Paula Tanner.
   The seventh sister / Paula Tanner Girard.
      p. cm.
   "A Zebra Regency romance" — Cover
   ISBN 0-7862-3503-9 (hc : alk. paper)
   1. Women entomologists — Fiction. 2. London
(England) — Fiction. 3. Sisters — Fiction. I. Title.
PS3557.I68 S38 2001
813'.54—dc21
                                      2001033734

THE
SEVENTH SISTER

One

Captain Bixworth Hawksby had no idea he was about to be ambushed. In fact as he exited the fine town house near Covent Garden, he was thinking if the weather on this crisp spring morning was any indication of things to come, it would be a most pleasant day indeed.

"By Jove, I feel great!" he expounded into the thin yellow fog. Had he not just spent the night in the company of one of the fairest and most promising jewels of the London stage, Miss Luciane Divine? Evidently the elegant actress thought his performance as inspiring as hers, for she had finally consented to be his mistress.

He still couldn't believe his good luck. "Divine!" he shouted. Then, taken aback by his own outburst, he looked furtively up and down the empty street to see if any other early risers had chanced to overhear him and think him twitty. That would never do. Never!

Hawksby had labored with great diligence and purpose to present to the outside world the portrait of a proud British officer—taller than average, broad shouldered, narrow hipped, back straight and unbending, every muscle and sinew toned to perfection. His fierce brown mustache and the sinister brows which shadowed his deep-set eyes like devil's wings only added to his warrior image. Wouldn't do to spoil it now. He tried his best to bring his brows together in their habitual scowl, but it was a dastardly difficult maneuver to accomplish when he was in such high spirits.

Ah, but what man would not concur with him? The dainty thespian was certainly the most divine creature on the earth, and she was his. "That is, as long as I am in London," he qualified aloud. "Can't blame her for saying if I am sent far away to a heathen land, I shouldn't expect her to follow me."

He'd agreed with her, of course, for after all she had her career to think about. An attractive woman like Miss Divine must share her talent with the world. She couldn't do that if he was dragging her all over kingdom come. It would be selfish of him to think otherwise. Of course, the theatre world hadn't yet recognized her full potential, but Miss Divine assured him she was making every effort to reach her goal.

He thought of the appealing picture Miss Divine had made sleeping upon her bed, her long blond tresses splayed across the pillow, one delicate hand under her chin. He paused a moment on the stoop to adjust his sword, then drew in a deep breath. Expelling it with a *swoosh* so strong it cleared a hole in the fog, he set off with a jaunty step toward the center of Town.

First off, he'd hike to his quarters, have Clugg give him a shave, spruce him up a bit, then head for the Guards' Club for a bite to eat. He reckoned that the *on dit* of their assignation was already on every man's tongue and he, for once, looked forward to basking in all the attention his victory would generate. Who would have believed that he, of all the little thespian's suitors, had won her favor?

Hawksby slapped his thigh and quickened his step. He couldn't recall all the men's names who'd begun pursuing Miss Divine after her benefactor, old Lord Davenport, had stuck his spoon in the wall a year ago. Despite his own dismal delay in starting his campaign to court the incomparable actress last year—a delay precipitated by an old war debt he couldn't ignore—he'd been happy to find that bit by bit over the last few months the legions of contenders had been pared down to that dandy Viscount Basilbone and himself.

Then, without a word to anyone, Basilbone had disappeared from the London scene. Last night, the lovely lady made her final choice quite apparent to everyone, clinging to Hawksby's arm when they left the theatre after the closing curtain. Had Miss Divine sent the fellow packing? Hawksby's chest swelled with pride to think that she had.

"Well and good," he could hear his fellow officers saying. "We always bet on one of our own." Hawksby did wonder, however, what exactly had turned the tide in his favor. After all, he was only a third son, possessing neither title nor great fortune, as had so many of her other admirers.

He did recall Miss Divine mentioning once in one of her fanciful moods that when he appeared in his well-tailored uniform, none of his competition had come up to snuff. Hawksby had puzzled over that and suspected she might have been quizzing him, for the regimentals of Wellington's light cavalry were unquestionably an undistinguished blue—not light, not dark. Rather dull, actually—somewhat like himself, he feared. Even he admitted that. His uniform faded into the background when placed alongside the scarlet coats and white breeches which usually caught the attention of the ladies.

However, invisibility had been exactly what he preferred in a uniform when he was about the business of war. But the fighting was over now. Ol' Boney was defeated.

Surely Miss Divine had been jesting. Hawksby always had a devil of a time telling. It must have been something else about his person which had drawn her attention.

He rubbed his stubbly chin. It couldn't be his humorous nature. He was sure he had none. He'd never fooled himself on that account, either. It had taken him a lifetime just trying to avoid making a donkey of himself. Besides, his family was silly enough on that score. Right now it was more pleasurable recalling what had transpired the night past.

Customarily, Hawksby rose before dawn. Today was no different. On this particular day, while the majority of London's higher orders lay abed, he marched smartly along the cobbles among the merchants, clerks, shopkeepers, and food vendors who were already bustling about on their way to work or setting up their stalls.

"Hah!" Hawksby burst out when his thoughts harkened back to his salad days. Early on, he'd learned that awakening with the birds and servants annoyed his father, the Honorable Clement Hawksby, and he'd used the habit to his advantage. The captain had let Papa think this restlessness was the reason he insisted on making soldiering his career. His father didn't know the real reason was Mama.

Of course, her son's choice of professions disappointed his mother, but for altogether another reason than Papa's. Mrs. Clara Bixworth Hawksby, of the prominent Westmorland Bixworths, wished her baby boy to make his livelihood as a clergyman. After all, she explained, his uncle, the Right Reverend Bixworth, was a bishop, was he not? "Just think, Bixie dear, if you choose the church, you certainly will be assured of a quick boost into a pulpit."

But *Bixie dear* was not persuaded. In fact, he was terrified. In all of his twenty-eight years, Hawksby couldn't remember once having any inclination to become a clergyman, especially at that green age, when he was still wet behind the ears. In desperation he'd badgered Papa beyond even that gentleman's good-natured patience into purchasing his son a commission in the army. No one could tell Hawksby he had not made the right decision, for those early lessons in tenacity had served him well on the battlefield.

He began to whistle, another uncharacteristic practice for someone whom his comrades considered rather stiff-rumped, to say the least, but forgivable when one realized that the captain had finally won the race for the beautiful Miss Divine.

The Frogs were beaten and Wellington had been appointed to command the army that was to occupy northern France. Hawksby had been told to take an extended leave until called back to duty. For the first time in years he reckoned he could sample some of the more pleasurable activities about Town, which would include parading his pretty ladybird on his arm.

Ah, yes! London in spring. Definitely the place to be.

Suddenly an inspiration popped into Hawksby's head. Before he returned to his rooms, he'd buy Miss Divine a gift. But what did one give to a beauty who made him the happiest of men? He wasn't a wealthy man, but he had enough of the ready to keep her well turned out. Lord Davenport had left her the town house free and clear, and she seemed to have funds for hiring a maid and transportation, so Hawksby would have no expenses there.

When he started out, his plan had been to head straight to his quarters, not up Bond or Oxford Streets. "Balderdash," he mumbled. "I'll have to retrace my steps."

With a sharp about-face, Hawksby quickened his pace back in the direction he'd come. It was going to take some getting used to, this business of being a man about Town.

They called her Maggie—that is, those who knew her best. Lady Margaret Durham, who preferred no one called her anything at this moment, was curled up on a velvet-cushioned window seat in her bedchamber in Terrace Palace off the Strand, not far from where Captain Hawksby trudged along the streets, grappling with the knotty question of what to buy his paramour.

While Maggie divided her time between reading a book, which now lay open on her lap, and staring out over the gardens below, her twin, Lady Mary, sat across the room in front of their dressing table mirror applying a masque of white paste to her nose to cover her freckles, an activity which was making it very difficult for Elsie, the maid, to secure her mistress's luxurious red locks in place.

"Oh, I am so happy we are back in Londontown!" Mary cried, twisting around so quickly that she sent another hair pin flying. "Maggie! You are woolgathering again. If you don't get ready immediately, you will make us all late for our trip to the milliner this morning. We are to go as soon as we've eaten breakfast."

Maggie didn't look up. If anyone wanted to know the truth of the matter, she would have been happy to be anywhere else than London. Especially anywhere else than a boring milliner, where it seemed she was destined to go with her sisters very soon.

"Oh, Maggie, you are such a spoilsport."

Both girls had inherited the blue eyes and carrot-red hair of their mother, the late countess, Gillian MacNaught Hendry Durham. Both girls had inherited their mother's freckles, too, although Mary did persist in numerous attempts to hide hers with powder or some sort of pasty mix which Maggie teased her about whenever she felt especially wicked. Both girls had been named after Scottish queens. *Lady Mary* suited her sister, Maggie thought, studying her twin surreptitiously through thick auburn lashes.

Mary had indeed gained a certain sophistication that had not been there a year ago, an admirable quality of fashion and address which their brother Daniel hoped all his sisters would acquire upon introducing them to Society the Season past. Maggie would be the last to tell her so, although she'd readily confess without remorse to her own insufficiencies in that field.

But even with her impressive grasp of proper etiquette, Mary couldn't quite eliminate the tendency siblings have of teasing each other whenever the opportunity presented itself. But, thank the lord, *Mary, Mary, quite contrary* was not as missish as she'd been when they left the borderlands a year ago.

Maggie welcomed the challenge by refusing to budge from her comfortable position. She brushed her thick unruly hair away from her face and boldly met the reflection of her sister's blue eyes in the mirror. "I already have half a dozen hats, and I see no need for another one." She would wear none at all if she could have her way.

"But we don't have any to match our new pelisses, which we are to wear calling this afternoon," Mary said in an admonishing tone.

Maggie shrugged and went back to gazing out onto the gardens at the rear of the house. It was barely light, and she was waiting for Elsie to finish combing her twin's hair, which would look like a furze bush on fire if it weren't tamed. The difference was that Mary had mastered the art of restraining hers. Maggie hadn't. In fact, Maggie would let her hair flow free around her shoulders and not confine it at all.

No, Lady Margaret didn't want to be in London. Of course, she would be the first to agree that Terrace Palace, the London mansion belonging to her brother, the Earl of Chantry, was magnificent and the gardens lovely, but already a year ago she was sure she'd found practically every kind of insect they had to offer. Her specimens were all preserved, pinned in rows in their wooden boxes, scientifically labeled, and stuffed quite neatly, thank you, underneath her dresses in her wardrobe. Dear Dr. MacDougal would be very proud of what his pupil had accomplished.

Durham Hall in Oxfordshire, the family country seat where they had spent the fall and winter months, had been very stately, too, with its surrounding farmlands, forests, and riding paths. But it had been a cold winter, and just as it was getting warmer outside, when she could have spent more time in the woods and gardens, they had returned to Town for the Season.

However, no matter how high-toned her brother Daniel's houses were, they were not home. Home was Knocktigh, the large, unruly manor house which perched like an eagle's aerie on a hillside overlooking the River Tweed, where the heather covered the rocky ground and sheep grazed willy-nilly among the Cheviot Hills in Northumberland. There, she and her sisters caught the wild donkeys and rode bareback whenever they pleased, not on an uncomfortable saddle where you had to sit straight, keep your balance without showing your stockings, or choke yourself with a ribbon tied too tightly under your chin to keep your hat from blowing off.

Home was where Maggie and her sisters had been raised by Lady Chantry until she died one night after a fall from her chestnut mare. They buried Mama Gillian there in her beloved hills.

The countess had been the third and last wife of the sixth Earl of Chantry, a father they seldom saw, and whom they knew less. He'd left his seven daughters to fend for themselves until their brother Daniel had ridden north to rescue them. If they had not had their half-sister Freddie to tell them what to do, they all might have starved to death.

Mary turned and glared at her sister. "Well, I hope you don't plan to collect bugs this year. I shall die of embarrassment. I am sure Dr. MacDougal has forgotten all about you by now anyway. After all, he hasn't seen you for over a year."

Maggie glared back. "He has not forgotten me. I write regularly to him in Edinburgh about my collection and my observations, and he writes me when he can. He said he is looking forward to the day I come back to Knocktigh."

"Well, don't you tell any of my beaux your name is Mary and then make them capture some horrid creature for you the way you did last summer. After that they avoided me like the plague."

"I just very well may," Maggie said, tossing her head. She knew how much Mary hated any creepy, crawly thing.

"Don't you dare," Mary cried, this time sending the comb flying out of Elsie's hand. "I'm going to tell Freddie if you don't behave."

"Hah," said Maggie. "Freddie may be the Countess of Chantry now, but if you remember, she's the one who suggested we snaffle our brother's clothes so that we could sneak into Vauxhall Gardens without chaperones last summer. Besides, I have already told her I want to go to a lecture on the flora and fauna of London at the Royal Institution in Albemarle Street this Friday next."

"You can't," Mary cried. "That is the night of the Lisbones' ball."

"Bosh and bother! I'd rather go to the lecture."

"Oh, Maggie, you will botch it for all of us. I just know you will. We swore not to get into trouble like we did last year."

Maggie was homesick. She didn't want another Season in Londontown; didn't want to go to balls, didn't want to sit sipping tea in the afternoons. She'd rather be at Knocktigh, perched atop one of the high wooden stools in the big manor house kitchen and stuffing her mouth with some of Mrs. Doone's shortbread. "No, it is not exciting," she said.

15

"You are impossible, Maggie. We will meet the most distinguished people in London Society at Lord and Lady Lisbone's house."

Maggie was about to open her mouth when they heard a knock and glanced up to see their elder sister Ruth stick her head around the door. "Freddie and I were passing and heard your voices," she said sweetly, a twinkle in her eye. "I thought perhaps Elsie could use some assistance."

The little maid bobbed humbly before Lady Ruth, as though her ladyship were an angel sent from heaven.

The tall elegant blond entered and crossed gracefully to the window seat. "Freddie has gone on down to the breakfast parlor. You know what an early riser our brother is. What are you reading, Maggie?" she asked.

"Some poetry by Sir Walter Scott," Maggie said in a mollified tone, for the eldest sisters, kind and gentle Ruth and Rebecca, always had a calming effect on their younger siblings.

"Well, I see Elsie has Mary's toilette well in hand. Perhaps I can help with your hair, little sister, and you can read to me while I comb."

Maggie obediently threw her legs over the edge of the window seat and turned enough so Ruth could start getting some of the tangles out of her hair. As she did, began to read:

> It was a barren scene, and wild.
> Where naked cliffs were rudely piled:
> But ever and anon, between,
> Lay velvet tufts of loveliest green.
> And well the lonely infant knew
> Recesses where the wallflower grew,
> And honeysuckle loved to crawl
> Up the low crag and ruined wall.

Maggie stopped and sniffed.

"That's the Cheviots he's speaking of, isn't it, dear?" Ruth said.

Maggie nodded. "I want to go home, Ruthie."

"If we always received what we think we want right away, we might miss out on better things waiting for us. You must learn to be patient. First, let's go down to breakfast. You'll feel better after you've eaten something."

Ruth was so sweet that Maggie could not protest any longer. "Do you really think so?"

Mary saw her sister's lips quiver. She knew if her twin cried, she would cry, too, and she couldn't stand that. Not on a day they were to go shopping. "I'm sure a new bonnet will make you happy, Maggie. You wait and see."

"But, Daniel, the Season has just begun. We cannot leave London so soon after we have arrived," Lady Chantry said in dismay.

Daniel Douglas Durham, the seventh Earl of Chantry, had just handed a letter across the breakfast table to his wife. A messenger had delivered it only moments before. "Can't be helped, my dear. The steward at my father's properties in northwestern Yorkshire has died. It is one of the holdings I inherited which I have not felt obliged to visit as yet, because Mr. Osborne was known to be a capital administrator. Now matters have changed, and I must go at once."

The earl took a quick sip of coffee and watched intently while his wife read the missive again. Nearly a year had gone by since the Earl of Chantry had taken a chance at being called a thick-skulled, dull-witted pea-brain for bringing eight young ladies to London for their debut into Polite Society at one time, only seven of whom he'd found to be his sisters. The eighth proved to be an impostor and not his sister

17

at all, Miss Winifred Hendry—Freddie—who now sat opposite him. His encounter with Freddie had been more of a case of the mouse swallowing the cat, he told himself. He'd had to wed the jackanapes for his own self-preservation or surrender his sanity. Happiness, yes. Tranquillity, no.

In attempting to marry off seven sisters, the earl had succeeded in launching only one, Lady Georgette. Even that matrimonial match had come at a great price. He'd lost his excellent secretary, the Honorable James Pettigrew. The newlyweds lived in Sussex. Daniel had yet to acquire another assistant, and the task still lay ahead of him to shuffle off the other six young ladies. Now another Season was upon them, and here he was having to leave the city.

A servant appeared at the entrance of the breakfast room. "Your man said he was instructed to have your hat and gloves brought in, milord."

One of the footmen rushed forward to hold the earl's chair.

"Daniel!" The countess rose with him, but before a servant could come to her assistance, she'd already darted after her husband. "You have had nothing but one cup of coffee. Where, pray tell, do you think you are going?"

"I have business at the bank," he said, taking his hat from the servant. "Then I shall walk to one of my clubs for lunch."

"You have just told me we are to depart from London, and now off you go as nice as you please. The girls' calendars are already filled. They will be devastated if they have to leave early. Why, we even planned on a shopping excursion to buy bonnets later this morning."

Escape from his wife wasn't going to be as simple as the earl had hoped. "I meant just us, my dear. I wouldn't think of disrupting their activities," Daniel explained, pulling on a glove. "We will leave the girls here."

"Alone?" Freddie cried, her brown eyes widening.

Daniel tried to hide his amusement. "I hardly consider a staff of thirty-seven people being *alone*. The household runs like a well-regulated regiment under Mrs. Vervaine. Nothing escapes her attention, as you well know."

Freddie nodded, but she still looked unsure. "How will the girls manage without me?"

The corners of Daniel's mouth began to twitch. "You forget that Ruth and Rebecca are older than you, Freddie."

"Well, yes, but I'm a married woman now."

"And that, I suppose, is to imply that you're wiser and better behaved?"

"I am always well behaved," Freddie said, gazing upward innocently at her husband of less than a year. "And your sisters have always been all that young ladies should be."

"Always? If I remember correctly, it took a large contingent of His Majesty's army to keep you all in line during your first Season."

"Oh, Daniel. You exaggerate and you know it. It was only a few of your friends who volunteered to escort us," the countess said.

The earl was not going to inform her of what it had taken to persuade a half dozen members of Wellington's elite aides-de-camp to champion his unpredictable sisters, whom he'd innocently let loose upon London Society the previous Season. If Daniel, then Major Durham, hadn't been of superior rank, he was certain the young noblemen would not have sacrificed themselves so easily. "It took some of Wellington's finest to keep you all in line, and you know it."

Freddie, Lady Chantry, raised her chin and pursed her lips. "Well, I do not think any of your sisters would do such nonsensical things now."

"That is because when I married you I took away their

19

leader." Her husband tapped her nose with his finger.

She laughed, a delightful sound which brought an answering smile to her husband's face. Then her mirth disappeared as quickly as it had come and she shook her head. "Except . . ."

"Except what? Come, Freddie. Something is bothering you. Out with it."

"Except for Maggie."

Daniel saw the concern in his wife's eyes. Sighing, he removed his gloves, took off his hat, and gave them back to the servant. Taking her hand, he led her back to the table. "I want to hear what is upsetting you. I promise I'll not leave until I hear the whole of it."

"Well, I don't fret by half about the girls' behavior now as I once did, but Maggie and Mary were at sixes and sevens again this morning," she said, repeating the squabble she and Ruth had heard through the bedroom door earlier. "Ruth went in to see if she could help smooth the waters."

"Then what is your concern?"

"Maggie doesn't seem to want to attend the sort of social activities which the other girls do. For instance, she insists she would rather be at the library than sipping tea in some lady's drawing room this afternoon."

"I see no harm in that. In fact, I'm quite in charity with her views on the subject. But surely a maid or footman can accompany her to a lending library."

"That isn't the problem. She insists she doesn't want to go to Lord and Lady Lisbone's ball because there is to be a lecture at the Royal Institution that evening. Such talks are often followed by receptions which are open to the paying public. You know the type: artists and scholars and actors of questionable character are often included. A footman cannot follow her into the rooms reserved for ladies, and a maid cannot lend her the consequence she would need in case she is accosted by an undesirable person. When they all go as a group, the girls look out for each other."

The earl looked thoughtful. "That is another matter altogether, but easily rectified. I shall just order her not to attend," he said with finality.

"But we will be away," she observed, "and you know what that means."

Daniel knew all too well. Nothing he ever said could possibly intimidate his sisters. "You are right, of course." He pulled out his watch. "We do need to set off from London as soon as possible, though, and there are things which I must tend to today. But I assure you, my dear, that we shan't go to Yorkshire until you feel *all* my sisters are content with their activities."

Freddie nodded. "If I leave a single one dissatisfied with her schedule, I shall not rest easy."

"Nor will I," said her husband. "I wonder why?"

"Ruth and Rebecca are reasonable, and the others will listen to their counsel, but I don't trust Maggie to follow their good sense."

"From what you are hinting, I don't either," he said, frowning. "I'll tell you what. We shan't leave until after the Lisbones' ball. No, we definitely won't. Does that make you feel better? Now you needn't fret any longer, my dear. I shall see to everything. I'm sure the right solution will present itself to me just when it is least expected."

Of course, Daniel hadn't the foggiest idea of what he'd do. He only prayed he was right. He signaled the servant to bring his hat and gloves once again. "Now I shall be off and out from under your feet for the rest of the day."

"You mean while I take the responsibility of informing the girls that were leaving."

"Well, that too," he said, trying not to look guilty.

"Oh, dear," she said, clasping her hands to her cheeks. "If we are to leave London, there is much I must do beforehand also. When you go out, would you please tell Beetleworth to have a carriage brought round for me right away? I shall have to visit the shoemaker this morning to see if the new boots which I've ordered can be finished sooner. Mrs. Vervaine can instruct the girls to go on to the bonnet shop without me. Telling them the news of our trip will just have to wait until I meet them back here for lunch."

Two

The collision was inevitable. Hawksby whipped around the corner without thought or caution. The sudden impact surely would have sent him sprawling onto the pavement had not two strong hands grabbed him by the shoulders and held him upright. There was no hope of escape even if he'd wished it.

"Devil take it! Captain Hawksby!" said a familiar voice.

It took Hawksby a moment to gather his wits. In the last hour he'd been first on one side of the street, then the other. He'd looked in a jeweler's window and thought of getting Miss Divine a pretty trinket of some kind, but she'd been showered with so much jewelry over the last year that another necklace or ring would have no outstanding significance.

He'd been attracted to a small porcelain figurine of a pug dog in a curiosity shop because Miss Divine had said she was sorry she couldn't have a pet, but he'd decided to look around a bit more before purchasing anything. Then he'd stepped off the curb and nearly been run over by a mad coachman who thought he had the right of it to ride his cattle over anyone he pleased.

Before Hawksby knew it, he'd been up Bond, down Oxford, in and out of the little side streets, and back round again. He'd just decided to return to the novelty shop to pick up the porcelain pug when he'd bumped into his old acquaintance.

"Major Durham . . . that is, Lord Chantry," replied

Hawksby, extending his hand to his former senior officer.

But instead of taking it the earl only tightened his grasp on Hawksby's shoulders. "I knew it, Captain! I told her something would turn up to solve our problem. I did indeed."

"My lord?" Hawksby queried. Suspicion was Hawksby's first reaction—and his second. He was sure he'd seen that look in his friend's eyes once before.

"Oh, just a reference to something I said to the countess this morning." The earl dropped one hand to grasp the captain's. The other still gripped Hawksby's shoulder. "Glad to see you are still in London."

Hawksby couldn't tell if camaraderie precipitated such spirited greetings or if it was a maneuver to keep him from bolting. Whatever, the ruse worked. Hawksby couldn't get away without seeming rude. "I thought perhaps you would have embraced the routine of the Quality now you have returned to the life of a peer."

The earl guffawed. "Not at all. The habit of lying abed all morning is not one which I seem to be able to accept, especially since I have taken to wife a woman who has always observed country hours, too."

Hawksby cocked an eyebrow. "Then Lady Chantry is well?"

"Very," Daniel said, stepping back so he could observe the officer better.

"I hear your sisters are again the toast of London."

"Ah, that they are," replied the earl, the gleam in his eye becoming more intense as his hold on Hawksby remained strong.

Hawksby's brows had lowered until they nearly hid his eyes altogether. He remembered the last time the earl had asked him and several other unsuspecting fellow officers to help him launch eight young ladies into their first Season in

London. Nothing but chaos had come of that. "I am pleased to know all goes well in the Durham household."

Daniel shrugged. "Well, there does seem to be a fly in the pudding. I must make a journey north as quickly as possible. I wish my wife to accompany me, but because of my sisters' popularity I'm in a bind. All of the girls enjoy the balls, routs, musicals, and teas . . . except one. Maggie . . . that is, Lady Margaret. Her interests run more . . . well, shall we say to more earthy things."

"You mean bugs," Hawksby growled under his breath.

If the earl heard the remark, he chose to pretend he didn't. "For instance, she expressed interest in some lecture coming up at the Royal Institution, and the other girls wished to attend another society function that evening." He held up his hand. "But never fear, I have taken care of that matter. There will, however, be other lectures coming up, and Lady Margaret may try to go by herself once my wife and I have left London. I need someone I can trust to keep her from doing something so foolish and perhaps dangerous. I'm sure you know what I mean."

Hawksby's spirits dipped lower with every word he heard. He remembered all too well. How could he forget? The brat had had him on his knees trying to follow her through the shrubbery while she hunted for some squiggly hopping thing. Perhaps six-legged creatures had their place in the scheme of things, but, damnation, in a man's pocket was not one of them.

Clugg had scolded him endlessly when he'd gotten back that afternoon. Not only had he torn a hole in his trousers, but his batman said he'd never get the stains out. Had to have another pair made, and they were not cheap.

"You shouldn't have thrust a child that green into Society so early," Hawksby said.

Chantry shrugged. "It was that or leave Lady Margaret and her twin, Mary, at home. They were seventeen. Many young ladies make their come-out even earlier."

"Lady Mary was at least docile. I'll give you that," Hawksby said. "But if I remember correctly, it was she whom you assigned me to look after."

The earl at least had the honesty to look chagrined. "How was I to know the twins were switching places all the time so they could sneak out of the house?"

"If I remember correctly," reminded Hawksby, "it was your wife, Lady Chantry, who was the leader of those shenanigans."

The earl laughed. "Yes, but by marrying her, I now have those tendencies under control."

I doubt it, thought Hawksby. Aloud he said, "So what is it you wish me to do? Escort Lady Margaret to a lecture?"

"That . . . and perhaps a little more."

The mention of *a little more* brought the captain back to attention. The last time Chantry asked a boon of him, it had led to disaster.

Hawksby brightened. "How about some of the other chaps? Byrd, for instance. He was supposed to be in charge of Lady Margaret last year. I'd say he needs to make amends for his neglect of duty to you, sir."

"He's with Wellington in Paris."

Hawksby rubbed the stubble on his chin. He needed to get back to his rooms so Clugg could give him a shave, and he still had to send something to Miss Divine before she left for rehearsal at the theatre. He was desperate to get away. "Heard Finch sold out now that he's a viscount. He may be available."

"Well, we did see quite a bit of him while we were at Durham Hall in Oxfordshire," the earl said. "Called several times in the autumn and twice in winter. Always seemed to be just passing by."

"All the way from Essex? Deuced long way to just be passing by."

Daniel guffawed. "I thought so, too. Well, he finally came to the point and said he wished permission to court Lady Rebecca. On the other hand, her twin Lady Ruth has turned down every man who has asked to address her. I don't know why. She's had three offers which I thought to be unexceptionable. Wouldn't even listen to them."

"No one asking for the other four?" Hawksby asked hopefully.

"None that I would accept," said the earl. "But now to the matter at hand. I don't think you need to worry overly much about Maggie . . . that is, Lady Margaret's deportment. My sisters had a rather unusual upbringing, but at least their mother raised the girls to respect the elderly," he said with a crooked grin.

"Elderly!"

It was the response Daniel had expected. "Oh, yes. Lady Margaret thinks you're quite long in the tooth, you know. I overheard her tell Ruth so. But I'm sure she will give you a little more consideration in lieu of your advanced years now that she has gained some Town bronze." Daniel chuckled when he saw Hawksby's eyebrows shoot up, knowing full well the captain was no more than a year older than himself. It must be the mustache that made him appear older to the girls. "If I remember correctly, she seemed a bit afraid of you."

Hawksby huffed. "That was Lady Mary."

"Yes, well, if it will make you feel better, my youngest sister thinks I am decidedly ancient also. And to go one farther, she thought Mr. Pettigrew, who is well past his thirtieth year, was close to extinction and was surprised when Georgette found him so appealing. Besides, you're the only one around who's fancy free at the moment."

"The hell I am, Chantry! I'm quite tied up—or down, whichever way you want to look at it," Hawksby sputtered, pulling himself up to his full military height.

"Captain, I'm only asking you to keep a sharp eye on Lady Margaret during a few daytime functions. Even if there is a late afternoon lecture, you can easily have her back at Terrace Palace early in the evening, then be on your way. After all, the crowd with whom you sport doesn't start its activities until well after midnight. Other evenings she will be accompanying her sisters to whatever social activities are on their agenda. Don't worry, you can have your nights for chasing your ladybird."

Evidently Chantry hadn't heard the chase was over, and it wouldn't be good *ton* to inform him of it himself, so Hawksby asked, "How long will you be away?"

"Not too long, I'm sure. The girls will be all right, I assure you. Ruth and Rebecca look out after them."

Hawksby cut him off. "How long is *long?*"

Lord Chantry coughed. "Oh, perhaps a few days . . . weeks. Depends on what the situation calls for in Yorkshire."

Hawksby let out a howl.

The earl pulled his trump card. "Must I remind you, Captain, that you may have paid me back for Salamanca but you still owe me for the incident on the Spanish border when we crossed into France?"

Hawksby backed off, but his frown remained. "That I do, Major." Chantry had saved his life more than once. He couldn't forget a thing like that.

"My wife will be beholden to you, as well, Hawksby. Lady Margaret, after all, is her youngest half-sister, as well as my father's youngest daughter and my half-sister as well."

Hawksby held up his hand as if to fend off the onslaught of explanations. "You needn't honeycoat it by trying to straighten out your father's progeny. It is enough to know he had three wives and seven daughters in fewer years than I can count on one hand. To set your mind at ease and to keep you from badgering me further, I shall keep an eye on the child while you're gone."

"Good. Good," the earl said. "And now do let me offer you lunch. We can set up a time for you to call and talk to Lady Margaret about her schedule."

"But Major—Chantry . . ."

The earl held up his hand. "No, no, I insist. We can be more private at Grillon's. Don't want our little arrangement to get about all the clubs now, do we?"

What a wrinkle, thought Hawksby. Best satisfy his lordship. He'd just have to pick up something for Miss Divine after they'd eaten. Clugg would really be in a double twist wondering where he was.

"What does your sister say about having a keeper?"

"Well, as to that . . . we haven't exactly approached the subject with her yet. That's why I'd like to discuss the details with you over lunch. Then I shall inform her of my plans."

"Hell! I'm out of here," said Hawksby, thinking of the last Durham sister fiasco, but the grip on his arm only tightened. Getting free of Lord Chantry wasn't to be.

"Shall we go to Grillon's, Captain?"

"Oh, no! Not Captain Hawksby, Freddie," cried Maggie, with all the indignation she could muster. "Mister Sobersides? The grouch?"

"He's no such thing," the countess of Chantry said, laughing.

"Captain Hawksby," Maggie repeated, plopping down in

less than ladylike fashion upon one of the leather couches which sat on either side of the fireplace in the library. Of all the wretched luck. She had just returned from a most boring trip to the bonnet shop with her sisters, and who should meet them at the door when they came back to Terrace Palace but Freddie, who signaled all six of them to follow her into the bookroom. Five obeyed immediately. Even Maggie began to rise. No one ever said *nay* to Freddie even before she'd become a countess.

"Now, dearest," the countess said, shaking her finger at her youngest sister, "don't give me that look. It will do no good. I told Daniel how much you wished to attend lectures and go to the special reference rooms in the museums." She took a moment to reread the message her husband had sent from Grillon's. "In this note, he says he chanced upon his friend in Bond Street, and when the captain heard of our plight, he graciously offered to be your escort. Let me read what his note says:

At this moment, Captain Hawksby is giving me his opinions on what I can do with this venture.

"There now," Freddie said with satisfaction. "I think that is very chivalrous of him, don't you?"

From where they stood nearby, five of the young ladies nodded in unanimous accord.

Smiling, Freddie thanked them for their good sense in agreeing with her before turning back to her recalcitrant sister. "Daniel says he will arrange to have Captain Hawksby call before we leave so you can renew your acquaintance and give him an idea of the events you wish to attend."

"Why didn't you tell us sooner you and Daniel were going to Yorkshire?" Maggie complained as she cast about in her brain for some way to get out of this unconscionable predicament and her brother's equally unacceptable solution. *A stuffy old military man breathing over her shoulder? She might as well be locked up in Newgate Prison.*

Freddie tried again. "I swear to you I didn't know about it until this morning. Daniel was up and out before he'd even finished a cup of coffee, and I had to rush to the shoemaker's to see if my new boots were finished. Since none of you were down to eat yet, I didn't have time to linger. I reckoned it best to wait until you came in from your shopping trip so I could tell you all at one time. If you remember, we have to be at Mrs. Hefflewicker's this afternoon. She's a simple-minded woman, but she is the sister of the countess of Lisbone nonetheless. With the ball only a few days away, it is sensible for you to keep a pleasant relationship with all members of Polite Society."

"We understand, Freddie," Ruth said in an assuring tone. "How soon do you plan to go?"

"Daniel wants to be off as soon as we possibly can. Oh, yes —I remember now. He said we'd wait until after the Lisbone Ball." Freddie hesitated a second to try to think of a plausible explanation of why her husband suddenly was so agreeable to attending one of the biggest galas of the Season when all his sisters knew he hated any sort of affair where they were threatened to be squeezed to death, where they'd be scrutinized, gossiped about, and where he would be expected to dance. She smiled broadly. "Your brother decided that we should have one evening together as a family before we leave Town."

As Freddie hoped, the girls brightened upon hearing the announcement . . . all except one.

"But there's a lecture I want to attend that night at the Royal Institution," Maggie lamented.

31

"I'm sure if the speaker says anything of significance he will be asked to make another."

Maggie was caught there. "Well, yes. In fact, he will be giving another in the afternoon of Tuesday next."

"There you are. Daniel has given you permission to attend such events as long as Captain Hawksby is free to escort you. Now aren't you glad your brother had the foresight to ask his friend to come to our rescue?"

More a gaoler, Maggie thought. She remembered occasions during their first Season, when all the twins thought it hilarious to switch places to confuse the young officers. Most of the men had been great guns about it, but the captain wasn't one of them.

Although she couldn't remember Captain Hawksby actually criticizing her outright, she couldn't recall he'd been overly cooperative, either, nor had he approached any of her insect collecting excursions with any great enthusiasm.

Being a soldier, she'd expected him to welcome having a go at such adventures. The picture of him which came to mind now was one of sweeping brows and critical frowns, and if she remembered correctly he was a large fellow. But when a man is down on his knees crawling around in the bushes it is sometimes hard to tell about his disposition. Had she been wrong in her analysis?

Maggie narrowed her eyes in contemplation. She had hoped to avoid going to the Lisbones' ball, as she was sure her brother had. She wondered what had made Daniel so agreeable all of a sudden to attending. Since that avenue of escape now seemed blocked, she decided to try another tactic to be rid of Captain Hawksby. "Why don't you stay home with us, Freddie? We'll miss you if you go. Daniel can take care of this estate business by himself."

"Now, Maggie," Ruth admonished, "Freddie's place is

with her husband. You will understand that someday when you fall in love and marry." The minute she said it, a becoming pink flush colored the fair Ruth's cheeks.

It seemed a mystery to Maggie why her elder sister should blush over the mention of a husband. Ruth wasn't even engaged, and she'd turned down every suitor who had asked their brother for her hand. "Well, I cannot think I ever will be so foolish as to prefer a man over my sisters . . . even Mary."

Freddie laughed outright. "We will just have to wait and see on that measure, young lady. Daniel speaks of Captain Hawksby as being an honorable gentleman. I take it he will call in the next day or two, so be a good girl and make things easy for your brother. He will be very concerned while we are away if he has to worry about his sisters not behaving themselves."

"Why can't Flora accompany me?"

"Flora may be well intentioned, dear, but she is a country girl and is much happier helping Cook in the kitchen. Maggie, why do you take such offense to the captain—that is, aside from the fact you think him too serious? I have an idea your brother may look upon that trait as a virtue in the man— particularly in your case. He is a gentleman and will certainly know which establishments are proper for a young lady, and he will not let you attend anything which would blemish your reputation."

"But Captain Hawksby is such a fuss-box."

Freddie's eyes widened. "Did he refuse to be polite or in any manner was he disrespectful to you during last Season? Your brother would certainly demand to know if he did something amiss."

Maggie shook her head vehemently. Although she couldn't in truth say the captain had ever used unseemly language in her presence, she was certain the words he'd mumbled under his breath hadn't been suitable for a young miss taking her first steps into Polite Society. She had the sinking feeling her chances of escaping the social folderol were becoming more remote than ever. "Well, he certainly objected to getting his knees dirty. And it was just a *little* tear in his breeches."

"Oh, Maggie," Mary said, clasping her face in her hands. "You didn't have him chasing after some bug, did you?"

Maggie glowered at Mary for tattling on her.

Freddie raised her eyebrows. "Well, Maggie? Out with it."

"It was only a bush cricket and Captain Hawksby's fault completely."

"Fault, Maggie?" Freddie pinched her lips together to keep them from betraying her by turning upward.

"Well, yes. If he hadn't tried to knock it off his neck just as I was about to grab it—which made it jump into the rhododendron bushes, you understand—he wouldn't have had to get down on the ground and crawl in after it."

"For shame, Maggie." Freddie chuckled. "I can only say that after having such an harrowing experience, I am sure we can trust Captain Hawksby to keep you from doing something so noodle-headed again."

Mary smiled shyly. "Well, I thought Captain Hawksby was quite elegant and a perfect gentleman, even if he was a bit overwhelming."

"You think every man in uniform is *elegant*," chided her twin.

Mary looked down her nose with what Maggie assumed was supposed to be a condescending air. "Well, it can be expected that I should mature faster. After all, I am the elder."

"Mama Gillian said you were born only a few minutes before I was," Maggie said, raising her nose a bit higher.

"Well, if we were males, that would be important enough to render me the heir to the title," Mary said, her nose tilting another inch toward the ceiling.

"Girls, girls, Freddie is trusting us to be ladies," Rebecca admonished, trying with great difficulty to keep from going into a fit of the whoops.

Antoinette and Babette, their dark curls swinging in synchronized harmony, nodded sweetly.

"I'm sorry, Freddie," Maggie apologized, folding her hands in her lap. "I shall endeavor to be prim and proper while you are away."

Freddie looked at her fondly. "I don't expect you to go so much against your nature as that, dear. Only try to regard the proprieties and not have half the household staff out searching for you in the middle of the night. I have assured Daniel that from all the instructions you have received you all know how to go about in Society now."

The countess then seated herself beside her youngest sister. "You have our Mama's fey spirit, Maggie—sometimes more than I. You are always here and there and never content to sit still, like a butterfly flitting from flower to flower forever seeking new excitement."

"Mary is too timid by far," accused Maggie.

Freddie patted her sister's hand. "Perhaps it is wiser to be cautious than to leap before you look, Maggie. You are twins —like two peas in a pod, the opposites of each other and yet the same. Daniel has undoubtedly gone to great lengths to acquire the assistance of a brave officer such as Captain Hawksby to escort you to places where you wish to go and your sisters don't. I want you to promise me you will behave while Daniel and I are gone."

Sighing, Maggie nodded. "When do you think Captain Hawksby will call?"

"I'll ask Daniel when he comes in this evening," Freddie said. Then, glancing at the clock, she clapped her hands. "Now hurry, everyone. We don't have much time to get ready to make our first call on Mrs. Hefflewicker."

The sisters were scurrying across the room when Lord Chantry slipped his head around the door. They came to an abrupt halt. "May I interrupt, ladies?"

Freddie jumped up. "Oh, Daniel, of course you may. Come in. The girls are eager to hear your plans."

Plans or no plans, Maggie had already decided what she was going to do. "I want to go back to Knocktigh," she said.

"I don't understand, Freddie," the earl said, turning to his wife. "Didn't you tell Maggie I'd made arrangements for her to go to her lectures?"

"I want to see Dr. MacDougal," Maggie said defiantly, still not budging from where she sat. "I miss him." And she did, very much. When the Scotsman came to Knocktigh, it was fun running among the high grasses to catch insects for him. It wasn't just insects she'd learned to appreciate, but all God's creatures. She could almost hear the dear man's voice as if he were in the room.

"I'll give ye somethin' tae think aboot," he'd say. "Did ye ever think tae wonder that such teeny tiny creatures can see and hear and eat and have wee bairns that grow up joost like their mamas and papas? Every one prettier than the other? Every one a miracle?"

Surely Dr. MacDougal was a miracle himself, Maggie thought, always encouraging her to do what she liked to do whether her sisters wanted to or not. "Don't treat me like a baby in leading strings, Daniel," she called to her brother from the sofa. "And before you do anything more about it, I want you to know how put out I am with you for even thinking of hiring Captain Hawksby to spy on me."

Daniel cocked an eyebrow. "My comrade wasn't for hire, my dear—and as to hearing your objections, I'm afraid it is too late for that. The captain is at this very minute waiting in the vestibule. I told him I had to find where you all were first. Now that I have, I've told Beetleworth to fetch him."

With that, he withdrew and could be heard saying, "Ho, there, Hawksby! You were here all the time and I didn't know it. Right this way. My family has just been saying how much they've been looking forward to seeing you again."

As Maggie watched her brother step to one side, Captain Hawksby's huge form filled the doorway. Her eyes grew larger. *Bless my soul!* The man was bigger than she'd remembered. A whole lot bigger.

Three

Challenging the enemy would have been less difficult. Instead Captain Hawksby found himself bending politely over each young lady's hand, repeating names, trying to recall faces and fix identities. They blurred before his eyes like the long rows of flower arrangements he'd passed in the corridor on his way to the library. Now the riotous colors and rare scents blended together as though he were taking a stroll in a garden—a deceptive perception, to be sure.

He remembered that the two cornsilk blonds were the eldest twins. Their clear melodious voices sounded like the chirping birds which had flown over Belgian fields before a battle was about to begin. "Lady Ruth . . . Lady Rebecca," he repeated.

With the next two introductions, he glimpsed dark curls and rose-petal lips that didn't need to speak to be heard and recalled the late Earl of Chantry's second wife had been a French noblewoman. "Lady Antoinette. Lady Babette."

A figure in a green frock and crowned with orange ringlets stepped out from the throng. As Hawksby bowed again, he cautioned himself not to lower his gaze too far or dwell too long upon what he remembered to be the outstanding attributes of the youngest Durham twins—the two with the flaming hair and figures not meant for females of such tender age. He was so intent on not making a cake of himself that he closed his eyes and thought of Miss Divine and didn't catch that twin's name. When he again raised his head and opened his eyes, another flash of orange registered somewhere in the vicinity of the fireplace. A young woman with similar charms sat looking daggers at him.

Hawksby lowered his brows until his eyes were mere slits. He didn't have to guess which one was Lady Margaret. More disturbing to contemplate was the question which was haunting him the most. How much was this delay going to cost him in his new relationship? Was his lovely Miss Divine asking for him at that moment? He'd left word with her maid that he'd contact her later, which he hadn't. He saw trouble looming ahead already.

"You don't know what a gift you are, Captain Hawksby," the little brown-haired countess said, startling him back to reality as she took his elbow and angled him toward the sofa. Damn, she was strong for such a little woman.

"Gift?" *Oh, Drat!* He'd forgotten all about Miss Divine's gift—well, not exactly forgotten it. The earl had rushed him to Grillon's, insisting he stuff himself with dish after dish of rich victuals, then drowning him in glass after glass of fine wine while telling him how desperately his lordship and the countess needed his assistance or else they wouldn't be able to leave Town with any peace of mind.

So busy was the earl in stating his own concerns that he hadn't listened to one single word Hawksby tried to get in edgewise about his own urgent business, which had to be attended to first. Subsequently he'd found himself kidnapped, hustled into a hackney carriage, and shanghaied to Terrace Palace. He might as well have been trussed up and gagged for all the good his protesting had done.

The devil take it. If Hawksby didn't want to find himself in the stew, it was imperative he send Miss Divine something . . . and soon. She'd be waiting to hear from him. Probably *was* waiting. Crying her eyes out, too—or, worse, throwing a tantrum because he was neglecting her. Miss Divine could be as sweet as sweet could be when it suited her, but Hawksby had seen her temper, too. His affair could be dashed to ruins before he really had a chance to have a go at it.

Now as the rainbow hues circled round him and he advanced closer to the bright spot of orange on the couch, an idea triggered itself in his brain.

Ah, that was it. "A mixed bouquet," he rasped, speaking his thoughts aloud without thinking and feeling quite proud, if he did say so himself, for coming up with such a sensible solution.

Surely he could find a flower lady on the streets and have a runner carry a few posies to Covent Garden for the nonce. He'd jot Miss Divine a little note telling her he was thinking of her and would bring her something more meaningful later.

"Why, isn't that a lovely thing to say, ladies?" the countess exclaimed, clapping her hands with delight. "Captain Hawksby has likened you to a bouquet of flowers."

He'd done it again, spoken his innermost thoughts too loudly. He tried his usual glowering from under his thick brows for a second, but it did absolutely no good. The little countess wasn't even looking at him.

"Please sit down, Captain," she said sweetly, oblivious to the discomfiture she'd caused. "Lady Margaret is eager to renew your acquaintance. While the two of you are doing so, I'm sure you will excuse her sisters to go freshen up for our afternoon round of calls. Ruth, dear, tell Mrs. Vervaine to have luncheon trays sent to your rooms. There is no time for eating in the dining room. Maggie will be up as soon as she has given the captain an idea of her schedule."

Everyone obeyed the little countess as any well-trained company of soldiers would their commander. But mutiny was more to Hawksby's way of thinking. He stood in front of the designated couch like a sword stuck in stone, eyeing the small space left him. The Friday-faced personage sitting in the middle of the cushioned seat—whom he now knew to be his target—didn't budge an inch, either.

"Oh, do make room, Maggie," hissed Mary, nudging her sister's foot with the toe of her half-boot as she passed. Then, with a shy smile and an approving glance at his face, she quickly passed between them, blushing.

Hawksby inclined his head toward the soft-spoken, pleasing-to-look-upon Lady Mary and wondered if the mustache had caught her fancy. With a flourish, his fingers smoothed out any hairs which may have gone astray. Mama always said women were drawn to a man with a mustache—not that Hawksby was the least interested in the sort of woman Mama wanted him to attract, but he supposed a mustache did have its advantages.

Lady Margaret gave her sister a dour look, but nonetheless obediently scooted over on the sofa without so much as a glance his way—or any way that he could observe. As soon as the other young ladies had filed out of the room, propriety as well as orders from the tiny countess dictated to Hawksby that he take his seat beside the girl he had sworn to protect, but who clearly was not as appreciative of his sacrifices as her twin.

Lady Chantry sat across from them. The earl moved out of the line of fire and stood in the background, his arm resting on the mantelpiece. Hawksby couldn't blame him. Confound it, but he wished himself in a coffee house with his comrades in arms or out for a ride in the country on his horse. Facing a line of cannons would be preferable to the scrutiny of seven young women taking his measure. He wondered how Chantry did it, living in a house with so many females.

41

Hawksby thought of sitting back so he could keep an eye on both ladies at the same time, but he wasn't about to take the chance of tilting the sofa. Wouldn't do at all to have the figure next to him come sliding down the cushion. After all, he did weigh a good fifteen stone, and Lady Margaret probably weighed . . . no, it wasn't proper for him to be making such calculations. She'd just have to remain a blob of green and cream and carroty hair out of the corner of his eye.

While the countess chattered merrily, Lady Margaret continued to stare straight ahead, and Chantry roamed about acting as if he weren't involved in the chicanery. *Coward.* Hawksby wasn't very good at small talk. Neither, it seemed, was the girl beside him. At least they had that in common.

Damned awkward situation, if Hawksby did say so himself. Why couldn't his lordship give him Lady Margaret's reconnaissance plans so he could be on his way?

Hawksby let his mind wander. This seasonal rigmarole— the marriage mart, as it was called—had nothing to do with him. Conspiring mamas dressing up their daughters to the nines and parading them in front of the establishment. Why all this subterfuge to get unsuspecting chaps to commit for a lifetime was beyond him. Didn't the young fools know they were stepping into the parson's trap? Surely they did. In his opinion, if they were that dim-witted as to what it was all about, they deserved what they got. But that was not the life for him, he thought pleasantly, and smiled.

The countess abruptly paused.

Out of the corner of his eye, Hawksby caught signals passing between her and the earl. An unspoken language, so to speak, as if one knew what the other was thinking. When he harkened back to his own childhood, he remembered his parents had just such a mystifying habit. No matter how secretly he and his siblings conspired, they couldn't get away with anything. Never could figure out how Mama and Papa did it. Something to do with marriage, he supposed.

However, since Hawksby hadn't tried to analyze the state of matrimony before nor had he experienced that state of idiocy which he'd witnessed in so many of his acquaintances, he couldn't come to any meaningful conclusion, could he? If there were men who were fortunate enough to escape such agony, Hawksby hoped he would be one of them. He'd not give up his freedom to gain the ability to read someone else's mind.

He felt a movement beside him—a dip, a little jiggle of the cushion. Perhaps Lady Margaret was about to say something. Yes, she surely was ready to tell him what he needed to know, and he could be off and about his business. But a quick sideways glance in her direction showed she still stared straight ahead, her hands clutched in her lap. The only change he observed was that she'd thrust her chin out a bit farther. Surely that was not enough to make the cushion bounce. Confound it! He must be the one not sitting still. He stiffened his backbone and dug his fingers into his knees to keep them steady. Demmed uncomfortable.

The countess chatted on. Hawksby fought the compulsion to yawn.

If the chit would just tell him where he was to escort her on which days and at what time, he could tell Clugg to mark it on his calendar and that would be that. But Lady Margaret seemed determined to keep him waiting on that subject.

He wondered who this Dr. MacDougal fellow was whom he'd heard mentioned when he was still in the hallway. He'd have to remember to ask Chantry before they left London. Hawksby didn't want any trouble from a jealous lover complicating his life. Definitely not. Damned nuisance.

Bored to the core, Hawksby went back to dreaming of

Miss Divine. He nodded his head at what he thought were the appropriate times. Yes, that was the thing to do, think of his little bird of paradise.

Miss Divine. Hawksby still couldn't bring himself to call her Luciane—or, heaven forbid, *Luci*—as he'd heard others refer to her. He supposed he was permitted now that they had an arrangement. He would ask her tonight after the evening performance.

He glanced over at the tall floor clock standing beside the library entrance. It was only half past two. If he were out of here in the next hour, there would still be time to send her a message before she had to be at the theatre. Surely this interview would take only a few more minutes. The corners of his mouth turned upward.

"Well, Captain, I can see by the pleasant expression on your face you are looking forward to escorting our little sister about Town," the countess said.

Hawksby blinked. He'd missed something.

"I am so delighted to have had this little talk with you," Lady Chantry continued as she rose. "You can't imagine what a relief it is to know our Maggie will have such an honorable gentleman to escort her while we are away."

Hawksby jumped up. He'd not heard a thing that had been said for the last several minutes. He chanced a quick glance in Lady Margaret's direction to see if he could catch a hint as to what the countess meant. He saw only the merest bit of the chit's profile and a great amount of orange hair, but looked away quickly before Lord Chantry should think him a fool for staring. He recalled how unhinged his lordship had become last Season when he caught men ogling his sisters in what he interpreted to be lecherous ways—which no doubt they were, because the earl had very attractive siblings. Only then did Hawksby realize the earl was nowhere to be seen.

Blast! When did Chantry leave?

The captain bowed deeply in the countess's direction.

She, in turn, placed her hand firmly on his arm and propelled him to the door. "So you will be expected at three o'clock come Tuesday afternoon, Captain."

Thank goodness she'd mentioned the day and time. Hawksby had no idea to what else he'd agreed. He'd just turn up that afternoon and go wherever.

"Come along, Maggie dear," Lady Chantry said to her sister. "When Daniel left I told him to tell Beetleworth to have tea and sandwiches sent out to the gazebo in the rose garden. Flora will accompany you while you are with Captain Hawksby. It will be much more pleasant out there and will give you a little privacy to discuss your engagements. I will extend your regrets to our hostesses this afternoon and tell them how devastated you are not to have been able to visit," the countess said, doing her best not to smile. "Now I must get ready. Your sisters will be wondering what on earth has been keeping me."

Hawksby asked himself where he'd been when all this communication had been going on. Well, he *did* know where his thoughts had been, but that was neither here nor there now. He started to thank Lady Chantry for her hospitality, but she was already skipping up the stairs. All he saw were the soles of her shoes and the hem of her skirt.

Somehow, someway, the earl had left the room earlier and Hawksby hadn't even been aware of it. *Blast!* You would have thought they were still behind enemy lines for all the stealth and secrecy he was encountering. How had he managed to agree to continue his encounter with Lady Margaret in the garden and not even remember? Next time he'd pay more attention when ladies were making plans. The earl must have a devil of a time ever getting a word in edgewise.

45

A footman handed the captain his sword, gloves, and hat, but left before Hawksby could ask that a message be sent to Miss Divine. Lady Margaret was already headed out onto the terrace.

Chasing after her was a plump cherubic dumpling disguised as a serving girl with a white apron and carrying a straw basket. No, 'twas the other way round. The rosy-cheeked cherub must be the maid called Flora.

She stumbled into the vestibule. "Wait for me, miss. Cook said whilst I was in the garden I might as well pick her some herbs. Oh, what a loverly day to be walkin' with a bonnie mon the likes of yer captain," she exclaimed in a light Scottish brogue. With a giggle she glanced back at Hawksby, her cheeks turning from bright pink to red.

"Do quit flirting, Flora, and come along," Lady Margaret threw back over her shoulder. "And mind you don't wander too far away from me."

"You know I always mind you, miss," the girl said with such good-natured laughter and hilarity that it caused her to trip over her own feet, tumble down the last step, and land her on her knees in the middle of the gravel path. Her basket flew off in one direction, her mobcap in another.

Hawksby had not even made it out onto the terrace before Lady Margaret came running back to help the clumsy girl. She tugged and hauled until she had her upright, brushed off her skirt, inspected her elbows carefully, retrieved the straw basket from the bushes, and collected her mobcap from the low limbs of a small tree. The latter she plunked on Flora's head, pulled it down over her ears, and patted her on the cheek.

By Jove, what an odd way for a lady to treat a maid, he thought. Yes, it most certainly was. Not one scolding word to the awkward servant did he hear from the termagant who had

46

given him nothing but dark looks since the moment he walked into the library.

But it was their whoops of laughter which truly brought him up short, warning him to remember his harrowing experiences of the previous year in these very same bushes. *Beware,* he told himself. Lady Margaret was not an ordinary young lady. Not ordinary at all—and that was what worried him most of all.

As quickly as possible, Hawksby sheathed his sword. He might need it. Then, tucking his hat under his arm, he did his best to pull on his gloves as he sped down the garden path after the two young women. This whole assignment was going to be a vexation. He could see that.

Maggie couldn't ignore the *crunch-crunch-crunch* of the captain's heavy boots behind her on the gravel path, sensing his presence as powerfully as she had when he'd sat beside her on the sofa. If her brother had his way, she was going to experience Captain Hawksby's presence from now until Daniel and Freddie returned from their trip to Yorkshire.

What was she going to do about Captain Hawksby? She hadn't decided yet. He certainly wasn't a man who could be easily overlooked, anymore than you could overlook a mosquito the size of a horse.

She had hoped that over time in her letters to Edinburgh she'd be able to persuade Dr. MacDougal to come to London. Then she was going to beg Daniel and Freddie to let her go back to the borderlands when the professor returned— back to Knocktigh. But with Daniel and Freddie going away, it seemed her chances of escaping the social Season silliness were more remote than ever now, what with the conspicuous cavalryman her brother had chosen to dog her every step.

Unless . . . unless Captain Hawksby might prove to be her

best voucher on that account. But before she could put any scheme in place she'd have to come up with a very convincing schedule to give him and Mrs. Vervaine.

She really didn't have any set plans for what she wanted to do other than the lecture at the Royal Institution the coming week. She'd told Freddie a Banbury tale about that, but she'd kept her fingers crossed when she did, so it didn't count against her.

Perhaps after she'd had more time to think about it, she'd see a way to handle the situation—or, more truthfully, how to handle Captain Hawksby. But for the present she'd leave well enough alone.

Maggie had managed a peek or two at Captain Hawksby in the library while he was greeting her sisters and afterward sitting beside her on the sofa, staring off somewhere into never-never land. His refusal to look at her had given her an opportunity to observe him from the corner of her eye. My, he was enormous, in both breadth and height—a man who could make their Knocktigh stableman, Loof, sit up and take notice. The old Scotsman was considered a giant.

Loof, however, smiled often. If her memory served her right from last year, the captain always looked more like a bear that had swallowed a hedgehog.

Then, to her surprise, right when he was sitting next to her, for a moment or two a most dreamlike expression had spread across Captain Hawksby's face. His clenched jaw relaxed and he lost that dogged expression. Right before her eyes, he'd appeared much younger than before. She thought it a most astounding sight.

Maggie had to ask herself how someone could look so old and forbidding one minute and like a happy young man the next—so handsome it nearly took her breath away. But, alas, the illusion lasted only a moment before Freddie was herding them out to the terrace and sending them off to the rose garden.

Now Maggie gave a quick glance back over her shoulder. "I declare, Flora, no matter how I twist and turn it over in my mind, it comes out the same. I'm afraid it's going to be quite bothersome having Captain Hawksby breathing down my neck for the next few weeks."

"What do you plan to do, miss?" Flora said eagerly, her eyes lighting up with anticipation at the thought of what mischief her mistress could possibly be contemplating.

Maggie lifted her finger to her lips. "Let me think. As soon as I believe my sisters have left the house, I shall endeavor to chase him off. Then, when we've seen the last of the captain, how would you like to go down to the old palace ruins on the Thames and watch the boats go by?"

"Oh, miss," Flora said, puffing her hands to her cheeks. "You know you're not allowed to go down on the steps along the waterfront, and if Mrs. Vervaine don't see us first, Beetleworth will surely stop us at the front door."

"You silly goose. When did we ever leave by the front door when we had exciting places to explore? After you have taken your herbs to Cook, fetch me your extra cape. Then we shall sneak out the old postern gate behind the hedge like we did last year. My sisters won't be home for hours, so who will know?"

The maid crushed her basket to her chest. "Oh, miss. It's been ever so long since we set off on one of your adventures."

"My thoughts exactly. You don't know how fortunate you are, Flora, not to have to sit on silk sofas and listen to some fancy-dressed peacock tell you about his new clothes."

She turned the maid off the path and pushed her toward a bed of mixed plants. "Now concentrate on collecting your herbs and I'll endeavor to rid us of Captain Hawksby as quickly as possible. There is the rose garden ahead."

Thank goodness, Maggie could see the tea tray awaiting her on the little iron table under the vine-covered arches of the gazebo. "I declare, Flora," she said, quickening her pace, "I'm starving to death."

Maggie skipped up the three steps and seated herself on a wrought-iron chair beside the table. She had her gloves off, her napkin spread on her lap, and had reached for the pot of tea by the time the captain entered the gazebo. He strode to the wooden bench which ran round the outer perimeter of the platform, as far away from her as the small structure permitted without his falling over the rail. There he stood at attention, a great hulk of a man, looking neither left nor right. He appeared to be as uncomfortable as she felt. "For heaven sakes, Captain, do sit down," she said. "You make me nervous hovering about."

He sat, placing his shako, the tall military hat which he carried under his arm, beside him. But since his sword now hung at his side, he had to perch sideways on the edge of the seat, which made him have to face the garden more than he did her.

That was fine with Maggie. As far as she was concerned, Captain Hawksby could wait a few minutes while she ate something before she wasted away to nothing. But she did remember her manners and held out a silver dish to him. "Will you have a biscuit or a jam tart, Captain Hawksby?"

He had to turn his head to see her. "What? Oh, no thank you, Lady Margaret." She started to offer him some tea, but his interest seemed centered on two servants who had just emerged from the long casement windows leading from the house carrying great baskets full of flowers. They marched down a path and across the lawn toward the back of the garden until they disappeared beyond the trellis covered with honeysuckle vines. Coming back by the same circuitous route were two other servants with empty containers.

Maggie shrugged, reached for a piece of gingerbread, and took a dainty bite, as a lady should. She glanced up at Captain Hawksby through her lashes. He still seemed completely absorbed in watching the servants cross the lawn, which gave her time to study him more carefully. There was a shadow across the lower part of his face, and she wondered if he planned on growing a beard. It would be a dark one—darker than his hair, more like his mustache. She told herself she shouldn't be concentrating on what Captain Hawksby looked liked. She should be thinking of what activities she could invent to get away from the silly parties she didn't want to attend.

On the other hand, she decided her health was more important to her immediate well being than either of the other two considerations, and she quickly popped the remaining piece of gingerbread into her mouth. She savored it for a moment with a happy sigh, took another hearty sip of tea, and swallowed.

While Flora snipped away at herbs among the flowers, Hawksby was watching another set of servants coming from the house with more plants. Odd. They followed the same path. Minutes later they were back, their baskets empty.

Lady Margaret ate with relish, saying nothing. Hawksby's spirits were sinking lower with every biscuit, every cucumber sandwich, every tart that disappeared down her throat. Damn, where did she put it all? A quick glance out of the corner of his eye only confused him more. What she had was very attractively arranged. Indeed it was—but that was neither here nor there. She was certainly taking her own sweet time to reveal her plans.

In the meantime, the maid hopped from plant to plant like

a fat little honeybee gathering her herbs. The servants kept up their march. Insects hummed, birds chirped. Hawksby continued to sit tall on the low bench, his knees nearly to his chin, bored, waiting. The longer he waited, the more he realized he really knew very little about what women wanted. Roses of every color surrounded the gazebo. Beyond that circle were more flowers of every variety and hue. What would Miss Divine think if he selected a single rose? Or should he send the mixed bouquet he'd envisioned earlier in the library?

A fly buzzed around Hawksby's face, threatening to land on his nose. He slapped it off and looked to see if Lady Margaret was coming any nearer to ending this interview. She seemed more interested in eating than in concentrating on the business they had come to the garden to conclude. Count on a woman to be thinking of something as elementary as food when a man had a serious problem to solve. But she was a female, and weren't they all basically the same—simple in their desires? Hers seemed to center on wiping the platter clean.

Hawksby cleared his throat. "Lady Margaret, may I ask you something?"

She looked up at him, her hand midway to her mouth, still holding a half-eaten crumpet. A crumb remained on her upper lip, and Hawksby was tempted to tell her so, but if he dared mention it he might embarrass her. That could throw her female sensibilities off-kilter and break the mood for what he wanted to ask. Time was ticking away. He could hear it as well as he heard the crickets in the shrubbery.

Damn! He was surrounded by more flowers than he'd ever seen in his entire life, and he couldn't even get away to purchase a few to send to his little buttercup. In fact, the possibility of obtaining even one flower was getting slimmer by the minute, which is more than he could say for Lady Margaret. He despaired of gaining her attention as long as there was one sandwich left on the tray, but he had to make the effort. Suddenly, he had an idea . . .

Four

"Lady Margaret, do you think Lady Chantry would mind if I picked a flower or two from her garden before I left?"

She raised a brow.

He thought he saw a mischievous twinkle in her eyes, which he couldn't quite interpret. At least it was a change from her indifference of the last several minutes.

"I see no reason why you shouldn't, Captain, but from my remembrance of your little encounter with an itty-bitty cricket, I must warn you there may be bugs on them. If you will tell Flora which two you want, she will be happy to pick them for you."

He could tell the chit wasn't taking him seriously at all. He'd approach his dilemma from another angle. "What I am trying to say is, if you were a woman . . . that is, I know you are a woman, but if you were a woman whose attentions a certain gentleman wished to secure and you should receive a flower from this admirer . . . this is just hypothetical, you understand."

She looked at him as if she expected to see butterflies fly out of his head at any minute, and his ears began to burn. He was presenting his point rather badly, but his range of possibilities on the subject were sadly stymied when it came to imagination. He cleared his throat. "Would you think more kindly of him if he gave you a flower instead of, say . . . a porcelain pug dog?"

Maggie waved the crumpet in a sweeping motion. "Why-ever would I want one flower—or even two—when I already have a whole garden full to look upon?"

"Oh, yes, I see what you mean," he said glancing forlornly about him.

"I have never been overly fond of pug dogs, either. But let me think," she said brightly, popping the remainder of the crumpet into her mouth. She chewed slowly.

"Yes?" Hawksby said hopefully. *She has pretty lips,* he thought, *as well as a nice chin. Nice but stubborn.* He waited for her to swallow.

Maggie's imagination never sat long on a short stick and she quickly warmed to the subject. "I suppose if this person doesn't have flowers to look upon every day and all of a sudden she should be given a whole garden at one time, understandably she would be quite taken by the gesture, don't you think?"

"Well, put that way—yes, I can see your point." Hawksby really didn't, but he didn't want to appear obtuse.

Maggie turned to Hawksby and nodded. "Excess, you know, Captain Hawksby. Excess impresses."

"Oh, I daresay—I *do* see what you mean," he said, looking out over the vast gardens of Terrace Palace. However, his comprehension only made him feel more downhearted than before. "But a person cannot be expected to find an entire garden which can be removed at a moment's notice, Lady Margaret. No, I don't suppose one can. Most people don't have entire gardens to be dug up and moved at a snap of their fingers," he said, watching two more servants hurry across the yard carrying containers with blossoms hanging over the sides, sprinkling a wake of colored petals behind them on the path.

"Besides, a person doesn't carry around a spade with him

every place he goes, and one would have to have a shovel of some kind to dig them up." He placed his hand on the hilt of his sword. "And this would be no good at all except for slicing a stem."

Maggie dabbed at her lips with her napkin. "Where is your imagination, Captain Hawksby? Don't you know you can do anything when it is just make believe?"

It had been a long time since Hawksby had had time to make believe. He'd never been very good at it anyway. "I suppose," he said, this time watching three more servants carry out baskets of flowers to the rear of the yard.

What the devil are they doing? Hawksby could stand it no longer. "Lady Margaret, can you tell me why they are taking all those flowers to the stables?"

Maggie bit her lip. "Would you believe me if I told you they are decorating the horses' stalls?"

Hawksby was beginning to think the Durhams as daft as his own family. "I wouldn't put anything past the earl after I saw his Scots Grey called Precious carrying a daffodil round in his mouth last year."

Maggie let out a hearty laugh, taking Hawksby by surprise. "Well, I shall have to confess the servants are doing nothing so handsome," she said, wondering if he'd known at all that she was quizzing him. "They are only emptying out the vases in the house, readying them for fresh flowers which they'll pick in the morning. They are taking them to the alleyway behind the mews. They do so each afternoon. Freddie likes fresh cuttings put in the house every day."

Hawksby studied the baskets more intensely. "They don't look all that bad to me. No, I don't see one wilted leaf—no faded blossoms."

"Some will be by tomorrow. It's easier to cut fresh. We have so many."

"And you say they just dump them in the alleyway?"

"No, no. Daniel pays a wagoner to cart them off. Sometimes he has them taken to a charity house. My sister, Freddie, says they should be sent somewhere so they can make those who are less fortunate happy. That's why she has them taken out every day while they still have several days more life and joy in them."

"I find that quite commendable. Indeed, I do." Hawksby knew for a fact that a member of His Majesty's army could use a little charity at this very moment. He rubbed his stubbly chin, its roughness only emphasizing how long it had been since he'd left Miss Divine's town house that morning. "Do you reckon he is out there collecting them now? The wagoner, I mean."

"Why, I suppose he is," she said. "The servants are quite regular in their duties. Mrs. Vervaine runs the house on a very strict schedule."

Hawksby jumped up and whirled so quickly that his sword barely missed knocking the teapot off the table. "Lady Margaret, if you have no more appointments scheduled at this time, may I have your permission to leave? I have a very important matter to take care of."

"Why, of course you may," Maggie said, with no little amount of surprise—but, if all were told, a great deal of relief. "Don't let me detain you."

The captain had not shown such enthusiasm during the whole of the afternoon. It was a characteristic she hadn't expected of someone of such stiff-rumped propensities, and she wasn't sure what had prompted the transformation. It made his face quite appealing, dark shadows, sprouting beard, and all. Yes, Captain Hawksby was quite an impressive man, quite well-looking in a rugged sort of way, she had to admit—that is, if she was attracted to tall, massive warriors who looked more like they belonged in the Middle Ages. Yes, he could be considered handsome—when he wasn't frowning.

"Then I shall see you Tuesday next? Promptly at three on the clock. Good-bye, Lady Margaret," he said, bowing. He backed down the steps, swung round, and bounded across the yard, ignoring the paths. He leaped over a bed of geraniums, took a low-lying juniper bush in one bound, and headed for the stables.

"Captain Hawksby surely is an odd one, miss," said Flora, approaching the gazebo. "He didn't even come on a horse, so why is he going toward the mews?"

"Why, I have no idea, Flora. Perhaps the alleyway is closer to his destination. Whichever, we can be grateful for it. I had begun to despair we should ever be rid of him," Maggie said, sighing with relief.

The Lisbones' ball had been in progress for several hours when they backed into each other at the edge of the ballroom. "Lady Margaret," said a deep, rumbling voice, one she hadn't expected to hear again until the following week.

Maggie whirled around. "You're Captain Hawksby!"

"That is who I've always considered myself to be," he said, with a hint of a smile.

"I mean what are *you* doing here?" Her hushed tone implied he shouldn't be.

"I imagine we share the same excuse. I was invited."

Maggie's eyes narrowed, and she whispered accusingly, "Are you spying on me?"

A muscle in Hawksby's jaw tightened almost imperceptibly. "Only when duty calls, my lady," he said, the good feeling disappearing.

When he realized he'd bumped into Lady Margaret, he'd

actually been in a mood to be charitable—actually was eager to tell her how well her suggestion in the garden had worked for him. *Excess impresses.* By Jove! She'd hit the mark right on the head and made his last few days excessively pleasant ones.

Overwhelming Miss Divine with flowers had done the deed. Of course, Hawksby had only planned to mention that the flowers had been given to a very worthy cause.

But now, with her accusations of his spying on her, he wasn't of a mind to speak of it at all. No. Not any of it. And it would have made a lively story, too, he thought with disappointment. He'd practiced it over in his mind so the telling would sound just right. He'd never been a good storyteller like his brother William.

He wouldn't tell her about catching up with the wagoner behind the mews either, nor about his offering the stout fellow a tidy sum for his cargo, nor that he himself had insisted on taking up the ribbons and driving neck or nothing across Town to Miss Divine's town house, leaving a trail of petals and blossoms all the way to Covent Garden and beyond. Knowing Lady Margaret's propensity for adventure, he thought she'd especially like the part about dozens of urchins running into the street to pick up the stray posies.

They'd arrived with the wagon just as Miss Divine was leaving for the theatre. Of course, he'd not planned on telling Lady Margaret the recipient's exact identity, nor could he tell her of the delight on the actress's face when he presented her with not just a single flower, not just a bouquet, but a whole conveyance piled high with blossoms of every kind and color imaginable. His little buttercup's thanks was more than Hawksby could have anticipated.

"Oh, my captain," Miss Divine had exclaimed, clapping her hands and twirling in a circle before bestowing a kiss upon his cheek. Even the neighbors and passersby were impressed with the excess, just as Lady Margaret had said they would be. Eyes bulged, hands flew to mouths, lads laughed. The driver helped the maid bring the flowers into the house and when every vase and every bowl—even the umbrella stand—were overflowing with blossoms, Hawksby paid the wagoner to carry the remainder to the charity ward at the nearest hospital. He was sure Lady Chantry would have heralded that benevolent action wholeheartedly.

Shortly after that, a hackney coach had arrived to take Miss Divine to the theatre. When Hawksby handed her up into the cab, she'd told him she would see him after the late night performance. Then, as the coach rounded the corner, she threw him a kiss from the window.

As he'd watched Miss Divine's coach disappear from view, he'd entertained the thought that perhaps his being assigned to watch over Lady Margaret might have its upside after all. She was, after all, a member of the Quality and she was a woman—or nearly so. He was not all that sure of himself as far as this new realm of charming a woman was concerned, especially one as pampered as his little buttercup. And he didn't want it to be known or cast about that Captain Bixworth Hawksby had never had a high-flyer such as Miss Divine.

It was not as though Hawksby hadn't been with women. Camp followers, yes, stray bits of muslin along the waterfront and a dalliance with a widow in Belgium, but nothing or anyone who would tie him down.

He just hadn't been round Town much and really didn't know how to go about it, not with the war and most of his time having been spent on the Continent sleeping in tents, riding a horse all day, and leading men into battle.

Hawksby's childhood had been spent in northern England. Mama had been a Bixworth, wealthy landed gentry with connections to the best Westmoreland families going back to Norman times. His grandfather Twitchell Bixworth had been knighted, and his uncle was, after all, a bishop. His sister Hortense had been exceedingly successful in her first come-out in London Society several years ago and had married a baronet. Mama was quite pleased with that.

Papa's family did not rise to the heights of those of many of the Bixworth relatives, but he had wealth and land and a knight or two in his family background as well. No, Bixworth Hawksby had nothing to hang his head about, so Lady Margaret had no business looking down her nose at him. Besides, she couldn't. He was much taller than she, he realized as she glared up at him now in the Lisbones' fine ballroom.

Lady Margaret didn't exactly impress him as being the best example of the first stare of fashion as her sisters, but she was a resident of the city and the daughter of an earl. And she did seem to have bang-up-to-the-mark ideas when it came to surprises. This one had worked very well. By George, it did! It was just the disappointment of not telling her about it.

Yes, for a moment there when he bumped into her, he'd thought of thanking Lady Margaret, but not now. Probably not ever, he told himself with a strange feeling of disappointment.

He gave her a slight nod, as much of a bow as was possible in the crush. "If my memory serves me right, Lady Margaret, my duty doesn't begin until I come to collect you on Tuesday next."

"My thoughts exactly, Captain Hawksby," she said absently, trying to peek around his wide shoulders to see if her brother was lying in wait for her to send her off onto the dance floor with another potential husband. Daniel was being a vexation of the worst kind this evening.

Hawksby watched her furtive movements guiltily. Appear-

61

ances were so deceptive it was hard to remember she was but a child. Not only their brilliant red hair set the youngest Durham twins apart. Dressing them in burlap bags would not have hidden the charms which they so abundantly possessed, and at this moment he was looking straight down upon them.

Had he misread her flippant remarks? Hawksby jerked his head up to a safer view above her head. "Is someone annoying you, Lady Margaret? If so, I shall send the beggar to perdition."

Maggie blinked. She had been thinking of other things. "Don't be silly. Of course not," she said indignantly. "I can take care of myself."

He didn't know why he felt protective of the chit when he was so annoyed with her. "Then I assume you have separated yourself from your guardians on purpose," he said stiffly. Although he was still not officially on duty, Hawksby took his promise to watch after her quite seriously—something the young lady didn't seem to appreciate.

Maggie's face grew warm. She had done exactly that, separated herself not from her sisters, but from her brother, who had steered toward her the unwanted attentions of a young peer, Reginald Drollop, an exasperating popinjay who closely resembled a panting puppy. Daniel had evidently thought him a promising candidate for her affections. Lord Reginald had bothered her last Season, and it seemed he was determined to make a pest of himself during this one as well. She had already granted him one dance, and that was all he was going to get.

Even the captain looked good to her at this point as a refuge of sorts, a perfect shield. Thank goodness he was broad and tall.

Maggie stepped closer into his shadow and tried to peer around one of those wide shoulders—so close she had to take hold of his arm. Sakes alive, it was like holding on to a log. Lord Reginald, a look of confusion on his long, thin face, was standing on tiptoe in his high-heeled shoes to try to see over the crowd.

Maggie ducked down. She'd calculated the distance between where she was and where four of her sisters stood surrounded by a covey of young swains. Rebecca had Lord Finch hovering about her. Maggie was sure that the two would be making an announcement before the Season was out. Ruth was the only one not among the group.

It was not difficult for Maggie to tell her two eldest sisters apart. Although most people confused the several sets of Durham twins, the girls themselves never did. Each sister was as diverse as are lambs to their mothers by voice, gesture, scent, or soul.

When Lord Reginald came very close to glancing her way, Maggie dodged back out of sight. Still grasping the sleeve of the captain's blue uniform, she dared once again to peer around. She spotted her brother and Freddie, but though they were much closer, she considered it risky to join them. Her brother would only send her right back out onto the dance floor.

Maggie decided the wisest course to follow was to join her sisters. Then Captain Hawksby's deep voice came from somewhere over her head.

"Do you wish me to escort you to your brother, Lady Margaret? Or is it your design to take permanent possession of my arm for the evening?"

Maggie jumped, bumping his chin. She'd forgotten all about him. She'd also forgotten her hand clutched his jacket. "Good gracious, no! Of course not." She stared aghast at the rumples she'd made in his sleeve. "I'm perfectly capable of crossing the room by myself," she said, as she tried desperately to straighten out the wrinkles she'd made with a slap here and a stretch there. However, she was doing a very poor job of it, she feared.

Hawksby rubbed his chin as he tried to pull his other arm out of her reach. "I am sure my man will be capable of ironing out the creases, Lady Margaret. If you will excuse me, I believe someone is signaling me."

Maggie looked in the direction Captain Hawksby indicated. She didn't think it necessary for him to sound so grouchy. There were people milling round, but no one in particular seemed to be looking their way.

At the entrance to the ballroom, which was now nearly empty, a new arrival—a tall, blond, slender gentleman—caught her attention. He was saying something to a servant at his side. She hadn't heard him announced and wondered who he was.

Despite leaning slightly on a cane, he was still taller than all the men around him and dressed in an elegant black cutaway coat and breeches and a white silk waistcoat and cravat, in the fashion of Beau Brummel. There was an air of aristocracy about him, and he was undoubtedly one of the handsomest men to have come into the ballroom that evening. But he was not even looking in their direction, nor calling. Least of all was he signaling to anyone.

What a clanker, thought Maggie. If Captain Hawksby wanted to be rid of her, why didn't he just say so? "You are excused, Captain Hawksby," she said, as primly as she could. Neither lost any time in heading in opposite directions.

Maggie had intended to march straight across the room and not look back. However, temptation got the better of her. As soon as she'd reached her sisters, she couldn't resist glancing back over her shoulder. Captain Hawksby was in deep conversation with the blond gentleman. So he did know him. But, Maggie argued to herself, the stranger certainly hadn't been signaling the captain, or she would have seen it.

Then the most surprising thing happened. Her sister Ruth, who was promenading about the hall with another young man, passed behind the captain and his companion. Captain Hawksby did not move, but the blond gentleman whirled around. His lips formed her sister's name.

Although Ruth kept herself aloof from favoring anybody, she was never unkind. So Maggie took notice when her sister gave the young man in black a snappy exchange, which turned his face brilliant scarlet. How unusual a reaction from her sweet-tempered sister. What had the young man said besides her name that would bring such a response from her?

Maggie then saw her brother, Daniel, separate himself from the group with whom he was chatting and charge toward Ruth and the stranger, daggers drawn. But Ruth had already walked past the gentleman in black and, with another remark in his direction, continued on with her partner.

For a short time, Maggie caught glimpses of Captain Hawksby, not that she was particularly looking for him, nor did she expect or wish him to ask her to stand up with him. She saw him dance with only two women, their hostess, Lady Lisbone, and her turbaned roly-poly sister from Durham, Mrs. Hefflewicker. After that she lost sight of him altogether.

Lord Reginald finally hunted her down again and had her agreeing to stand up with him before she realized what she'd done. When he returned her to Freddie's side, Maggie found the earl and countess in another discussion of their most consuming subject of the evening—who would make promising husbands?

With a sigh, Maggie seated herself beside her sister and hoped no one else would ask her to dance.

"It's unfortunate Ruth cannot find someone as suitable as

Lord Finch," Daniel said.

Freddie looked at her husband with amusement. "You complained enough about Finch's attentions to Rebecca last year. You didn't even like the way he looked at her."

"Well, yes, I admit I was wrong there." He sighed. "I suppose if I keep turning away all the fellows that come bowing and scraping to me, I'll never get the girls married. But I'd hoped to find three or four promising candidates this evening."

"I told you it was not sensible for you to think you could wind up all their betrothals in one evening, especially when you have been so persnickety about the men they saw over the last year. Besides, it is very late," Freddie said, trying to stifle a yawn. "You said you wanted to start for Yorkshire at dawn."

"You are right, as always," Daniel said. "I suggest we go home, my love."

"I called for our carriage half an hour ago," Freddie said. "You look quite battle weary, dearest."

"Yes, well, it's true. I've been crushed and mangled enough for one evening."

Maggie quickly agreed with her brother. "Oh, yes, Freddie. Do let us go home."

"Then you will both have to help find your sisters and persuade them to leave," Freddie said. "I will express our thanks to Lord and Lady Lisbone."

"There is Ruth now," Maggie said. "That tall gentleman in black has stopped her again. The one who came in late. I don't think she likes him."

Daniel jumped up, growling, "I shall get Ruth. You both see to the others." Before he had finished his sentence, he set off for the other side of the room.

"Whatever was that all about?" Freddie asked. "Daniel

just said he was going to look more favorably upon possible suitors for you girls, and now that the best-looking of all appears, he charges out like he's ready to do battle."

"Hmm. I saw Ruth speak to the gentleman—or perhaps it was Captain Hawksby whom she addressed. No, I'm sure it was the other man," Maggie said. But whoever he was, it did seem her brother had taken a definite dislike to Captain Hawksby's acquaintance and was bent on rescuing Ruth.

"Well, you may be right," the countess said. "Anyway, we needn't be concerned anymore. Ruth has seen Daniel and they are now coming our way, so all is well."

Maggie's eyes crinkled in mirth. "Perhaps he doesn't want a brother-in-law who is handsomer than he."

Five

As planned, Lord and Lady Chantry left for Yorkshire on Sunday. At half three o'clock on Tuesday afternoon, Captain Hawksby arrived at Terrace Palace to escort Lady Margaret to her lecture. He was early for his appointed time by thirty minutes.

He found the young lady ready. It was not clear who was the more surprised—or pleased—that he was as early as she was.

Hawksby was ahead of schedule because he didn't know what arrangements had been made to carry them to the lecture hall. He didn't own a carriage, and he knew he would have to take time to stable his horse in the mews behind the mansion. All Lord Chantry had told him was that transportation would be provided.

Maggie was ready because she saw no sense in changing into a different dress from the one she'd put on that morning and only her sisters had seen. Besides, if she stayed in the same clothes, she could get in some extra reading.

Her twin was not as understanding. "At least wear your new bonnet, Maggie. It will blend nicely with the blues in your pelisse."

Maggie refused the bonnet which her sister suggested, because she already had her plain brown straw bonnet with the green ribbon on her head and the bow tied under her chin by the time her sister got the new one out of the hat box.

"Oh, Mary, will you never understand? I'm going to be with people who are more concerned with what's in a person's head, not on it."

Mary sighed. "At least let me tuck in some of this white lace and these pink silk roses into the band. I think that gives it a more stylish look," she said, stepping back to survey her handiwork.

Maggie pulled them out and left them on the dressing table. "Just because I'm going to a lecture on plants," she declared, "doesn't mean I have to look like one. Anyway, I will only knock your folderols off getting into the coach." A comfortable pair of gloves thin enough to enable her to grasp a pencil and a serviceable canvas bag large enough to hold the tickets for the lecture and her note-taking materials were all the necessities she considered appropriate for the afternoon. "I'm ready," she said.

Her five sisters and Mrs. Vervaine, Beetleworth, and Flora all saw Maggie and Captain Hawksby off in one of the family carriages. Hawksby felt as though he was being inspected for an audience with the Prince Regent for all the attention their departure received. All of her sisters, of course, were beautifully coiffed and elegantly dressed for an afternoon of making social calls.

However, of all the Durham siblings, it was his charge's face which shown the brightest and happiest as she sat on the edge of her seat, an ugly bag clutched on her lap, her nose pressed to the window, the riot of red curls sticking out every which way from under that ridiculous straw hat. Where had he gotten the crack-brained idea that she could show him how to acquire a bit of Town bronze?

There wasn't a thing wrong as far as Hawksby could see with Lady Margaret's eyes or vocal chords, though. He swore she didn't miss a thing that was going on outside, chattering constantly about the people, the trees, the birds, the bees, and the little boy who ran across the street in front of the coach. She even mentioned that missing cobbles from the roadway were the culprits which made the carriage bounce about, giving them such a bumpy ride. She didn't seem to mind the jolts, though, and Hawksby wondered how she could tell the coach was lurching. She bounced about so much on her own.

Hawksby, on the other hand, sat back and folded his arms across his chest, preparing himself for a boring afternoon. His responsibility for the keeping and care of Lady Margaret Durham had begun.

He tried to keep in mind he was supposed to be annoyed with her. He hadn't expected to see her at the ball. He'd only come for a few minutes that evening to pay his respects to Lord and Lady Lisbone and to pick up an old friend who was to accompany him to the theatre.

If Lady Margaret hadn't been so determined to use him poorly—like some sort of fortress in the middle of the floor —he'd have been in a more charitable mood and thanked her for suggesting an excess of flowers. Oh, he could tell when she bumped into him she'd been hiding from someone, but she'd denied it. How was he supposed to protect her if she was going to lie to him? For a mere girl, she had a grip like a Cornish wrestler. His twisted jacket had proved that.

He had spent the evening of the Lisbones' ball with his friend, as it wasn't often he came to Town. Because of it, Hawksby had not been able to spend the night with Miss Divine. Clugg was not convinced of his master's excuse for his wrinkled coat when he arrived home, however, and wanted to know if he'd been wrestling with a bear to have such creases. The batman didn't know how close his guess had been.

"We're here," Maggie cried, making Hawksby's jolt back to the present rather nerve shattering.

The footman had the door opened and the step lowered as soon as the coach came to a halt. Hawksby scrambled out first and extended his hand to help her down.

She caught him unawares. "How many times have you been to the Royal Institution, Captain Hawksby?"

"Never have, my lady."

"What! You have never been *ever?*" Maggie draped her carpet bag over his hand, rendering it useless to assist her. She leaned on the quick-thinking footman's arm instead and descended to the pavement.

Hawksby looked helplessly at the bag and gritted his teeth. Damn! She made it sound as though there was a big hole in his education.

She shook her head. "As old as you are? I cannot believe it."

His eyebrows lowered until his eyes were mere slits. "I am not doddering yet, Lady Margaret."

The look she gave him made him wonder if he really was. She was on the pavement now straightening her bonnet, which had gone crooked when she knocked it to one side getting out of the coach.

"Well, I hope not, but in any case," she said brightly, taking back her bag, "since we have arrived early I shall have time to show you some of the exhibits in the basement before the lecture begins."

She was already up the steps and into the entrance hall before he'd had time to give instructions to John Coachman.

Hawksby caught up to her halfway across the rotunda, heading for the stairwell to the basement. "Hurry, Captain. We don't have much time to spend before we must go into the auditorium."

"I am sure there will be plenty of seats, Lady Margaret."
He couldn't imagine anyone coming out on a fine summer
afternoon to hear a lecture on the *Effects of Industrialisation
and Overpopulation on the Flora and Fauna of London*.

Maggie entered the first room at the bottom of the stairs.
"We will start with the exhibit of household inventions. These
are the newest of kitchen stoves, roasters and broilers, and you
know Lord Rumford invented a drip coffeepot. There is a min-
eralogical exhibit upstairs, too, but I'm sure there won't be
time for you to absorb all of that. I just can't believe you have
not been here before," she said, shaking her head.

She talked to him as though he were a schoolboy. It was
true Hawksby had never set foot inside the Royal Institution
before. In fact, he'd never been in any of the historical
museums, art galleries, or lending libraries which London
had to offer. He'd attended a few routs and soirees at the invitation of his cohorts in arms, many from noble families, and
been invited to their fine Town residences. Hawksby had
friends enough in the upper tiers of Society to make him
accepted in most of the finest clubs in St. James's Street. But,
devil take it, young officers on leave didn't spend precious
time in educational pursuits.

Wounded pride spoke for him. "I've been fighting a war,
madam!"

Maggie's mouth dropped open in a big silent O.

Hawksby let his breath out in one big *swoosh*. That was
more like it.

The corners of her mouth began to twitch. "Cry even?"
she said.

Hawksby looked at her quizzically. He hadn't heard that
expression for years. "Cry even," he replied, extending his
arm. "Shall we go find ourselves seats for the lecture, Lady
Margaret?"

On the first floor was a semicircular lecture room with rising, cushioned seats. To his amazement, Hawksby estimated there to be about nine hundred on the main floor with accommodations for some two hundred in the gallery. Already half of the seats were taken. By the time the lecture began, at least three-quarters of the seats were filled.

The lecture was given by a professor of chemistry from Liverpool. Although he wasn't a great speaker, Hawksby did find some merit in his statistics of how ground movements of citizens affected the displacement of plants and animals— very much like the war on the Continent. But aside from having enough plant and animal life to put food on his table, trees to give him shade, and horses to ride, Hawksby had little interest in the subject.

He found it more amusing to watch Lady Margaret's face as she hung on the professor's every word. Part of the mystery of her big canvas bag was solved for him, too, when she drew out her pencil and pad to record much of what the speaker said. What did she hope to accomplish by it? She'd be married someday managing some man's home, bearing his children, and arranging balls, not checking on how many beetles were chewing up the elms.

After the lecture was over, Hawksby thought they would leave. He was wrong. Neither was he ready for the surge of people pouring toward the dais to talk to the professor or to form little circles of their own to discuss the lecture.

Lady Margaret, he found, was not in the least reticent about putting forth her own opinions. Several times he lost track of the inquisitive brat. If he hadn't been taller than most of the people in the hall, he'd have lost her altogether. Damn, but she was an elusive little witch. Each time he found her and tried to steer her toward the exit, she'd slip away from him and be back talking to someone or another about the effects of coal smoke on the environment and how the growth of the population was ruining the habitat of birds and bugs and other creatures.

Hawksby heard her mention Dr. MacDougal several times in her conversations, which reminded him he'd forgotten to broach the subject of the Scotsman to Lord Chantry before he left.

The captain's thoughts had been on other things during the last few days. He'd found out the reason for Lord Basilbone's sudden departure from London. It seemed Basilbone's father had ordered him to take a wife. Hawksby had heard the banns had been read in the prospective bride's parish church in Shropshire and the wedding had taken place a few days ago. That should well enough take care of any competition for Miss Divine's attentions from that corner, thank goodness, because it was going to be all he could do to keep tabs on Lord Chantry's youngest sister.

It seemed Hawksby no sooner got near Lady Margaret than he'd be shut out by a swirl of people moving about the hall. Fortunately, he only had to follow the sound of her voice to find her. At least Lady Margaret didn't have one of those sweet trilling, lilting voices that irritated a man's eardrums. Yes, he could say that for her.

The middle-aged man she was now speaking to had a thick accent. Sounded German. Curly-haired fellow, not much taller than she. Hawksby thought the man was standing too close to her—didn't like the way he was looking at her, either. *Good lord*, he thought. *I'm beginning to sound like Chantry.*

Hawksby recognized Dr. MacDougal's name again. She was telling Curly-head she knew the professor. Hawksby elbowed his way through the throng, which wasn't too difficult with his bulk and tenacity. One scowl from him and people automatically gave way.

Hawksby nearly knocked a woman's hat off and turned to apologize. Oh, drat! He'd lost sight of Lady Margaret again. Couldn't take his eyes off the child an instant or she'd disappear.

"Just a few lectures—that sort of thing," the earl had said.

"Damn and blast! Why me?" Hawksby mumbled. The whole of Wellington's finest would be needed to keep track of this one brat.

Hawksby finally found himself in the press behind her, near enough to hear snips and snaps of the conversation, but not near enough to grab her.

By all that was holy! The bugger was talking to her about the reproductive habits of a ladybird named *Coccinella*. A young girl shouldn't even know about that side of a man's life, let alone discuss such goings-on. And there she was—it wasn't hard to hear her—telling him of hunting alone in the Cheviot Hills with this professor from Edinburgh. No wonder Curly-head thought he could speak of matters which should be private.

The earl had been right that his sister would need protection at such gatherings as this. Hawksby would have darkened the man's daylights right then and there if he hadn't been in such a crowded gathering. Instead, he could do no more than take her firmly by the arm. Just before he pulled her away from the jackanapes, he met the surprised cad nose to nose, lowered his imposing brows, and hissed, "Bounder. I will not have you talking to Lady Margaret in such a manner."

"Whatever do you think you are doing?" Maggie said, trying to shake her arm loose from his hold. She found taking back possession of her limb from Captain Hawksby was not as easy as she thought.

Hawksby marched her out of the lecture hall.

"Where are you taking me, Captain Hawksby?"

"Home where you belong," he said in such a way that for once Maggie didn't argue. She'd ring a peal over his head later after she'd caught her breath.

Hawksby lowered his head like a charging bull and made for the entrance. It seemed the blame for such misguided ideas that had been put into this young lady's head fell squarely on this MacDougal fellow. Had Lord Chantry really checked the man out? Hawksby was beginning to wish he could meet up with this professor from Edinburgh and let him know what he really thought of him.

"Am I to believe what I think I heard, that you were permitted to go off into the hills alone with this Dr. MacDougal person?"

She glared at him. "Of course. Many times. He persuaded me it was very important for me to assist him. My sisters didn't take as much interest in catching specimens for him as I."

Hawksby snorted. He had no idea that this business of playing duenna would be so difficult. Wily fellows seemed to wait round every corner to seduce gullible lasses, and he had one of the most gullible on his hands for the devil knew how long.

As soon as they entered the coach, Maggie settled back—or, more accurately, plopped back—on the seat, clutching her bag to her chest. My goodness! A gentleman couldn't even finish a sentence to her before Captain Hawksby was ready to accuse him of some sort of dastardly intentions.

"You were very rude," Maggie said. "I didn't even get to finish what I was saying."

"Your brother would be extremely angry should I let a man, a stranger no less, speak so plainly of . . . of such matters with you."

76

Maggie stared at Hawksby. "That was Herr Wehrhahn from Germany."

"Well, that explains it, then."

"Explains what?"

"Blücher may have been a brilliant general, but he was no angel, you know. They think they won the war for us at Waterloo. Now they think they can win our women."

"Your women? I didn't know I was your woman."

Hawksby cleared his throat. "Well, of course not. I mean, you belong to Lord Chantry, and I'm standing in for him while he is away."

"I didn't get to hear all of what Herr Wehrhahn was going to say."

"And you will not if I have my way." Hawksby lowered his voice. "You don't even know what he was suggesting, do you?"

"Of course, I do. He wants to go visit Dr. MacDougal. He thinks they will have much in common."

"I don't doubt they will."

"Herr Wehrhahn is a great admirer of Dr. MacDougal. He said he'd give anything if he could travel to Edinburgh to meet him."

"Good," said Hawksby. "I hope he goes."

"I do, too," said Maggie, "because I told him if he does that, I'd like to travel with him."

Hawksby nearly jumped off the seat. "You did what?"

"You need give it no nevermind. I will get to hear what he was going to suggest. I invited him to call on me tomorrow afternoon."

"You didn't."

Maggie stuck out her chin. "Yes, I did. I told him of the insects which I have found in London parks that I have not been able to identify. They are in the special box which I keep in my wardrobe. He wants to see them."

"He wants to see your insects? And you believed him?" Hawksby hit his forehead with the palm of his hand. "I've never heard that tarradiddle used before on an innocent young woman. Well, I won't permit you to receive him."

"You will do no such thing. Herr Wehrhahn is a noted entomologist from Berlin. It would be bad diplomacy to turn him away."

He knew she spoke the truth. The government didn't need a national incident with one of their allies. What a rumble. Tomorrow Hawksby had planned on taking Miss Divine for an afternoon walk in Hyde Park. "What time is Herr Wehrhahn to call on you tomorrow?" He knew what she was going to say before she said it.

"I told him to come round about four o'clock." Maggie had made sure that the visit would fall right at the time her sisters were to attend an afternoon of musical entertainment by Lady Dipram's niece, who attempted to play the pianoforte and sang with a voice which sounded like highland bagpipes.

Hawksby sighed. He'd have to think of something to tell Miss Divine. "I will be there," he said, sitting back and folding his arms across his chest.

"You will not. You weren't hired to chaperone me in my own house, just when I go out of it."

Hawksby knew he had to speak to her somehow, warn her about older men like Wehrhahn. But how could he do that? Nor could he ask her sisters. They weren't much older than she. What she needed was a mother or an older woman. As long as he was with her, he could protect her. But how could he trust she'd be all right when she had only her sisters or servants around?

They rode in silence the remainder of the trip back to Terrace Palace. By the time they'd arrived, he knew he had to say *something*. She was too trusting, too gullible, too likely to fall into the man's evil clutches.

The captain cleared his throat. "Lady Margaret, before you get out of the coach, there is a matter of some delicacy of which I must speak, since Lord Chantry is not here to advise you." He cleared his throat a second time, deeper. "I want you to think of me as a brother."

He was not looking at her directly as he said this, so Maggie couldn't see his eyes. In fact, Maggie realized she'd never really had a chance to look into his eyes. They were always shadowed by those woolly wings.

Maggie watched his forehead crease, the great brows flare up then down, and the muscle work in his strong jaw in such a way that she knew Captain Hawksby had something of great import to relate. She tried to imagine him as Daniel, but she got nowhere doing that. She looked down at her hands in her lap and waited.

Captain Hawksby stared straight ahead at the back of the seat across from him. "Herr Wehrhahn was speaking to you of things that aren't proper conversation for a gentlewoman's ear. Didn't I hear him speaking of his . . . that is . . . a lady-bird?"

Maggie raised an eyebrow. "Why, yes, he did," she said.

"A . . . a Miss Cicconella, I believe?"

Maggie blinked. *"Miss?"*

"Well, he didn't exactly say Miss. I was just trying to be polite."

"It is *Coccinella*. C-O-C-C-I-N-E-L-L-A. He wanted to know if I had seen the ladybird *Coccinella*. Quite common."

"I am quite sure she is, Lady Margaret. You don't need to

spell her name out to me. But the fact is that a gentleman doesn't speak in Polite Society about ladybirds, especially to a young woman of good breeding."

Maggie peeked up at him. Something was amiss here. "The *Coccinella* we were speaking of is a little red beetle with black spots, Captain Hawksby. There are many of them in our gardens. You thought I was talking about something entirely different, didn't you?"

Hawksby had the uncomfortable feeling his ears were turning cherry red. "No, no," he said, casting about desperately for some way of saving himself. "I just didn't think you'd have any left. You know . . . what the professor said. The coal dust and all. I thought they'd have all been killed by the smoke by now. If in fact . . . you do have some left in your garden perhaps you'll be good enough to point them out to me sometime." He let out his breath in a big *whoosh*.

Now Maggie glanced fully up at him, a questioning look in her eyes, but he was pushing open the door of the carriage. "I'd be glad to anytime, Captain Hawksby."

Hawksby hurried Lady Margaret to the door and made his departure as quickly as was possible.

That evening after dinner Maggie drew Ruth aside. "Ruthie, what is a ladybird? And I don't mean the beetle."

Lady Ruth looked askance. "Wherever did you happen upon that word, dear?"

"Oh, I just overheard some men talking."

"Well, I wish you had not. It is a subject gentlewomen aren't supposed to know about. Some men make . . . they make acquaintances of women not of our social standing. That is to say, they cannot marry them, so they develop a . . . friendship instead."

"I think that sounds quite nice, Ruthie," Maggie said. "I

don't know why all the classes cannot be friends. We were at Knocktigh."

"I know, dear, but we are in London now. It is nothing that need concern you, and I hope you don't eavesdrop again."

Six

Hawksby drove his horse neck-or-nothing westward along the Strand. By Jove! He was going to make certain he was at the front portico of Terrace Palace at half four o'clock, thirty minutes earlier than Lady Margaret had said.

As he leaped off his mount, Hawksby threw the reins to a houseboy and rushed up the steps. He'd promised to protect the earl's sister. Yes, he had, and protect her he would . . . even if it meant he'd had to fib a little to get Miss Divine to excuse him from taking her for their stroll in Hyde Park.

Beetleworth greeted the captain with a wide smile. "Lady Margaret asked that you be shown into the library as soon as you came, Captain. She said you'd be early, sir."

Well done, Hawksby congratulated himself. The little minx was learning that the officer her brother had appointed to advise her in his stead was not some dimwit she could throw off guard easily. Hawksby handed his shako and gloves to a servant and followed the butler down the long corridor which led to the book room. He kept his sword. It would be well that Herr Wehrhahn know from the beginning his adversary meant business and would tolerate no dallying with Lady Margaret.

The one thing Hawksby had not contemplated when he'd accepted this commission was having complications from other men. He had been thinking more along the lines of girlish escapades such as trying to scamper off unchaperoned to Vauxhall Gardens or skinning her knees by falling off the garden wall. For someone so young, Lady Margaret certainly was beginning to show a tendency for attracting members of the opposite sex like moths to a flame. By all that was holy, her hair was the right color for it, too.

That Scot MacDougal had not concerned him overly much. He was four hundred miles away. But now having to add a German to the pile was outside of enough. Hawksby wondered if the termagant had any other admirers hidden under rocks somewhere that he didn't know about.

He looked round as he marched into the room and smiled smugly. Hah! Just as he had planned, he'd arrived before Curly-head.

Lady Margaret came forward holding out her hand. "I'm so sorry you missed Herr Wehrhahn," she said.

Down came the sweeping eyebrows. "You said he was expected at four o'clock," Hawksby barked, trying at the same time to erase from his mind what a pretty picture she made. For once her hair was neatly in place, as if someone with some sense of style had a hand in its arrangement.

However, his glower of displeasure didn't wipe the smile from Lady Margaret's face, for she went right on with her cheerful report. "Herr Wehrhahn sent round a note saying he would have to come an hour or so early. Last night members of the Royal Society asked him to go on a lecture tour in southern England for the next couple of weeks. Only this morning, he found out the hired post chaise on which they ticketed him was leaving at three o'clock this afternoon. He has just now left. I thought surely you'd pass each other coming and going."

Hawksby tried to collect his thoughts. Damn and blast! She'd done it again on purpose, he reckoned, deliberately foiling his well-thought-out stratagem. He stopped just short of shaking his finger in her face. "I made a pledge to your brother, Lady Margaret. The purpose of my being here is to make certain you behave in a fit and proper manner. These occurrences cannot be repeated, or I shall have to notify his lordship."

"Whatever for?"

"Do not play the innocent with me, my lady. You know it is not acceptable that you should be alone with a man like that."

"Mrs. Vervaine was here," Maggie said, looking back over her shoulder.

A tiny stick figure dressed in deep blue-gray bombazine stepped out of the shadows on the far side of the room. "Good afternoon, Captain Hawksby," came a dictatorial voice accompanied by a cacophony of jingles and jangles set off by the variety of keys, gadgets, and household tools which swung from the chatelaine wrapped around her waist.

No one ever questioned the authority of the pint-sized housekeeper of Terrace Palace, and the fact she had been present relieved Hawksby of a great deal of anxiety in knowing Lady Margaret had been foiled of any attempt she may have had in circumventing the proprieties.

"Hah!" he expostulated. "Then Herr Wehrhahn's visit came to no other outcome than to say good-bye."

"Oh, you are wrong there," Maggie said. Picking up an ornately decorated wooden box from a tabletop, she opened it and stuck it under his nose. The lid and sides were carved with such intricately designed Celtic symbols that a person would think it a jewelry box. Instead it held five rows of insects, one a butterfly of exquisite colors that could readily be called a gem in itself. But the others? As far as Hawksby could ascertain, they looked like any number of the ugly creatures which had crept and crawled into his boots and bed at night in his tent during the war.

"These are the insects I've not been able to identify. Herr Wehrhahn named some of them, which he recognized as European, though not usually found in England. However, there were two he couldn't identify at all. He was quite baffled and asked if he could take my sketches of them with him on his journeys to see if he could find someone who might know their names. If they prove to be insects which are harmful to crops and perhaps have come in on ships from the Orient or elsewhere, my find may be very important to the importation business."

The minx's eyes glittered so as she spoke that if Hawksby hadn't seen the bugs himself, he would have thought she'd discovered a pirate's chest of jewels. He could think of no response that would have sounded sensible, so he said nothing.

It didn't matter, because Maggie was intent on having her say anyway. "Herr Wehrhahn also said he would take the time for me to run up and get another box of insects which I wished him to see. I keep all the containers in my wardrobe pushed back under my dresses. Mary hates to see them sitting about even though I latch them shut. She is certain the specimens are not at all dead and will crawl out in the night." This sent her into another fit of hearty laughter.

As soon as she could control her merriment, Maggie opened the second box, which was made of much plainer wood. She would have stuck that under Hawksby's nose, as well. But he was aware of her intent and managed to grab the box from her hands before he was assaulted. He held it out at arm's length. He'd had enough of insects when he'd been on campaign on the Continent.

"Herr Wehrhahn was very complimentary about my presentation, but he also was sharp-eyed enough to point out that one of my grasshoppers had lost a leg. See," she said. "I shall want to find another with all its appendages to replace it before I show them to Dr. MacDougal. 'Twould never do to have a five-legged grasshopper in my collection." This sent her into another peal of laughter.

It certainly didn't take much to amuse Lady Margaret, Hawksby thought. He tried to focus on the beautiful scroll-work around the first box to avoid looking at its occupants. What he didn't like was hearing about MacDougal again. At least he was rid of Curly-head. "It is too bad Herr Wehrhahn must leave London so soon," he said, not in the least sorry to hear the man had left.

"You needn't be sorry," she said. "You shall be able to see him again. As soon as his tour is over, he has been invited back by the Royal Society to give some lectures here in London. He said he'd be very flattered if I would attend. Isn't that splendid?"

The best news I've heard all day, Hawksby thought.

Maggie closed the box and placed it beside the more ornate one on the table. "Herr Wehrhahn said he has always wished to meet the famous Dr. MacDougal to compare their research." Maggie sighed. "I told him how much I wanted to return to Knocktigh. That's my home on the Scottish border. It means hill house—but of course you know that."

He didn't, but he nodded anyway. He wasn't about to let her in on anything else which could give her more fodder to proclaim him a dunce.

"Herr Wehrhahn was very sympathetic about my wanting to go home," she told him. "That's more than I can say for the members of my family. In fact, he said if he can arrange to go to Edinburgh, he would be willing to escort me to the border."

Hawksby's hands clenched at his sides. *I'll just bet he would.*

Maggie clapped her hands. "So I think I shall write to Daniel and tell him of Herr Wehrhahn's generous offer and ask him if I may go."

"Over my dead body," mumbled Hawksby. His hand moved across his body to come to rest upon the hilt of his sword.

"Are you all right, Captain Hawksby?" Maggie asked. "You don't look quite the thing."

Hawksby was saved from answering that question by Ruth, who at that moment stuck her head into the room. "May I come in, dear? You didn't forget, did you, that you said you'd accompany us this afternoon?"

"Do come in, Ruthie. Of . . . of course, I hadn't forgotten. Captain Hawksby was just leaving."

Hawksby could see she'd forgotten her promise to her sister, but he was just as glad to have the excuse to go. "It is my fault entirely, Lady Ruth," he said, bowing. "I'm afraid my call has disturbed your afternoon."

"Not at all, Captain," Ruth said, sweetly. "It is just that Mary is going with Babette and Antoinette to an exhibition of china painting and since Maggie had no other plans she promised she would accompany Rebecca and me on a ride in Hyde Park. Lord Finch should be arriving any moment with his family's barouche. You are welcome to accompany us. There will be more than enough room for another gentleman."

A quick glance at the floor clock told Hawksby it was barely four o'clock. If he hurried, he might have a chance of finding Miss Divine at home and still persuade her to take a walk—but not in Hyde Park. Perhaps in the smaller, relatively solitary Green Park. Not that he was afraid of running into any of the Durham family. No, not at all. He'd be proud to promenade with someone as beautiful as Miss Divine upon his arm, but perhaps another day for Hyde Park would be better. Strange that he'd forgotten about her, but Lady Margaret did seem to have a jarring ability for putting him off his direction.

He hadn't gotten to the front door before he heard his name called from behind. "Captain Hawksby, don't forget that we are to go back to the Royal Institution on Saturday."

He managed to skid to a stop before knocking into Beetleworth, who was holding the door open for him. "The Royal Institution, Lady Margaret?" What could she mean? There weren't any lectures that he recalled. In fact, he'd received no list at all of any more excursions.

"You are very forgetful, Captain Hawksby. You must write down my schedule if you can't remember any better than that. You said you would like to see the gem collection."

"Oh, yes. Right. Right. And that was to be at?"

"Call for me at ten o'clock in the morning, Captain. I prefer to be there before it is too crowded. There was also an item that you said you wished to look up in their library reference room. You do remember?"

Hawksby groaned. The little minx was fudging to get out of something else. He knew it. But one look into those pleading eyes and he gave in, fool that he was. He'd barely be back at his quarters by that time of the morning. He had looked forward to a long pleasurable Friday eve with Miss Divine after the final curtain. There were to be two performances on Saturday and one on Sunday, and his little buttercup said she'd be too tired to entertain him on those nights. Monday rehearsals were starting for a new play, and she needed her rest for those if she was to have a good chance of capturing a major role.

Since he couldn't see Miss Divine, Hawksby had promised Spencer that he'd accompany him on Saturday night for a round of the men's clubs. Now this pickle.

"You do remember, don't you, Captain?" Maggie repeated.

Lady Ruth stood behind her, smiling at him.

He glanced out of the corner of his eye at the butler. His eyebrows were raised in expectation. Hawksby clicked his heels together. "I look forward to it, Lady Margaret. Ten o'clock it is," he said, bowing again.

Then before the widgeon could trick him into anything else, he made a smart turnabout, shot out the door, bounded down the steps, and, grabbing the reins from the boy at the curb, leaped upon his horse and clattered into the street.

Damn you, Chantry. Why couldn't you stay home and take care of your own? I shall be wasted away to nothing by the time you come back.

The fashionable set was out in full array, promenading and bowing and prancing by on their horses for everyone to observe and gossip and see who was with whom. The day was lovely, enticing the Durham sisters to walk instead of ride, so the coach was stopped along the carriageway and a footman helped them down.

The only reason Maggie had been so agreeable to coming was the promise of a hike along the Serpentine where the grasses grew tall around the lake and presented the possibility for her to find herself another grasshopper with the proper number of legs. She had brought an extra handkerchief in her reticule in which to wrap it if she could find the right species.

But to her disappointment, her sister Ruth was not in accord with her plans. She soon made it known she had a scheme of her own.

To allow Rebecca and Lord Finch to have a bit of time together, Ruth feigned feeling very warm and said she wished to sit for a moment in the shade of an oak tree, urging the young couple to go ahead without them.

"Maggie and I shall catch you up in a few minutes," she said, yanking Maggie down upon the bench beside her.

"But I want to . . ." Maggie started.

"No, you don't, dear," Ruth said, placing her finger upon her younger sister's lips before she could protest. "Allow them to go ahead. They find so little chance to be alone. The footman will be only a few steps behind them, and we can keep them in sight."

"Oh," Maggie said. A dawning look played across her face as she watched the couple walk away, oblivious to everyone around them. "Do you think it is possible to find men as nice as our sisters have done?"

Ruth was silent.

Maggie didn't take notice, for she had her own questions rising in her mind about this strange behavior that was striking the members of her family. "I've noticed that if Daniel gets out-of-sorts, Freddie only has to smile or whisper something in his ear and he's agreeable again."

Ruth murmured softly.

"I wish Mr. Pettigrew were here to escort me," Maggie said, bobbing her head to emphasize her predicament. "He is always nice and he likes all kinds of intellectual things."

"Well, he isn't . . . nor is Georgette," Ruth finally said, a hint of a smile finally appearing on her lips. "They are happily married and settled in their house in Sussex. I don't think they would be the least bit interested in chaperoning you."

Maggie conceded that point. Two of her sisters had made very good marriages, indeed, and it looked as if a third would soon be added to that list.

"Well, I am glad *you* are not being so foolish," Maggie said, giving such a definite nod that her bonnet fell over one eye. She pushed it back up and waited for Ruth's agreement.

Her sister was looking down at her gloved hands, which were folded in her lap. "There is a young man for whom I hold great regard," she said, blushing profusely.

"Oh, Ruthie. You are in love with someone? Why did you not say so? I would not have gone on as I did. Is he someone I know?"

Ruth turned sad eyes toward her. "You may have seen him, but I don't think you have been formally introduced. He has been at some of the musical entertainments to which we've gone and he attended the play at the theatre in Drury Lane last week."

"There were so many gentleman who came to our box. Let me guess which one he was."

"No, he didn't come to the box."

"For whatever reason? He surely likes you, doesn't he? I cannot imagine he is not madly in love with you," Maggie said, teasingly.

Tears glistened in Ruth's eyes.

Maggie felt terrible that she could have hurt her sweet sister with her teasing. "He isn't married already, is he?"

Ruth shook her head.

"Then what can be the problem? If you like each other, why hasn't he asked Daniel for your hand?"

"Our brother seems to have taken a dislike to him. I cannot imagine why, because I know Daniel isn't cruel."

"Cruel," cried Maggie, forgetting all about her sister's troubles. "If you don't think foistering that dribble Lord Reginald on me at the Lisbones' ball wasn't outside of enough, I don't know what is."

Maggie looked so genuinely discomforted that Ruth couldn't help but laugh. She patted her hand. "Forget what I said, dear. I'm sure it is just a passing fancy on my part. Here come Rebecca and Lord Finch. Just seeing the happiness in their eyes when they gaze at each other is enough to make me to rejoice."

Now that she had heard Maggie tell Captain Hawksby she didn't have anything planned until Saturday, Ruth would not hear any excuses from her sister for not accepting an invitation to Mrs. Hefflewicker's on the following afternoon.

"Rebecca is attending because she knows Lord Finch will be there. The other girls are invited for drives in the Park, and their abigails will be going with them. I shall be glad for your company."

"Mrs. Hefflewicker is a skitterbrain, Ruthie. Remember when we first met her at the Crown and Hare Inn last year on our way to London? She caused such a hubbub the first time she saw us. She screamed and told her husband she was going blind. She found out later, of course, that we were all sets of twins and she wasn't seeing double. I don't know why you accept so many of her invitations, even if her sister is the Countess of Lisbone."

Ruth smiled as she recalled the incident. "She may seem silly, but she means well and enjoys entertaining in the lovely apartment she and the squire are given in the Lisbones' palace. I don't suppose her house is nearly so grand in Durham. So when she comes for the Season she must save up enough memories to last her for the remainder of the year, when she returns home. She said she really is disappointed that you haven't accepted any of her invitations."

Maggie looked guiltily at her hands. "I have only been thinking of myself. I'm sorry, Ruthie."

"Perhaps you might feel more willing to go if you hear she often is visited by Mrs. Sylvester Wrenn, who is known to be quite an authority on the birds of London. She has written a book on the subject and is now making a study of all the counties."

Maggie's eyes lit up. "So she must know something about insects. For if it weren't for insects, we wouldn't have half as many birds—or flowers."

Ruth smiled. "I'm sure she does. I also heard she is a member of the Society for the Encouragement of Arts, Manufacture, and Commerce."

"They allow ladies in such societies?"

"Yes, some of them do. And now that the Society is not meeting for the rest of the summer, I believe she will be there."

"Oh, my," Maggie said, "I should like that." All of her objections set aside, she went eagerly to Mrs. Hefflewicker's drawing room that afternoon, where she soon found herself immersed in deep conversation with several ladies and gentleman who had something more on their minds than the latest fashion.

Mrs. Hefflewicker, looking very much like a large soufflé in black lace, was easily distinguishable from the rest of her guests. Her silver hair was always piled high for her special gatherings, and her dark eyes shone like ebony buttons set in plump cheeks which turned rosier as the afternoon wore on. The famous refreshments were more than most of the *beau monde* would see in a week of such calls. In fact, her buffets were as much a feast for the eyes as for the stomach.

She bounced about the room with surprising agility for someone as big around as she was tall, urging everyone to eat, while introducing the most unlikely people to one another. So it was that she appeared suddenly at Maggie's elbow. "Here you are, my dear," she said with a throaty laugh. "I've been looking all over for you. There is someone who wishes to meet you."

Before she knew it, Maggie found herself being pulled to the other side of the room.

"Lady Margaret, may I present Sir Spencer Packard," Mrs. Hefflewicker said, smiling widely. "Lord Lisbone's nephew. He is visiting from his home in Hampshire."

The man turned his head slightly in a most beguiling manner, and Maggie found herself looking up at the handsomest face she'd ever seen—the same face she'd seen at the Lisbones' ball, the man who had been dressed in black then and was still. The man who'd said something that brought her sister to anger and a dark look to her brother's countenance. Without thinking, she placed her hand in his. He brought it to his lips.

"I am honored, my Lady Margaret—with hair the color of an autumn sunset."

One glance at the blond locks spilling over his forehead, caressing her fingers, and Maggie looked about frantically for Ruth. But it wasn't slender Ruth who appeared. It was a great blue wall. "Captain Hawksby," she gasped, pulling her hand away abruptly from the gentleman in front of her. "Whatever are you doing here?"

"You seem to have a habit of asking me that," he said, in his usual gruff manner. "If you must know, I've come to accompany my friend to the Guards' Club. Do you mind?" he asked, placing his hand firmly upon Sir Spencer's shoulder.

"Of course, I don't," Maggie said, too surprised to realize she was blushing.

"It's about time you got here, Hawksby," Sir Spencer scolded. "I thought I should have to go it alone if you didn't turn up soon."

"Never," Hawksby growled.

Grumpy as usual, Maggie mused. As the two men walked away, she saw Sir Spencer leaned heavily on his walking stick. He limped alongside the captain and turned to him with a laugh. "You always do appear at the most inopportune times, Hawksby. Good day to you, ladies," he threw back over his shoulder with a devastating smile.

"Well, I never," spouted Maggie.

Mrs. Hefflewicker didn't appear the least perturbed by the outlandish behavior of the two men. In fact, she seemed quite amused by the whole conundrum. But before Maggie could say anything more, Ruth was at her side. "I think it is time, sister, to thank our hostess for a lovely afternoon. Lord Finch and his mother have been kind enough to see Rebecca home."

"Do come again. You don't need to wait upon a formal invitation, my dear," Mrs. Hefflewicker said, laughing jovially in Ruth's direction. "You know you are always welcome."

Maggie waited until they were seated in their coach before turning to face her sister. "Oh, Ruth, I'm so sorry I acted like such a ninnyhammer. But I vow I was too taken by the rake to put him in his place. He is the man who insulted you at the Lisbones' ball."

Ruth turned her eyes away from Maggie's gaze. "He is the earl's nephew, remember. That is why he was there."

"But Captain Hawksby . . . they seemed so friendly."

"They served together in the war."

"Hmph. Well, that explains why they make excuses for each other."

"Yes. Well, they do go out together quite often, I hear."

"That is no reason for his remarks."

"What remarks?"

"Well, not so much *what* he said, but the way he stared at me."

Ruth turned back to Maggie. "Why, what do you mean?"

"I can't explain it, Ruthie. His eyes looked like an endless ocean. It was as though he could see right through me."

"My dear," Ruth said, "didn't you know? Sir Spencer could not have seen you. He is blind. He lost his sight when gunpowder exploded in his face during a battle in Spain."

Maggie's hand flew to cover her mouth. "Oh, my goodness. I had no idea. But how did he know the color of my hair?"

"You are a very pretty girl, Maggie. I'm sure someone has mentioned it to him."

"Of course. What a fool I am, Ruthie. And the limp? Was that also a wound?"

"He lost a leg at the same time. He is both crippled and blind. That is why Captain Hawksby comes, I hear. Sir Spencer is too proud to be led about by a servant, but he will allow another soldier to guide him."

Maggie thought about Captain Hawksby's hand on his shoulder. That was to let him know he was there. The way Sir Spencer cocked his head toward the person speaking was to hear better, she supposed. "But I still don't understand why he would say something to make you angry, Ruthie. No one who knows you wouldn't like you."

Ruth patted Maggie's knee. "There are some things we aren't meant to understand, dear. Eventually we find there is a lesson to be learned."

Seven

Maggie took a critical look at the list she was attempting to write. She'd managed to think up quite a few activities which would allow her to be excused from making wearisome morning calls. She put down the British Museum, the Tower Menagerie—they had a new tiger—the research library at the Royal Institution. But she needed more.

Ruth asked if she could be of help. Between the two of them, they came up with a longer, more comprehensive list of interesting places to go.

Maggie loved to dance. Now that their brother Daniel was not around to make a pest of himself, she could pick her own partners, so she didn't object to attending the numerous balls in the evenings or going to see the lively performances at the theatres with her sisters. However, to find excuses for avoiding those dull morning calls, she needed to find more destinations acceptable to Mrs. Vervaine and Captain Hawksby.

To her great surprise and happiness, Ruth asked Maggie if she would object should she want to accompany her to the Birdcage Walk at St. James's Park. Nothing could have pleased Maggie more than to think that her favorite sister was becoming more interested in natural things than in spending her afternoons listening to squeaky violins or foppish suitors reciting dull poetry.

The only exception would be to go to Mrs. Hefflewicker's. Maggie delighted in the jolly lady and her humpty-dumpty husband. "I thought Mrs. Hefflewicker favored you, Ruthie. Why have you not received an invitation to attend any of her gatherings lately?"

"She told me her husband was going to take her to Brighton for a few weeks," Ruth replied. "She hinted it was to celebrate the twenty-fifth year of their marriage. She seemed very excited."

Maggie laughed. "I am very fond of Mrs. Hefflewicker, too, Ruthie. But I declare, I have not seen such a pair in my life. Squire and Mrs. Hefflewicker are both as big around as they are tall. Do you remember when we first ran into them at the Crown and Hare and they got stuck in the doorway of the inn?"

"How can I forget it?" said Ruth. "And after we got to London, we didn't know who was the greater tittle-tattler, Mrs. or Mr. Hefflewicker. It was the squire who let the cat out of the bag about the Earl of Chantry having so many sets of twin sisters."

"And now you are telling me she is romantical after twenty-five years? I don't believe it."

"Mrs. Hefflewicker declares her husband to be the most dashing man in England and he tells everybody how fortunate he is to have had such a beauty fall in love with him. That may sound absurd, but I find it rather sweet," Ruth said, dipping her pen in the ink pot once more.

When they finished the list, Maggie made two copies. After giving one to Mrs. Vervaine for her approval, she had the other sent round to Captain Hawksby with a note cautioning him to be careful not to lose it.

Miss Divine declared that she was too tired to see Hawksby for nearly a week and begged his forgiveness. She had told him excitedly she had been given a lead part in a dramatic new play written by a promising new playwright. It was called *The Orange Girl of Tothill Fields*, starring the great Sarah Siddons as a dying countess. If it was successful, the aspiring author would be acclaimed by the theatrical community, and she could become the Toast of the Town. If it were not, she sobbed on his shoulder, she would throw herself off the London Bridge. And that was why she did not dare have any distractions while she learned her part.

Hawksby told her he understood and had a bouquet of flowers sent round to her town house every day. He hand-picked them himself at the market to let her know he was thinking of her. Roses one day, violets the next, some white-petaled things with yellow centers and a mixed bouquet the next. He was back round to roses by the sixth day and worried his buttercup might be getting bored with his offerings. But he didn't trust himself to select a piece of jewelry for her, nor was he sure of what other folderols a woman as particular as Miss Divine preferred. Hawksby was running out of ideas, and he didn't think the *excess* charade would work a second time. The element of surprise would be gone.

As far as his obligation to Lord Chantry to watch his sister, she seemed too busy with her goings and comings in the Fashionable World. Hawksby wondered if she were getting frivolous like the other young ladies of the *beau monde*. He didn't know why that should bother him.

He hadn't had any summons from Terrace Palace for some time, although he had received a list of possible—or impossible, in his opinion—assignments. He'd read her note, too. He should have been relieved when he saw the first date was a week away. He'd given the list to Clugg, telling him not to misplace it. He didn't want Lady Margaret blaming him if it got lost.

Sir Spencer Packard was still at his uncle's. Sometimes he

accompanied Lord Lisbone to his clubs, but even on those occasions, Spencer insisted Hawksby come along to assist him. That took care of a few evenings. Other times Hawksby took him to the theatre or more often to the Guards' Club, where both men felt more at ease with their military cronies.

The last time Hawksby had seen his sweet Miss Divine, she'd complained that she needed new frocks. "Fashions change, my darling. You don't want me to look shabby in front of my friends, do you?" Of course he didn't want his little buttercup to come up second to any. But this business of keeping a mistress was getting more expensive than Hawksby had planned.

Hawksby could understand how such a delicate little woman like Miss Divine was exhausting herself. All those visits to the modiste, keeping up with her rehearsals for the new play, and, unfortunately for him, although her part in the current production was a small one, she had to be at the theatre every evening for the entire performance.

He'd gone down a few times to the rehearsals of *The Orange Girl of Tothill Fields*, but she said it made her nervous for him to watch her as she learned her part. "Be patient, darling," she cooed.

He tried to be, but he was having a difficult time finding things to do during the day. Although he was welcome in the drawing rooms of many fine houses in London, he was not interested that much in the activities taking place during the social Season. When he was surrounded by young ladies of Quality, he didn't know what to answer to their chattering. Besides, if he attended any of the soirees or routs, he might run into a redhaired vixen who would most likely accuse him of spying on her.

To pass the time, Hawksby even visited the Royal Institution by himself one afternoon—just out of curiosity. Just to see what was in all those rooms in the basement he didn't get to finish seeing when he'd taken Lady Margaret to that confabulation about trees and bees dying. Looked into the reference library, too, and spent some time going through some books on fishes. When he ran across the importance of the insect realm to their diet, he quit. Sat at one of the reading tables and tried to figure out what women wanted, too, but didn't get very far coming to any conclusions on that account. The only solution to his dilemma was to be patient and wait.

In the meantime, he rode his horse in the country to get out of the city, sparred with a few of his friends at Gentleman Jackson's—though that wasn't very entertaining, because with his size and his strength he couldn't find many who wanted to challenge him. He tried to hold back, but one good facer and the blokes went down like skittlepins. He didn't gamble because he never won—never had—and besides, he didn't have the blunt. Miss Divine's new wardrobe had taken most of what he had on hand.

Captain Hawksby was rewarded handsomely in the end, though, for being so understanding. Miss Divine finally found a free evening and had a note delivered by messenger inviting him to dinner at her town house. When Hawksby arrived, the maid showed him into the parlor, where he found a table spread for two. Shadows danced in the candlelight while the mingled aromas of food and perfume would have conspired to send any young man into a world beyond earthly expectations.

Miss Divine swept into the room in a shimmering dress of green silk threaded through with silver, her blond hair swept up like frosting on a cake. Emerald teardrops swung saucily from her ears when she moved her head from side to side. She glanced up through long lashes, made a moue, and without a word took a goblet already filled with wine from where it sat on the mantelpiece and pressed it to her lips. Then she kissed him.

Afterward when he was satiated with good food and fine wine, she modeled her new wardrobe for him, running in and out of her chambers to change, giggling and flirting with him from behind her fan. It was when she was sitting on his lap that she told him he could call her *Luci* now.

Everything he'd spent on her was worth it.

Even though they didn't spend the evening together intimately, Hawksby returned to his quarters a happy man—so much so that he didn't even growl much when Clugg awakened him the next morning to remind him that he was to escort Lady Margaret to St. James's Park in an hour's time.

The minute Captain Hawksby came round to collect her, Lady Margaret was already in the foyer, waiting to tell him that her sister Ruth would be joining them. She was glad he didn't object to escorting two young ladies. In fact, for some reason he seemed quite agreeable to taking on the double responsibility.

When Beetleworth opened the front door for them to exit, Maggie's eyes widened. It was not the carriage which they had used previously awaiting them under the portico, but a more splendid one with a strange crest upon the door, a coachman, four horses, and two livened footmen.

"Lord Lisbone has offered us the use of his family coach," Hawksby said, as if it were most ordinary for him to have at his disposal the equipage of one of finest families in England.

He offered his arms to both ladies and escorted them to the coach, where a footman opened the door. The other stood ready to assist them up.

Ruth entered first.

Not until Maggie had her foot upon the step did she see

another person already seated on the far side. She came just short of gasping and looked quickly at Ruth for what to do. Her sister set the example of propriety. She said nothing.

Captain Hawksby spoke. "I know you both have met Sir Spencer Packard in Mrs. Hefflewicker's drawing room. He said if he could come along, he knew he could obtain the use of his uncle's family coach. And since you ladies will have each other to walk with in the park, I shall be able to escort my friend." He said it firmly and that was that.

Dear Ruth sacrificed herself by moving to the far side of the coach to sit across from Sir Spencer so Maggie didn't have to be knee to knee with the handsome rascal. However, that left her Captain Hawksby to face, which didn't fadge anyway for all the attention she was apt to get from him.

Surprisingly, Ruth suggested the change in venue by asking if the gentlemen would mind stopping at a small art gallery off Bond Street instead of going on to St. James's Park. Their sister Georgette, she said, had written from Sussex that her husband the Honourable James Pettigrew, now becoming considered an accomplished artist, was sending some of his watercolors for the exhibition. She was not sure of the exact date they were to be shipped, but Ruth suggested that they stop to see if they had arrived.

Maggie knew all her sisters had agreed to go together later in the week. But as the coach advanced westward along the Strand, Ruth had acted very odd, sitting stiffly upright, her lips primly sealed, her eyes avoiding the man across from her even though she knew he couldn't see her. Maggie suspected Ruth didn't want to be seated across from Sir Spencer any longer than need be. Captain Hawksby had no disagreement to the change of plans and informed John Coachman of their new direction.

The paintings were there, twelve of Mr. Pettigrew's watercolors. Captain Hawksby admitted to knowing little about art. Maggie professed she was not much better informed. And since Sir Spencer was not able to see, that left it to Ruth to lead them round the gallery describing and explaining each work. Mr. Pettigrew's paintings were soft, gentle, thoughtful landscapes depicting the countryside where he and Georgette now lived. Sir Spencer followed closely behind, one hand on his cane, the other on Hawksby's shoulder, listening so quietly, so attentively to every word that Ruth said. Maggie almost forgot that she and Ruth were supposed to be leery of the rogue.

Afterward they found the Lisbone coach awaiting them in Bond Street at the end of the little alleyway, but as they walked toward it, a window display in a little novelty shop that specialized in women's accessories and decorations caught the captain's eye. The store looked familiar. They were nearly to the coach when he stopped. "Lady Margaret," he said, "may I take the liberty of asking you to go back to that little shop for a moment? I would like to seek your advice on something I saw in their window."

Maggie looked anxiously at Ruth, who was now left alone with Sir Spencer walking toward the coach. Ruth, when she heard the captain's request, nodded her permission and graciously placed her hand on Sir Spencer's arm to keep him from stepping into the street. But Maggie could see from the expression on her face that it bothered her to have to touch him. Maggie didn't feel comfortable until she saw both of the Lisbone footmen quickly come to her assistance to help them into the coach.

Hawksby was right. It was the same window where he'd seen the little porcelain pug dog. It was still there, only in another corner sitting on a pile of lace-trimmed linen handkerchiefs, surrounded by all sorts of feminine doodads: fichus, silver-handled combs, fans, and ivory-clasped reticules all beaded in intricate designs.

He cleared his throat. "Lady Margaret, were you to choose something from this display, what catches your eye?"

She wondered why he hadn't asked Ruth. Her taste was far more fashionable than hers. Maggie didn't know why, but a strange little shiver went down her back. She let her gaze scan the fancy accessories. "Why, the beaded reticule with the design of butterflies and bees buzzing around the flower, of course," she said.

"Of course," said Hawksby, trying to hide the disappointment in his voice. He really liked the pug dog, but now he wasn't sure.

"Whatever is wrong with butterflies?" Maggie asked defiantly.

"Nothing. Nothing whatsoever," he answered. "I just thought . . . no, give it no nevermind. Butterflies are far more ladylike insects, I suppose, than . . . other things."

The *things* on Maggie's mind were not in the window. They were back at the curb. She hurried toward the coach. What had she been thinking? Her sweet and trusting sister had been inside alone with Sir Spencer for at least five minutes now. Poor Ruth.

They had spent far more time than Hawksby had realized in the little gallery. Lady Ruth had seemed determined to look at and explain about not only Mr. Pettigrew's work, but every painting in the exhibit. True, she had a way of opening up a window to the vision of the artist he'd never realized existed, but Hawksby's evening of overindulgence was catching up with him. Thank the lord they'd decided to postpone the trip to St. James's Park until another day.

"It is really a pity, isn't it about the trees?" Maggie asked.

Hawksby had hoped if he turned his face and appeared to be watching the scenery outside, he could lay his head back against the squabs and rest a bit. But that was not to be. He was being forced to make an observation, which meant he had to open his eyes and look out.

The carriage was joggling along a tree-lined avenue, past a small city square crisscrossed with little paths bordered by plants of all types—big and small, some of riotous hue, some just green. Hawksby could see lots of green.

"My goodness, Captain Hawksby," Maggie chided. "You haven't been listening to a word I've said. You must remember the professor's lecture on problems caused by industrial smoke and the cutting of trees. Have you never asked yourself why so many of the trees in London are now plane trees?"

No, he hadn't. Unless they were an evergreen or decid-uous, a tree which dropped its leaves in winter, Hawksby didn't know one tree from another. "No, there is nothing unusual about them that I can see. They all look like plain trees to me, Lady Margaret." He closed his eyes again.

"Not *plain* trees, Captain. *Plane,*" she said. "P-L-A-N-E."

His eyes shot open. She was doing it again, spelling at him.

Sir Spencer sat in the seat beside him with a silly grin on his face. Hawksby was sorry his comrade couldn't see the scowl he threw his way. Lady Ruth was another matter. She was making little wheezing sounds into the handkerchief which she was holding to her mouth while she stared out the window. Evidently the bad air disturbed her, as well as the trees.

Hawksby drew his lips into a tight line and pondered his predicament. He hadn't been given any options. He'd made a promise to Spencer and he was obligated to Chantry. His friend didn't come to London that often and Hawksby wasn't about to desert a fellow officer in need.

He could see Lady Margaret wasn't exactly overjoyed at having Spencer along, but at least she hadn't put up a fuss, he told himself. To avoid looking across at the aforementioned termagant, he turned to stare out the window again. As usual when the chit had found a subject that warmed the cockles of her heart, he should have known she wouldn't let up until she'd had her say. She was staring straight at him, which meant he couldn't get away with closing his eyes, either, so he lowered his brows and glared back.

"Most of the trees here in Town are a hybrid of the Oriental plane and trees brought to England from our Virginia colony. They call it sycamore in America. Surely you know that."

Well, Hawksby didn't, and he'd just as leave not pursue the matter any further if she was going to continue to spell things out for him. He thought if he didn't answer, she'd eventually run down. However, Lady Margaret obviously was too wound up to do that. Perhaps he could persuade the Royal Society to send her out on a lecture tour.

"The soot and coal smoke blasting out of chimneys over the last hundred years has killed nearly all the native trees in Town. I shall point out some plane trees to you if we pass any. There are some splendid specimens in Berkeley Square, and the avenues in Green Park are lined with them—and there are several in front of St. James's Palace."

Suddenly an incident which had happened a year ago snapped into Hawksby's memory. The corners of his mouth twitched. An *on dit* about one of Lord Chantry's sisters had been spread about the quarters where he was sequestered at the time. If he recalled, it had caused quite an uproar in the staid corners of the *beau monde*.

"Ahah!" he spouted, shooting a look of triumph across at

his tormentor. "That is why you know where the plane trees are. If I remember correctly, it was in front of St. James's Palace that you were caught up in the boughs when you first came to Town. Looking for birds' nests, you said. Your escapade caused quite a scandal, too, if I'm not mistaken."

She didn't even have the grace to blush. "Well, yes, I suppose it did," she said, a mischievous glint in her eye. "But Queen Charlotte forgave me. Now that I know it is frowned upon for a lady to be found climbing a tree in a good dress, I shan't do it again. I shall wait until I go home to Knocktigh."

Hawksby heard a choking sound from Sir Spencer's direction, but he ignored it. "It is *never* proper for a young lady to climb a tree, Lady Margaret. In a good dress or bad."

"And how, pray tell, was I to get up to the top? I had no ladder, nor wings with which to fly. I had to climb."

Hawksby tried lowering his voice. "Well, believe me, you will do no such nodcock thing while you are in my charge."

Her chin came up a notch. "I thought you are only supposed to protect me from harm."

"What if you had fallen and broken your neck?"

"Don't be absurd. I've never fallen out of a tree in my life."

Hawksby could see that protecting Lady Margaret from herself was going to be the greater challenge. "Out of curiosity," he asked, "did you find one?" That got her attention.

"One what?"

"Did you find a bird's nest?" He avoided looking directly at her when she spoke to him.

"Yes, I did. The plane trees resist insects. That is why they last so long. But even though the birds don't find any food there, they still build nests in the limbs. The only crawly things you'll find are some big, fuzzy caterpillars of the vapourer moth."

He shouldn't have asked.

"If I ever come across one, shall I save it for you? I mean the caterpillar, of course, not the moth. The moth flies away. The caterpillar tickles when it creeps up your arm," she said, wiggling a gloved finger across the palm of her hand and up her wrist. She was sure she saw the captain shudder.

With a great deal of satisfaction, she glanced over to see if her sister had noticed Captain Hawksby's reaction, but to her disappointment she had not. Sir Spencer had evidently made some untoward remark to Ruth, for she seemed overcome with a sudden attack of the shakes and sneezes. When Ruth began to cough uncontrollably, Maggie reached over and banged her on the back, for all the good it did her. Captain Hawksby, the blackheart, did nothing to reprimand his friend. Maggie glared back and forth between the two of them. One, of course, couldn't see her displeasure, but the other could. There was no excuse for upsetting her beloved sister like that.

Eight

When Maggie and Ruth found they had arrived home before their sisters, Ruth asked Mrs. Vervaine to have tea and sandwiches served to them in the library.

They sat on the same sofa where Maggie had entertained Captain Hawksby centuries ago, it seemed. "If you don't like Sir Spencer, Ruthie, I shall just tell Captain Hawksby that we won't tolerate his company."

Lady Ruth reached over and placed her hand upon her sister's knee. "Oh, Maggie. Is our playacting so well done that we fool you as well?"

Maggie was taken aback by that question. "You like each other?"

"We love each other, dearest. I met him last year at the Lisbones' gala. Do you not remember? No, I suppose you don't."

"Then why do you pretend?"

"Didn't you see the way our brother reacted when Spencer came into the Lisbones' ballroom the other night?"

"I wondered about that. It isn't at all like Daniel to treat someone who has . . ."

"Someone who has lost his sight and a leg?" finished Ruth. "No, our brother would be the last to count a man off who has given so much for his king and country. It has to be something that goes farther back into the past. I asked Spencer if he knows. He cannot understand it, either. They were school

110

chums. Daniel even spent one Christmas holiday with the Packards in Hampshire when he would have had only the servants to keep him company if he'd gone to Durham Hall in Oxfordshire. Spencer said his sisters liked Daniel exceedingly well, although he was shy and didn't join in with their games and jollity as they would have wished."

Ruth bit her lip and fiddled with the lace on her sleeve. "Our brother doesn't know it, but Spencer and I have met more than once at his aunt's house. I beg you, Maggie, please don't let on to him. I fear if word should reach Daniel that I am seeing someone behind his back, he shall think I am doing it to defy him," Ruth said.

"Ruthie, no one could think that you would do anything defiant. You really do like Sir Spencer, don't you?"

Ruth blinked away a tear. "Yes, I do. Very much."

"Then I know I shall like him, too, and I shall not tell Daniel."

"Thank you, dearest. I've been praying everything will work out all right."

Maggie leaned a little closer so she could whisper. "But there is something which bothers me. You say you have not seen him since last Season, and we were at Durham Hall all the rest of the year. How could you know him well?"

Ruth's eyes twinkled. "There was no magic in it. We exchanged letters all winter. At first they started out as friendly discourses and grew into a closer relationship."

Maggie looked at her, unbelieving. "But how can that be, Ruthie? He is blind. How would he be able to see if his words ran off the page or know that his lines were straight?"

"Spencer tells me his sisters were as excited as he that their favorite brother had fallen in love. They devised a way of etching lines across a thick sheet of foolscap to guide him, and one kept his pen filled and told him when he began to stray from the line. They promised not to read what he wrote to me—but he said they are so full of vinegar and giggled so much while he was composing his thoughts that he knew they were probably reading as much as they could through his fingers. But Spencer doesn't seem to mind."

"But someone had to read your letters to him."

"I knew his sisters would have to read my letters to him, so I was much more circumspect in what I wrote. He understood. He is a dear and has such a good nature, Maggie. He says when he sinks into the dismals his sisters keep his spirits up by teasing him unmercifully. Spencer has had a lot of love and support from his family."

Maggie took a moment to think about that. "Captain Hawksby seems to like him well enough."

"Yes, they seem to have a close bond. Spencer said they served together in Spain at the beginning of the war, but he doesn't like me to speak of it—the accident and all. He has adjusted remarkably to his disabilities, I think."

Maggie nodded. "I can tell you have accepted it, too. Haven't you?"

Ruth blushed. "Yes," she said. "As have Lord and Lady Lisbone and the countess's sister, Mrs. Hefflewicker."

"Well, I must say, Mrs. Hefflewicker has certainly taken a liking to you. Does she know about you and Sir Spencer?" Maggie asked, scrambling to assimilate all she was hearing. True to her nature, she didn't wait for an answer. "Of course she does. That is why Mrs. Hefflewicker told you to come as often as you wished. She knew Sir Spencer would be there."

"Yes, Mrs. Hefflewicker is very romantical. She loves matchmaking," Ruth said. "Now you can understand why I have become so fond of her."

"I declare. And all this time she has been conspiring to bring you and Sir Spencer together."

"Perhaps the Hefflewickers may not appear to be the handsomest of couples, but they see something in each other we cannot," Ruth said dreamily. "I believe they love each other very much. Squire Hefflewicker dotes on her, and she claims her husband to be a combination Romeo and pirate prince."

"Well, I won't call her silly anymore, but, oh, Ruthie, can you really picture them as Romeo and Juliet?" Before she could say more, Maggie doubled over with laughter.

Ruth sighed happily. "I agree. Who can explain love?"

Maggie's gaze took in Ruth's soft yellow hair, her blue eyes, her laughing lips—her lovely, lovely sister who turned all men's heads. "But, Ruthie," Maggie lamented, "if Sir Spencer is blind, he will never know how truly beautiful you are." She clapped her hands over her mouth. "I should not have said that."

"Spencer's eyes may not be able to see, dear, but it is almost as if he has developed a sixth sense. He knows what others are thinking without having to see the expressions on their faces. He knows who is telling the truth and who is not."

"Like Granny Eizel," Maggie exclaimed. "Freddie always was the one who went to old blind Granny Eizel at Knocktigh after Mama Gillian died. She said Granny Eizel had the *sight*. Is that what Sir Spencer has?"

Ruth had to smile. "Perhaps it is something like that. Or maybe it just tells us we all need to learn to listen better."

Maggie's bright face turned grave. "It speaks well of Captain Hawksby, too, doesn't it, Ruthie, being such a stalwart friend?"

"Yes, it does, dear," Ruth said, giving her young sister a searching look. "Captain Hawksby is indeed true and faithful. He is a bit stern perhaps but that may be due to military life or his upbringing."

Maggie frowned. "Has Sir Spencer mentioned anything about Captain Hawksby's family?"

"Spencer said that in Spain the captain spoke of the Pennines and how some of the landscape reminded him of the rolling moors. So he may be from Yorkshire or Durham County. Otherwise, he said the captain rarely speaks of his family and circumvents any direct questions about them. I cannot but wonder if they perhaps seldom conversed with one another. You know if children are seldom spoken to or if their parents are absent a lot, the offspring may learn little toward how to interact with people."

"That would be terrible. We don't have that trouble, do we?"

"Not at all, I'm afraid," Ruth said, her humor returning.

"Do you know if Captain Hawksby has any siblings?"

"Spencer wasn't sure, though there seemed to be a reference that the captain once made which led Spencer to believe he had an older brother. If there are others, they must not have been close."

Maggie threw her arms around her sister and hugged her. "Why, whatever could he be fearful of? I'm not afraid to talk about my family."

"None of us are, but some men dread appearing sentimental, and therefore foolish, so instead of speaking aloud they will keep everything inside their heads. They feel safer that way."

Maggie thought that over. "Do you suppose when they have repeated it so many times to themselves they fully believe they have said it aloud?"

"You know, you may have the right of it, Maggie. Sometimes I believe men think about things so hard that I can actually see the little wheels turning in their brains like clock-works," Ruth said, making little circles in the air above her ears.

Maggie's eyes grew rounder. "Truly, Ruthie? Isn't that amazing? You must have the *gift* if you can do that. Can you teach me?"

Ruth laughed gaily, her good spirits completely restored. "Not really, dearest. I am bamming you. Men give away their thoughts in a million ways, no matter how they try to hide them. I suppose it just comes with experience and observation."

Maggie didn't hear her. Her mind was skipping over hill and dale contemplating the possibilities.

The following weeks gamboled along with amazing swiftness. Maggie found herself free to participate in the activities she liked, free to visit whatever, free to go wherever she chose as long as it passed muster with Mrs. Vervaine and Captain Hawksby. She went over her list with Ruthie first before giving it to the housekeeper and the captain. Ruth had offered some suggestions on places to go, which proved prophetic now that she and Sir Spencer were accompanying them to so many of those destinations. It was as if Ruthie knew that she would be going—but, of course, how could she have known that unless she had the *gift?*

Maggie was finding it to her advantage to have a tall, fierce-looking man in uniform hovering over her. With his impressive shako of fur, gold trim, leather, and its impressive plume sitting upon his head, Captain Hawksby appeared seven feet tall. Not even the meanest of ruffians would dare challenge such a formidable warrior with a sword swinging at his side.

Even Mary admitted, grudgingly, that being guarded by Captain Hawksby gave her sister much more consequence than being followed about by an abigail or even a livened footman. She wished she'd thought of having Daniel appoint an officer to watch over her, too.

Maggie began to feel proud that the captain was there. All he had to do was lower those great bushy brows and even the nastiest of guttersnipes stepped aside to let them pass. And he didn't complain when she said she preferred to walk to their destinations within London whenever it was possible, unlike most of the young men she met. She missed her long hikes in the Cheviot Hills. Thank goodness, Captain Hawksby wasn't one to want to hail a hackney to go two blocks to the bookstore.

There were the afternoons when they went to see the menagerie at the Tower, and on another they visited an art exhibit given by the Royal Academy at Somerset House. They obtained tickets for the British Museum where, through Lord Lisbone's influence, they were able to have a private conductor take them into one of the closed rooms where Sir Spencer was allowed to examine the newly arrived Roman friezes and artifacts with his hands.

Four of the sisters preferred to join the promenade in Hyde Park in the afternoons, so when Maggie wanted to explore the smaller parks, such as Green Park and St. James's, Captain Hawksby found himself again called into service. And when he was, Sir Spencer and Lady Ruth more often than not accompanied them.

But Captain Hawksby had set down his own rules. He forbade Lady Margaret to ever pick up an insect when in his charge, a restriction she thought wholly unfair. In fact, he forbade her to even mention insects should any eligible young man try to engage her in conversation. He knew where his duty lay. Chantry was never going to get the chit married off if potential suitors kept having bugs stuck under their noses every few minutes. There was nothing more likely to turn them off. There surely wasn't.

Chantry would probably want a detailed account of his youngest sister's activities, too, when he returned from Yorkshire. So Hawksby found himself scrutinizing everything Lady Margaret did—monitoring every word she uttered, or might say, before she said it. That pretty little mouth could say the most shocking things.

And it wasn't just the pretty little mouth that attracted men. Her eyes would light up, and her laughter caught the attention of every male within one hundred yards and turned their heads in her direction. That was before they saw her orange hair flashing like a lighthouse beacon, beckoning them. Hawksby would watch them come closer, lingering about, hoping to gain her attention. The bolder ones sought an introduction.

Viscount Woodbridge did just that when their little party was enjoying the Birdcage Walk alongside St. James's Park. Hawksby had met him at White's. He was older by ten years than himself, if Hawksby judged right, deep in the pockets, good bloodlines. Hadn't been leg-shackled yet. A good catch, according to the *ton*. Hawksby thought the earl would probably approve. If Hawksby could make the match, perhaps Chantry would consider himself paid in full for saving his life and not ask another favor of him.

But would Lady Margaret make a good wife? She couldn't even follow orders. Hawksby had seen her only minutes before snatch some big brown flying creature off a flower, and he knew she now held it prisoner in her gloved fist. He knew exactly what she was going to do—or thought he did, anyway.

The viscount stood admiring her, looking as if he wanted to eat her up. For a moment Hawksby's stomach roiled. Perhaps he should let the termagant open her hand and scare the lecher off.

Hawksby stood nearby, paying little attention to their light banter until he heard the viscount ask, "What are your interests, my dear?"

Before he knew what he was doing, Hawksby found himself answering for her. Found himself spewing out some tiddily nonsense about needlework and bonnets and raising flowers. Then he had an inspiration. "Butterflies!" he boomed. "Yes, she likes butterflies."

Lord Woodbridge nearly bent over backwards with the blast.

Hawksby pulled himself together with Herculean effort. Before he should make more of a fool of himself than he had already, he took Lady Margaret by the elbow. Woodbridge was told, in terms a little harsher than Hawksby planned, that he must excuse them. He had to escort Lady Margaret back to where her sister was waiting, he said brusquely, leaving the startled viscount with a bemused expression upon his face.

She'd looked at Hawksby aghast, and as soon as they were away she attacked him. "That is not what I was going to say," Maggie spouted, trying to catch her breath as he hurried her along. He came to a halt when they reached the waiting coach and pulled her back. Ruth and Sir Spencer were already inside.

"No, I know it was not, but it may be better that you *did* say butterflies when a gentleman asks you where your interest lies. Or birds are even better, I think, for they spread over a larger range, and you are more likely to find a man who will admit to liking birds than saying he likes butterflies."

Maggie cocked her head to one side and looked at him strangely. "You make no sense at all, Captain Hawksby. Do you know that?"

Hawksby was afraid that he was doing that a lot lately—making no sense. He couldn't explain the peculiar phenomenon. Perhaps he'd made a mistake. Butterflies. That was the problem. He should have bought the little pug dog instead.

Sir Spencer Packard told Hawksby of the rumor being spread about the clubs that Lord Basilbone was back in Town without his new wife, boasting it had not taken him long to make sure the next little Lord Basilbone was in the basket. His duty done, he'd seen no need to rusticate in the country for the rest of the Season.

If the gossipmongers were also correct in their assumptions, Basilbone's consuming occupation now seemed to revolve around liquidating his wife's dowery as quickly as possible. Toward that goal, he expended the bulk of his energy in the most disreputable gambling hells in the lower east side, where Hawksby refused to go. He had no fear that their paths should cross on that account.

From what else was bandied about, Packard told him, the bounder was likely to run through his new source of income as quickly as he had done his own allowance and the inheritance his grandmother had left him, an obsession which had put him in dun territory in the first place and forced him to marry.

The bets were being laid at White's as to how long it would take Basilbone to be stripped of his blunt, dipping the hands of the moneylenders deeper into his pockets. That circumstance would surely hasten Lord Basilbone's retreat from London a second time and perhaps forever. Good riddance, as far as Hawksby was concerned.

The second bit of news was not so pleasing. Packard told him he had to leave London shortly, and asked if Hawksby would look after Lady Ruth for him while he was gone.

"Yes, of course," Hawksby said. He was going to miss his best friend, but on top of that he now had two Durham sisters to guard.

★ ★ ★ ★ ★

A week passed before he saw Lady Margaret again, a week which seemed strangely peaceful and relatively quiet as far as Hawksby's nerves were concerned. Yes, a rest from Lady Margaret's antics was as purely restorative as a visit to the mineral waters at Bath, but just as boring. He'd tried them once on a dare.

Luci's play had opened to resounding hurrahs from the critics. *The Morning Chronicle* proclaimed Miss Divine the new darling of the London theatre. Hawksby had to fight every night after a performance to rescue her from her adoring public. But she said that was what she liked about him—he looked like a gladiator and kept the undesirables at bay. Hawksby reckoned that was a compliment.

She claimed she adored him. She claimed she adored everyone. But he was the one she permitted to escort her home each evening, though he was not allowed to stay as long as he would have wished. That was a disappointment, of course, but she needed her rest. He understood that—or tried to, anyway. And . . . she needed more money. "There are little personal items a woman needs, darling," she cooed. He gave her all he had on hand.

Hawksby received another missive, this one from Lady Margaret. She wrote that Herr Wehrhahn had returned and was to be giving a lecture at the Royal Institution on Thursday next. However, she said, on that same evening the entire family of Durham sisters were invited to attend a dinner party at Lord and Lady Payforths before going on to see a performance of *The Orange Girl of Tothill Fields* at the Theatre Royal Drury Lane. Had he seen it yet?

Hell! He'd seen it five times. Of course, he wouldn't object to seeing his little buttercup perform one more time, but he'd planned on meeting some former members of his regiment at a coffee house in the afternoon, then on to dinner and a few drinks before collecting Luci at midnight after the performance.

Here Lady Margaret was saying she needed his help. Hawksby could see trouble right there. He read on down the page. Her sisters and Mrs. Vervaine said she would be permitted to attend the lecture instead of the dinner if she was already dressed for the evening and only if Captain Hawksby were free to escort her to the Royal Institution, and then carry her directly to join them at the theatre.

This may be the last time I will be able to see Herr Wehrhahn.

Well, that was a bit of good news. He could deliver Lady Margaret to the Durham box at the theatre and still have time for a few hours with his chums. He penned her a note saying he would be honored to attend her and had Clugg send it off with a messenger.

The lecture was not as boring as Hawksby thought it would be. Lady Margaret sat silently, as quiet as the color of her apparel this evening. She wore a plain grayish cloak which covered her dress underneath, and she refused to take it off during the lecture. It was not what most ladies chose to wear to the theatre. She did let the hood fall back to reveal a nicely arranged coiffeur of ringlets and ribbons, rather like a pretty confection all decorated with colored sugar bits one might savor at a country fair. A moment of nostalgia threatened his warrior image. He didn't know why that picture came into his head. He hadn't thought for years about the sheep auction days his family used to attend when he was in short pants.

He cast a glance at her now and then to see if she was up to some mischief only to find her looking at him—or, more to the point, like she was trying to stare holes through him. He drew himself up stiffer, squared his shoulders, and faced forward.

Even after Herr Whatsiz began his program, Hawksby could feel her gaze upon his face now and then. When the lecture concluded, he permitted her a few minutes with Curlyhead, whom he suspected of showing far too much jubilation than was proper upon seeing Lady Margaret. Only after Hawksby reminded her that her family awaited her at the theatre did she agree to leave.

"Herr Wehrhahn has great hopes he'll be able to get the funding to travel to Edinburgh before he returns to Germany," she told Hawksby. "He says he has been trying to get in touch with Dr. MacDougal. He sent him his history and hopes he can obtain a speaking engagement at the university."

Either way, Hawksby could see he would soon be rid of the charming German. "Then he may be leaving soon?" he inquired pleasantly.

"He has another lecture. I told him we would certainly come."

Hawksby noticed she said *we*. He looked at her sparkling eyes. She said it so naturally. She also was greeting everyone —friends and strangers alike—whom they passed on their way out with, "I hope to see you again soon." She even told several people she was going to see the famous Miss Luciane Divine at Theatre Royal Drury Lane tonight.

He gave his head a little shake. What was happening to him? He wished he weren't so confused about the female gender. But whether he liked it or not, he had to admit that he was learning more and more about the flora and fauna of London—as well as kitchen stoves and steam propulsion— than he ever thought possible.

Outside the Royal Institution in Albemarle Street a cabriolet hack, its undercarriage painted bright green, caught Hawksby's eye. He raised his arm to signal the driver. The large gray cob pulling it maneuvered the smart two-passenger equipage over to the curb just past them. Written across the back of the boot were the words JACK WRIGHT DOES IT RIGHT. Coattails flapping, the young man leaped to the ground, and with a flourish whipped off his hat and bowed.

"Jack's the name, guv. How can I serve ye?"

Hawksby threw a suspicious glance at the large horse in the harness left alone to stamp his feet and nod his head up and down and around in circles.

"Don't ye worry about me Bob," the lad said. "He's a grand 'un. Knows how to behave. Just bobbin' his head to say *how-dee-do*. Hope t'have me own line sumday with a string like 'im."

After giving the driver their direction, Hawksby handed Lady Margaret into the vehicle.

For a while, she wriggled and wrestled with her cloak. Hawksby could only surmise she was trying to remove it, but then it seemed she put it right back on again. In the close quarters of the hired hackney, it was hard not to be aware that she was struggling, but too close for it to be proper to help her. If he did so, he would have to put his arm around her, and that would never do. He continued to sit looking straight ahead. Finally she settled down, and with a sigh leaned back against the squabs. But even from that angle he was aware that her gaze was once more fully upon his face.

He could stand it no longer. "Lady Margaret, is there some reason you have been holding me in such regard?"

Maggie jumped, her eyes widened, and her hand flew to her mouth. "Oh, dear. I just wanted to find out if I could see them."

Hawksby felt as though he were being examined by a

doctor for spots. He turned his head ever so slightly away from her. "See what?"

"The little wheels. Ruthie said it is easy to see them whirling round in men's heads and know what they are thinking."

His brows lowered. Could women really see what men were thinking? They would soon be at the Theatre Royal Drury Lane. What if Luci should look up and see him with Lady Margaret in a box reserved for the aristocracy? There was no telling what she would think. He didn't know what to think himself, so how could women know more?

Hawksby shook his head. No matter what he'd told her, he was afraid the explanation he'd given Luci about Lady Margaret would not fadge. He'd told her he was made guardian to a friend's little redheaded sister barely out of the classroom while the friend was away on a trip. Luci had kissed him on the cheek and said she thought it very sweet that he liked children. Now that he was beginning to see Lady Margaret in a whole different light, Hawksby knew there wouldn't be a man in attendance at the theatre who could think of her as a child. What would Luci say when she saw him with the *little girl* in a peer's box? He took a deep breath. "And what did you see?"

Maggie shook her head, quite convincingly. "I didn't see any wheels or pins or springs whirling at all. No, indeed I didn't." She sounded disappointed.

Hawksby breathed a sigh of relief. For a moment there the little beggar had him churning. She didn't have a clue about his relationship to Luci, but he would have to watch himself round Lady Ruth. She saw far more than was meant to be seen.

Nine

The curtain at the theatre went up at six o'clock and wouldn't go down again until the final act, around midnight. The two performances preceding Luci's play were a farce, followed by an illusionist who performed a magical trick show with a dancing monkey and a singing dog. They would be late for those.

Hawksby and Lady Margaret arrived at the Theatre Royal Drury Lane just before the second show was ending. Hawksby hoped he would be able to deliver his charge to the Durham box before the crowds of revelers streamed into the magnificent Corinthian rotunda to seek refreshments or to make their way to pay their respects to friends in the other boxes. Some young bucks had already begun to exit the pit area, and he feared the eyes of every gentleman—and those not so gentlemanly—followed the young lady on his arm as they made their way up one of the double staircases.

Not until he handed her down from the carriage did Hawksby realize Lady Margaret had turned her plain gray cape inside out. It was now a shimmering garment of silvery-white, pinned with a gold clasp at the neck. The moment they entered the vestibule, she threw the cape back over her shoulders, revealing a gown of cobalt-blue sarcenet with puffed sleeves and long white-lace gloves—a mouthwatering morsel of silk, ribbons, and lace.

But not until he helped her remove her cape from around

her shoulders at the entrance to the box was he fully aware she was revealing too much of everything. How was it that her look-alike sister, Lady Mary, wore an identical gown and still appeared prim, proper, and all that she should be? She had saved a chair for her twin at the front of the box right along the railing, which Lady Margaret was quick to capture as soon as she greeted her other sisters and paid her respects to Lady Payforth. Hawksby followed her down with her wrap. He would see her seated and then make his departure.

Maggie sat down in the comfortable chair and looked at the boxes across from her, then at the galleries, and finally down at the revelers in the pit. To see those who sat below their own box, she had to lean out over the railing to peer down. Mary pulled her back. "Oh, Maggie, do behave."

The box was soon invaded by admirers. Lord Finch was the first to arrive, followed by a whole platoon of males trying to crowd into the little enclosure.

In the squeeze Hawksby found it impossible to escape unless he chose to catapult himself over the railing, which would only cause greater chaos were he to fall on top of the rowdy patrons in the pit, probably breaking his leg in the maneuver. He would wait until the troops retreated.

Hawksby had forgotten—at least it had slipped his mind —the sensation the Durham sisters had provoked among the *beau monde* the previous year. Now seated neatly and prettily in the box Lord Chantry had reserved for them at the beginning of the Season, they drew the admiration and the envy of all those in the theatre. Two blonds, two with black ringlets, and two redheads. Anybody would have to admit they made a striking picture—a veritable summer bouquet. "Hah!" he expounded. That same analogy had led him into trouble once before.

The box was still crowded even after all the visitors had

returned to their seats and the heavy velvet curtains at the entrance of the box were pulled shut. Lord Finch had decided to stay and was standing behind Lady Rebecca's chair, blocking the only way out. Besides, Hawksby would have to tread on several toes if he were to try to leave.

"My dear boy, you are going to stay to see the play with us, surely," Lady Payforth said, seeing his indecision.

"I believe Captain Hawksby has already seen the play," Ruth said. "Perhaps he doesn't wish to see it again."

"Do tell us what the story is about," begged Mary. Babette and Antoinette nodded silently.

Hawksby was going to have a devil of a time saying no to a bevy of beauties. But the magic of the play was the expectation built up in the audience's mind, that the plight of the little Orange Girl, Luci's part, could only end in tragedy. But in the final fateful moments of the play she was saved from a fate worse than death by the only man who ever loved her—a man she had never noticed—who reunited her with her dying mother, the role played by Sarah Siddons.

"If I tell you the story, it would only spoil it for you."

No amount of teasing could make Captain Hawksby break his resolve not to reveal the ending.

And so the play began. As their parts came up, the players made their entrances onto the stage. Of course, Sarah Siddons' acclaim brought a long and deserved ovation, but none received such a round of calls and shouts as did Miss Luciane Divine. The uproarious applause lasted a full twenty minutes before she could say her first lines. Hawksby sucked in his breath. He saw Luci searching the audience against the lights for him. What would she think when she didn't see him standing in his customary spot on the main floor? What would she think if she should look up and see him standing in a box with six beautiful women?

That made him look at Lady Margaret. She was leaning over the railing again waving at someone.

"Aren't you cold?" Hawksby barked. He grabbed the cape from off the back of her chair as he spoke and tried to wrap it around her shoulders.

"Good heavens, no," Maggie said, with a hearty laugh.

His arms were still wrapped around her. Before he had the chance to release his hold, he realized half the eyes in the theater had turned their way.

"I do believe that Miss Divine is acknowledging me," Maggie said, breaking away from Hawksby. "She is looking right at our box and waving her arms about in the air." Maggie smiled and waved back. "Isn't she magnificent? Oh, do look, Captain Hawksby. Don't be such a stick-in-the-mud. Admit that at least one woman is worthy of your attention."

Damn and blast. He'd really be in the suds with Luci now.

The next day, the critic for *The Morning Chronicle* reported that not since they had seen Sarah Siddons play Lady Macbeth had they witnessed such a passionate performance as Miss Luciane Divine's. *If her acting denotes her future, she is indeed slated to become one of the most sought after dramatic actresses of the London stage.*

The following week the Durham sisters were deluged with callers. Even Maggie was pressured by her sisters to help entertain. So Rebecca's request that Maggie and Ruth accompany her and Lord Finch to Hyde Park for a carriage ride was a welcome relief. Since Sir Spencer had left London, Ruth was not her usual self, and Maggie was determined to bring a smile back to her favorite sister's face.

None of them were averse to Maggie's suggestion that the coachman drop them at the Lancaster Gate on the north side of the Park near the Long Water, instead of joining the more populated south side for the Promenade.

The day was bright and sunny and just right for a leisurely stroll. While Rebecca and Lord Finch walked ahead, and Ruth enjoyed the fountains and flowers, Maggie kept her eyes open. She had her own reasons for wanting to be on this side of the Park. North of the Serpentine, and beyond the road bridge, the Long Water, with its tree-lined banks, its high grasses, and its brambly bushes, promised a great assortment of wildlife—just the place to find a fine green grasshopper.

"Ruthie, will you please hold my reticule for me?" Maggie said, handing her sister the bag. "There's a wildflower by the lake I wish to examine."

"All right. Don't take long, dear, and try not to get your feet wet. Remember, you ruined a good pair of shoes on our last outing when you stepped off the path. I shall be waiting ahead for you with Rebecca and Lord Finch."

Maggie circled a tree and crept round the bushes, down to the edge of the water. *Swish, swish!* Her gloved hands slapped at the tall grasses. Several grasshoppers flew into the air, as well as a pair of grebes and a heron. Patience, she told herself, and whipped out a lace-trimmed linen handkerchief she'd stuffed it in the top of her glove. Her sharp eyes, keen responses, and swift hands had their reward. *Smack—hop—jump—grab.* The grasshopper was in the handkerchief. Maggie carefully peeled back a corner of the lace to examine her catch. A beautiful specimen, with all six legs.

"Maggie, do come, dear. We have to leave," Ruth's voice penetrated the brambles.

"I shall catch you up in a minute," Maggie replied. Carefully rolling the handkerchief into a ball, she fisted her prize. But her route back was cut off by the brambles. Remembering Ruth's admonition, she tried not to muddy her half-boots too badly. She had to follow a circuitous route along the bank until she spotted an opening and began to climb back up to the path.

The voice she heard was familiar, but not the one she expected. "Captain Hawksby," she exclaimed, startling both him and his companion.

Clinging to his arm was the renowned Miss Luciane Divine. She was even lovelier than Maggie had thought her onstage. Gone was the ragged Orange Girl. In her place was a vision in a raspberry-colored walking dress with silk trimmings, fluted gold cord, and a shawl of Indian silk. Her broad-brimmed bonnet was the largest Maggie had ever seen, decorated with silk flowers and a large white ostrich plume. Maggie was quite overcome with awe. "I had no idea you were acquainted with Miss Divine, Captain Hawksby. Why did you not say so when I told you how much I would like to meet her?"

For a moment Hawksby could do nothing but blink. Why should he be surprised to see Lady Margaret rise from the lake looking like a sea nymph—her bonnet askew, mud on the toes of her shoes, her hair looking as though it had caught on a branch somewhere and pulled loose from its pins, and that saucy little grin? No, he should not be surprised at all.

"You shouldn't be alone, Lady Margaret," he snapped.

"Ruth and Rebecca are about somewhere," she said, laughing. "I had to climb up to the path another way. Ruth said she'd scold me if I got these shoes wet as well." She smiled brightly at Miss Divine, who clung tightly to Hawksby's arm, her eyes narrowing to mere slits.

"Miss Divine is getting angry with you for not introducing us, Captain Hawksby, as am I," Maggie scolded. "I want to tell her how much I enjoyed her performance the other night."

Hawksby introduced them.

"You are even more beautiful than I imagined, Miss Divine. See, Captain Hawksby, I told you she was worth your notice."

Miss Divine, never immune to high praise, relaxed her hold on Hawksby to acknowledge Lady Margaret.

It was then that Maggie saw the beaded reticule with the butterflies and bees in Miss Divine's own dainty kid-gloved hand.

Hawksby realized Lady Margaret recognized it, too, the minute he saw fireworks go off in her eyes.

"What an interesting reticule, Miss Divine," Maggie said, reaching out her hand. "May I see it?"

The actress could do naught else but hand it to the young noblewoman.

Maggie turned away and held the bag up to the light as if to examine it. Her eyes were misting for some silly reason, and she didn't understand why. She only knew she didn't want either of them to notice. She studied the shiny beaded butterfly, fingered the smooth ivory clasp which moved up and down, then handed it back. "It is lovely. Thank you," she said. "I must be going now." And she walked away.

"Maggie, where are you?" Lady Rebecca rounded the curve in the path just then. Upon seeing her sister, she took her firmly by the arm and pulled her along the path, scolding her as they headed back to where she saw Ruth and Lord Finch waiting. "Freddie and Daniel would be most displeased to see you speaking to . . . to that sort of person." Maggie watched her sister's face flush becomingly. "Here," Rebecca said, leaning over. "You have dropped your handkerchief."

"But that was Miss Divine," Maggie said, confused over Rebecca's remark.

Lord Finch stepped forward and extended his arm to Rebecca, hiding his smile as best he could.

Maggie looked quizzically at Ruth.

"Rebecca is just upset over her concern for you, dearest. You must not disappear like that. A young unmarried lady venturing out alone can lead to gossip and censure from the *ton*. Daniel and Freddie would not be pleased. Come now, the carriage is waiting."

Lord Finch had just handed them up when they heard the screams. A woman's screams, one after the other, coming from the footpath behind them—somewhere in the direction of the Long Water.

"My goodness," Lady Rebecca exclaimed. "Whatever could have happened?"

They listened.

"I'm sure it is nothing for us to worry about," said Lord Finch. "See, the cries have stopped."

Maggie sniffed. Rolling up her empty handkerchief with a certain sense of satisfaction, she stuffed it down into her reticule.

Hawksby had no choice but to take Lady Margaret to Herr Whatsiz's next lecture, because he was obligated to Lord Chantry. Since the Durham sisters were going to need two carriages that same afternoon, Hawksby told John Coachman he would hail a hired hackney to carry them home after the lecture.

Closemouthed, formal, and cool best described the atmosphere which surrounded them like a fog during the lecture. He hadn't liked it one bit either when she told him, "Herr Wehrhahn called on me yesterday to return my sketches." He still hadn't been able to find anybody, Curly-head had told her, who could identify all the mystery insects. Hawksby gritted his teeth when Lady Margaret said she'd also told the professor she wished she could go with him to Scotland to present her research to Dr. MacDougal.

"Whatever made you say such a noodle-headed, poppycockish, foolish thing?" he said, with a great deal of exasperation.

"Well, you don't have to snap off my nose. I just want to show him all the work I've done," she said, her voice trailing off. "I want to take my collection in person to show Dr. MacDougal. I'm sure Daniel would say it's all right."

Hawksby disagreed with that, but he already felt like a brute for taking out his frustration on her. He did allow her to talk to Herr Whatsiz for a few minutes afterward, however, to make up for his here-and-therian outburst. Wouldn't do to make a scene in such a public place. Hawksby stayed as near to the brat as he could, but only caught snatches of their conversation. Curly-head did most of the talking, he noted. Lady Margaret did a lot of head bobbing. And a head-bobbing chit who didn't interrupt was suspect in Hawksby's eyes.

It certainly didn't take much to bounce Lady Margaret's spirits back up though, for she came back smiling after their little talk.

"Herr Wehrhahn said he received permission to go to Edinburgh. He's going to meet Dr. MacDougal. Isn't that wonderful?"

"By Jove! That is great news," Hawksby answered, with the first bit of enthusiasm he'd expressed all afternoon. *Maybe they'll both be caught in a butterfly net by a nearsighted student and stuffed in a box.*

Once again Hawksby spied the familiar equipage with the green undersides and the big gray cob outside in Albemarle Street, and waved it down. As soon as Hawksby had Lady

Margaret settled inside and had informed Jack of their direction, their conversation tapered down to nothing. Hawksby wondered at the silence, but was thankful for it nonetheless.

They had been carried as far as Haymarket when the carriage stopped. Jack leaped to the ground. There was some thumping and jumping and a bit of profanity, some snorting and stamping and threshing of the cob's head, before Jack came back to speak to his passengers. "Sorry, guv. You'll have to step down. M'horse has thrown a shoe. Won't go another step, I'm afraid. Bob's a bully goer and I dun't dare have him cum up lame. He's me livelihood."

Jack saw Hawksby reach into his pocket and shook his head. "No need to pay, guv. I didn't take you to the destination wot I promised."

Hawksby climbed down. He opened the young man's fist and slapped a coin into it. "You're going to need the blunt to pay the smithy, Jack. You're a plucky young man, but if you refuse the fare for your services, how are you going to get that line of carriages?"

"Shoosh!" Jack's eyes widened as he saw the coin in his hand. "Thank y'guv. I won't forget you and yer lady. Anytime either of you need a favor, you just ask any hack driver for Jack." He threw Maggie an appreciative look.

Maggie was no sooner in the street than she asked, "May we walk back to Terrace Palace down along the river instead of hailing another hackney, Captain Hawksby? There is something I'd like to say to you."

Since he was feeling quite amiable after her announcement of Curly-head's impending departure from London, Hawksby agreed readily. He, too, felt the need for stretching his legs after sitting for two hours.

He nodded and offered her his arm—which she didn't take. Lady Margaret was already off and away.

Hawksby was not quite sure how they ended up sitting on a stone wall alongside the Thames watching the river traffic go by. But there they were, side by side, skipping flat pebbles or throwing sticks in the water, to see how long it took them to bobble and dip about in the current until they were sucked under a vessel of some kind.

The property was the Farley Mansion at the west end of the Strand. Now an old pile of what once was a magnificent palace with a ballroom one hundred feet long, the grounds were overgrown with weeds and high grasses. Water stairs led down to the river, where wherries and rafts picked up paying fares to cross to the other side. Hawksby had the feeling that the grounds were familiar to Lady Margaret. She seemed to know right where she was headed when they arrived at the rusty entrance gate.

Hawksby was surprised and secretly delighted to find Lady Margaret preferred to walk instead of taking the hackney carriage. Not many young ladies of the Quality cared to expend such energy.

Maggie wriggled a little, then lobbed a flat pebble into the water and watched it skip three times before sinking. "I want to apologize for last week in Hyde Park." She waited, studied the side of his face, watched the little twitch as the muscle in his jaw tightened. "I said I'm sorry," she blurted out. Fascinated, she watched his ears grow red.

Hawksby kept his sights on the river. "Then, dash it, why did you put the grasshopper in her reticule, for lord's sakes?"

Maggie looked down at her hands. "I don't know," she said. "I suppose it was when I recognized it."

"Of course you did. It was the one you picked out. I thought you said you liked it." He sounded exasperated.

"I did—above all others."

Hawksby shook his head. "Now it's you who isn't making

any sense." It was the truth. Females! There was no rhyme nor reason in their brain boxes. He'd taken her suggestion and now she was mad at him.

"I said I was sorry."

She was so quiet that Hawksby took the chance of glancing at her. He shouldn't have. She was staring at him in a dangerous way—dangerous because she appeared ready to ask another question. He quickly turned his gaze to a safer sight —the river.

"Ruth told me a ladybird is a gentleman's friend. Does that make Miss Divine your ladybird . . . your friend, that is?"

Hawksby swallowed hard. It wasn't difficult to figure out she was still staring up at him and her mouth was somewhere just below his ear. Lady Margaret didn't exactly have a missish little voice.

"For my part, I'm glad you have a good friend like Miss Divine, Hawksby. But it seems a funny thing to call her. Why, she isn't spotted at all. In fact, I thought her very elegant and her clothes the latest fashion."

They should be, thought Hawksby. *They cost me a pretty penny.*

Maggie chewed her lower lip in deep concentration. "I don't know why Rebecca said it wasn't proper for me to make her acquaintance, or why you told me I shouldn't talk about such things."

Hawksby could picture her stubborn little chin thrust out.

She went right on. "It's always comforting to have someone to tell your troubles. I have my sisters, but they all seem intent on finding husbands. Well, I don't know about Ruth." She remembered her promise to Ruth that she wouldn't speak to anyone about her *tendre* for Sir Spencer. "Perhaps Ruth and I can live together someday when all the others have homes of their own."

Hawksby looked at her then. She obviously didn't know about Spencer and . . . no, he wouldn't tell her. "But what if Lady Ruth marries?" he asked, wondering what her answer would be to that.

"Then I will go home to Knocktigh alone." Her tone perked up when she mentioned the name. "It means house on the hill you know. I like to be up high near the sky. You can see so much more, don't you think?"

"Oh, yes. Definitely," he said, not seeing anything clearly at all at that moment, except her large blue eyes, her freckled nose and parted lips, her chin, her neck. Hawksby dared not let his gaze go lower, but his traitorous eyes did. For a second he thought he'd stopped breathing altogether. He should have remembered the dangerous effect the redheaded Durham twins' figures had on the male population.

She cocked her head and stared at his face. "Why, Captain Hawksby, your eyes are blue—like mine. No wonder that I never took note of them. You are always frowning so much," she said with candor. "You ought to let people see them more often—smile more. You can't smile and frown at the same time. Just try it and see," she said.

Her face twisted into such a silly grimace that Hawksby nearly laughed.

Then she leaned toward him so she could see his face better still. "They are quite nice eyes. Do your parents have blue eyes?"

"My mother," he blurted out. His mother's eyes. The Bixworth eyes. The same large blue eyes which were windows revealing every blasted thought that blew through her head. Her brother, Matthew Tredworthy Bixworth, the Right Reverend Bixworth, Bishop of the Church of England, was no different. His parishioners were devoted to him. They might be perfect eyes for a clergyman, but they weren't the eyes for a fierce and terrible warrior. Not one of his other siblings got them, not even his sister Hortense, the tricky one. A person never could figure out what she was going to do next.

"Hawksby . . . may I call you Hawksby?"

The request caught him by surprise. He nodded because he couldn't talk at the moment. His voice seemed not to be a part of him anymore. Hawksby took a deep breath.

"I'm sorry I put the *omocestus viridulus* in Miss Divine's reticule," she said, looking down demurely at her hands.

She now had Hawksby's full attention. "What . . . what did you say, Lady Margaret?"

She grinned. "The grasshopper. I was seeing if you were listening."

Hawksby shifted his gaze to the traffic on the waterway. Safer that way.

"I think you can call me Maggie under the circumstances, don't you?"

Hawksby jerked to attention. "What circumstances?" He looked around, sniffed, took a deep breath. The air was ripe with the smell of water. A wherry floated up to the water stairs and let off three people, two gentlemen and a lady. They mounted the steps and headed up the wide path which led to the Strand. Lord, what had he been thinking of? Lady Margaret could have been seen sitting alone with an officer.

When he'd started out from the lecture hall he'd planned to head straight back to Terrace Palace. But she loved to walk —would rather walk than take a coach, she'd said more than once. It was a nice day, and she wanted to tell him something. Lord! If he were found like this with her, Lord Chantry would have his head—or worse, he'd make them tie the knot. After all, he'd trusted the captain to look after his youngest sister.

She was nodding in his direction. "Now that I am calling you Hawksby, I think it perfectly all right for you to call me

Maggie, at least when we are with family." She cocked her head to the other side to study him. "Was she very angry?"

Hawksby jerked around. "Who? Who's angry?"

"Miss Divine. You know," she said.

"Oh. Oh, the *omocestus viridulus*."

Maggie thought she detected a slight smile under the mustache. "You remembered its Latin name."

"The grasshopper, yes." Did she think him a dolt? "You will find I have excellent recall, Lady Margaret. As to Miss Divine, well, she was a little upset."

He'd actually forgotten all about Luci for a moment. Perhaps because he didn't want to think about the rage she'd flown into when she'd put her hand into her recticule for a handkerchief and out jumped that green monster, or the length of time it took for him to calm her down. But the promise of another gift had worked wonders—so why had she completely popped out of his thoughts for the last hour?

As soon as he'd left her town house, he'd gone to the novelty shop and purchased the china pug dog. The price far exceeded what he had contemplated, but the proprietor insisted it was a rare antique. However, nothing but the best would do for his little buttercup. Hawksby planned on giving it to her after her performance tomorrow night.

Lady Margaret was giving him a look he couldn't interpret. Was she angry that he'd refused to call her Maggie? He couldn't tell. She never erupted like a volcano unexpectedly at every provocation, as Luci did, and he thanked her for that. He didn't think he could take any more screaming.

They sat together in silence for some time looking out over the water, watching the watercraft make their way up and down the Thames.

"Cry even?" she said.

He looked down at her as if he were discovering her sitting

there beside him for the first time, and recalled the inappropriateness of their questionable situation. Her bonnet had fallen back, held on only by the loose ribbons. Her hair was sadly askew, but then it was most of the time. Her gloves were dirty from picking up stones from the ground, and now she wanted to address him familiarly as *Hawksby*. What would Lord Chantry think if he should hear of it? No, it would never do.

"Cry even," he replied, rising. "Now it is best that I escort you home, Lady Margaret, or Mrs. Vervaine will have my head—or worse."

"Worse than what?" she said, laughing her delightful laugh as she ignored his hand and slid off the wall without his assistance.

"Good lord!" he said, observing the smudges of earth and moss stains on the front of her gown where she'd wiped her hands, and on the back of her pelisse where she'd been sitting on the ancient stone barrier. What would the gabble-tabbies say?

Hawksby cleared his throat. "Lady Margaret, I fear you have smudged your frock." She immediately rubbed at the dirt, making the damage worse. Hawksby groaned.

"Give it no nevermind," Maggie said. "No one will see us."

He could do nothing but walk closely behind her to hide the damage. Thank God they didn't have far to go and they encountered no other pedestrians who recognized them on the way.

They both fell silent after that and said no more until Terrace Palace came into view. However, instead of following the carriageway to the front portico, she led him around the perimeter of the property. Suddenly she dipped her head and disappeared into the high shrubbery.

"Damnation!" Hawksby held his hat to keep it from being knocked off his head and plowed in after her, only to discover a hidden gate opening into the back of the garden. By the time he'd fought his way through the thick brush, the chit was already halfway across the lawn and heading toward the house.

Hawksby waited to make sure she was safely in through the French windows off the Terrace before he headed for the stables. She hadn't even said good-bye. Guarding Lady Margaret was one thing, but being alone with her in the overgrown gardens of an old deserted palace was another. She'd looked so forlorn after the lecture that he'd forgotten all reason for a moment. It was very easy to forget convention when one was around Lady Margaret.

An uneasy feeling went through Hawksby. A quiet Lady Margaret was a Lady Margaret plotting no good. That worried him.

Ten

The next day brought no respite, even at the male bastion of White's, when Clugg arrived bearing news that a footman from Terrace Palace had reported Lady Margaret missing.

He should have known better than to trust her out of his sight. Hawksby would be glad to wash his hands of her. Let the chit run away to her lover. Good riddance.

Then why, he fumed, was he pulling on his coat, grabbing his sword, and yelling, "Clugg! Have my horse out front immediately!"

Clugg proved his worth. Not only did he have his captain's horse ready by the time he got to the curb, but the batman had his own mount.

"Where do you think you're going?" shouted Hawksby as he swung himself onto the back of his horse.

"With you, Captain. We been a pair through a long war. I reckon you have another important battle ahead of you, and you might find me to be of assistance in this one as well."

Hawksby didn't have time to argue the point. He kneed his horse and raced eastward toward the Strand.

"How long has she been gone, Mrs. Vervaine?" Hawksby asked of the housekeeper the minute he'd stepped inside Terrace Palace.

"She wasn't in her bed when Lady Mary awakened, sir. The girls thought she'd eaten early and was out in the garden somewhere, hiding because she didn't want to go to the musical program Mrs. Payforth's niece is giving. Lady Mary stayed here, she was that upset, and the other girls went on to Mrs. Payforth's so there wouldn't be any talk."

"That means Lady Margaret has already been gone half a day. Why wasn't I notified sooner?"

"We did send a note to your lodgings, Captain Hawksby, as soon as we realized she wasn't to be found. The housemen have been out looking for her and the young ladies sent inquiries to friends' houses, where they thought she might have gone."

He didn't want to say Clugg had finally caught up to him at White's, where he'd gone for lunch and to play cards with Lord Finch. "Have you questioned the stablemen to see if she took a horse or carriage out?"

"Beetleworth said she took neither horse or carriage. Knowing the young lady, she could just as well have walked away from here."

Walking about with him as an escort was one thing, but walking out alone was a completely different matter altogether.

"We also questioned all the servants," the housekeeper said. "Especially Flora Doone, the girl they brought with them from Northumberland. She often accompanies one or another of the ladies when they go shopping or to the lending library. But she swears she hasn't seen anything of her mistress since yesterday after you brought her home. Very quiet she was, which isn't like that young woman at all." Mrs. Vervaine pursed her lips and jingled her keys. "Of course, there are other ways of getting away from Terrace Palace than the front door."

The postern gate. Everyone had been aware of the gate in the hedge except him—until yesterday. "I know about the gate in the wall, Mrs. Vervaine. May I talk to Lady Mary? And I'd like to speak to the maid, Flora, too. She may know something we don't."

As soon as Mary appeared, Hawksby asked her to find out what Lady Margaret might have been wearing and whether any other garments were missing. They were twins, after all, and would have basically the same wardrobe.

"I believe she also has some wooden boxes." He asked if Mary knew where she kept them.

Mary made a face.

Hawksby asked if she would check to see if they were still there, and especially would she look for one box in particular —one intricately carved with Celtic designs.

A couple of dresses, a small portmanteau, and her comb and brush were gone. All the boxes were at the back of the closet except the carved one. Flora provided the information that one of Maggie's capes with a hood was also missing.

It had to be the German. She'd run away with him. He should have known the vixen was doing too much nodding after the lecture. Curly-head was luring her into his web, the villain. Or was she the wily one, using old Whatsiz to get to her true love, the Scot? Whichever it was, the chit would be ruined. Hawksby slapped his forehead, paced the floor, and was just finishing a long string of unmentionable words when Lord Finch came hurrying in.

"Can I be of help, old chap? You rushed out of the club so fast I had to hire a hackney. Came as quickly as I could."

"You know members of the Royal Society, Finch. Can you find out where Herr Wehrhahn was staying?" Hawksby nearly choked on having to say the bugger's name. "And if and when he left?"

"Will do," Finch said, exiting as quickly as he'd arrived.

Clugg was sent to The Bull and Mouth, a City inn whose

proprietor provided the horses for the Great Northern Road mails. "Find out if Herr Wehrhahn or Lady Margaret was on one of their coaches and, if so, when did it leave? And get a schedule for the Edinburgh route."

By now all the sisters had come home early. It didn't take long for Lord Finch to return. He'd found a member of the Royal Society who told him Herr Wehrhahn had planned on leaving the previous night on the eight o'clock evening mail coach to Edinburgh.

Clugg came in a while later with the schedules. The coach had left on time with seven passengers—six men and one woman. The German professor's name was on the roster. The woman was a Mrs. Reever, a thin elderly lady. Even if she'd wanted, Lady Margaret could never disguise herself as thin.

If Lady Margaret were to catch Herr Wehrhahn up along the High Road, she would have needed a faster mode of transportation. Then it struck him. Jack Wright. Why hadn't he thought of the hired hackney driver sooner? Devil it. She probably talked the young man into taking her on a wild-goose ride. "But she would need money," Hawksby said.

"She's been hoarding her allowance," Mary volunteered. "She never spends it on anything except books and lectures."

"That's it, then." Hawksby bowed to the sisters, told Finch to hold down the fort, stuffed the mail schedule inside his jacket, grabbed his hat, and headed for the stables. "Come Clugg. We have one more place to check. If I am right—and I'm sure I am—we shall have Lady Margaret home before any harm is done to her reputation. But be quick about it. We must hurry."

Hawksby's surmise had been correct. A woman had appeared at the mews before dawn that morning and hired

Jack Wright to carry her somewhere. No, no one heard where. No one saw her face. She had a hood over her head.

"Wait a minute," Hawksby said, looking at a big gray behind a rope. "That's Bob, Jack Wright's cob."

"So he is, guv," the stableboy said. "The mort insisted he take one of the other hacks. Said she had to catch up to someone and they might be gone for a good time. Didn't want *Mr. Wright,* she called him, to have to worry 'bout leaving his horse at a posting inn."

Hawksby's fists clenched at his sides. Just wait until he caught up with the little devil. A short time later, he and Clugg were tearing along the turnpike going north.

So accurately did the mail coaches run that the towns surrounding the posting inns could set their clocks by the sounding of the guard's horns as they pulled up to their stops.

The undercarriages of government mail coaches were always red. Strict records were kept of stops and passengers, so it should be easy enough to find out if Herr Wehrhahn got off or stayed overnight at an inn.

Jack Wright's cabriolet with its green undercarriage and large sign on the back would surely draw attention to its occupants. Lady Margaret was as well as snared before she started.

Coming and going, all hours of the day, the road was filled with travelers, fine coaches, soldiers, and cattle drovers driving their livestock to London markets. But with the highway being as much as thirty yards across, Hawksby and Clugg made good time, stopping only long enough to make inquiries and to pick up fresh mounts.

The German was less than eleven hours ahead of Lady Margaret. The mail coaches had several stops to make, and Curly-head might have chosen to lay over after a full day's ride. Maybe that was what they'd planned. Then when she joined him, they would catch a later coach. If Lady Margaret had the blunt to pay for the exchange of horses for the cabriolet, she could catch up to the professor in half a day's time. Hawksby pressed onward.

Then it suddenly occurred to Hawksby that in only a few hours he was supposed to collect Luci at the theatre. "Damn and blast!" Tonight he'd planned on giving her the porcelain pug dog.

It rained. Not hard, but enough to wet Hawksby and Clugg through. They'd been on the road all that night and the next day. The German hadn't gotten off except to grab food to take back on the coach. The cabriolet was easy to follow. They'd gone straight on, too. Either Jack Wright had the stamina of a soldier or else they were trading off on driving the carriage. He wouldn't put it past Lady Margaret. Hawksby and Clugg were used to three-day marches in rain or snow, but she was a lady, the daughter of an earl. If he'd underestimated her before, he never would again.

The rain stopped, but the road remained muddy. It was chilly because the sun had been down for hours. They needed a change of horses. Aside from a short nap at noon under a tree, after they'd lunched on bread and cheese and a bottle of wine, they'd had no sleep. His regimentals had dried but were in a despicable state, his face was black from not having shaved for over twenty-four hours, and his great bushy brows looked ready to fly off into the sky. So Hawksby wasn't in the best of moods when he stepped into the common room to buy some ale and order two hot meals while Clugg saw to the horses.

That was when he heard a shout and saw a tall, gangly, loose-jointed lout pound his companion over the head with a box—a particular carved box Hawksby recognized only too well.

" 'Tain't jewels, you knucklehead. You stoopid, lame-brained, ignoramus! It's nuthin' but some stinkin' bugs. You collected us a bunch of stinkin' bugs."

"Don't hit me, Spindle. How was I t'know? The way that she-devil fought over thet box, I thought it had t' be sumthin' 'pensive."

"Well, it weren't, you dumbbell! An she's probably a witch and will put a curse on us."

Hawksby had never moved so quickly in his life. One hand closed on the box, slamming it to the table. The other encircled the scrawny man's neck.

It was then that Clugg came upon the scene. Hawksby shouted for him to stop the shorter, stouter thief from fleeing the inn. Clugg grabbed a tankard off a table and gave the man what-for on his noggin. The thief went down for the count without a sound.

Hawksby commenced to pound the daylights out of Mr. Spindly-legs. The crowd grew larger as they pressed into the room to witness the fight. Taking note of Hawksby's regimentals, the proprietor decided an officer in His Majesty's service was more likely to have the right in the matter. He stepped back and encouraged him to proceed with all diligence with whatever punishment he felt the brigands needed.

"Captain," shouted Clugg over the din, "I were just coming in to tell you that the cabriolet with the green undercarriage is in the stableyard."

The proprietor added his voice to the melee. "Those men brought that carriage in, sir. 'Bout an hour ago."

Hawksby looked at the fellow dangling at the end of his fist. "Where did you leave them?" he growled, giving the bounder an extra shake.

"Captain," shouted Clugg, "I don't think he can hear you."

"Then I'll squeeze it out of him," Hawksby said. But before he could carry out his threat, another commotion was heard at the entrance of the inn.

Two travelers were half carrying, half dragging a bundle of mud and rags between them. "We found this poor chap alongside the high road. Said he'd been robbed and was trying to get help. We think his leg's broke."

Hawksby sped quickly to his side and scooped up the lad before he slumped to the floor. Spindle collapsed in a heap behind him.

"By Jove! It's Jack Wright, Clugg. He needs something to revive him. Spirits," Hawksby called to the innkeeper's wife. He then carried the young man into the front waiting room and lowered him onto a wooden bench.

Hawksby grabbed the mug of beer thrust into his hand and held it to the boy's lips. "Mr. Wright, can you hear me? Where is La . . . where is your passenger?" He didn't dare let anyone know her true identity.

Jack groaned and drank and choked and tried to open one of his swollen eyes. "Cat'n a wall."

"That's wot he kept saying when we found 'im on the side o' the road," the first traveler said. "Couldn't get more out o' 'im."

"Damn and blast!" expounded Hawksby. "Cat'n a wall. That don't make any sense."

"But, sir," said the innkeeper's wife, "there is a Cat-on-the-Wall Lane. 'Tis an overgrown country track about a mile up the Great Northern Road. Takes off to the west. Used to lead to an old manor thet fell t' ruin years ago. The acres lay fallow and 'tis nothing but marsh and overgrown weeds now."

Hawksby was up and heading for the door.

"Wait for me," said Clugg.

"No," ordered Hawksby. "You stay here with Mr. Wright. Send for a surgeon or barber who can set his leg," he said to the innkeeper's wife. "And have someone summon the authorities to take care of those two thieves," he barked at the proprietor. "I'll get my horse and take a lantern from the stables." With that, he grabbed up his belongings and charged out the door.

Hawksby found her sloshing through a field about two miles off the highway. No telling how much territory she'd covered by then. He was too glad—or too mad, he couldn't tell which—to say one word to her. He'd ridden along Cat-on-the-Wall Lane, holding the lantern high and calling her name loudly, so loudly his voice was hoarse and he could barely speak.

Then he'd heard a "Halloo!" and there she was, waving her arms at him like she was on a Sunday stroll in the park. He spurred his steed up the embankment and galloped to her side. He handed her the lantern and told her to place it upon the ground. Hawksby didn't know where he found the strength, but he reached down and swept her up onto the saddle in front of him. She flung her leg over the horse and settled back against him with a sigh.

"You're all right?" he asked, not knowing what else to inquire of a young woman of noble birth after she'd been abducted and robbed.

"Of course," she answered.

It was only a short stretch back to the lane. The horse would find his way from there. They rode in silence for a few minutes. She was shivering, so he held her closer. Her hood had fallen back and his chin rested in the wild nest of her hair.

"We were pounced upon and robbed, Hawksby. Jack tried to protect me. He jumped on the back of the carriage after they dumped us in the field and rode off with them."

"Mr. Wright is safely back at the inn, Lady Margaret. Some travelers brought him in. He was hurt." He heard her quick intake of breath. "He'll be all right. I left Clugg with him."

"You were worried about me, weren't you, Hawksby?" She sounded pleased.

He didn't say anything. Yes, he supposed he was, and he didn't know why that surprised him. His arm tightened around her. "You are a spoiled young lady and should be locked in your room until you get some sense in that head of yours."

Maggie leaned back against his chest. "Hawksby . . ."

"What?" he growled.

"I'm glad you came. I didn't know where I was." She smiled when his big gloved hand rubbed up and down her arm to warm her.

Hawksby noted she didn't say she was frightened. But he'd been. Lord! He didn't remember ever being so frightened about anybody so much in his life, except perhaps when Mama had her accident. "Your family was very worried about you."

"Oh, I did not mean for them to be. I didn't think."

"Well, it's about time you start thinking and begin to worry about the consequences of your actions."

"What consequences?"

"That your reputation will be ruined and you will find no man of high station who will have you for a wife."

"Why should that bother me?" she asked.

"Then you don't intend to marry, Lady Margaret?"

There followed what sounded to Hawksby to be a *snort— gurgle—hoot.*

Hawksby was surprised by her reaction. "But I thought it

was the desire of all young ladies to find a husband."

"And what is the gain for me, pray tell?"

"Why, a woman cannot carry on alone."

"I certainly don't see why not. My sisters and I did quite well for four years by ourselves when . . . after our father died."

"On cabbage and eggs?"

"We snared a rabbit now and then."

"I see why your brother assigned me to protect you."

She harrumphed. "Why did he?"

"He thought you needed to have someone take care of you. Guide you."

"Well, you've not been doing a very good job of that, have you?" Maggie yelped. "You are squeezing me to death, Hawksby."

He loosened his hold.

She sighed and lay her head back against his chest again. "I meant it when I said I was glad you came, Hawksby. It was getting very soggy and dismal out here in the wet grass and muddy field."

She smiled as his arm tightened even more around her, gently this time.

"Well, it would serve you right if I did squeeze the day-lights out of you," he said, grumbling several unintelligible phrases after that.

"They stole my box of insects," she said.

She sounded as if she'd lost the crown jewels. Hawksby was of a mind not to tell her, but he could never stand the sound of a female so down in the dismals. "I took them from the bast . . . beggars who robbed you."

She tried to turn her head to look at him. "Oh, Hawksby! You are a game one. Did you know that? You really are. I hope you gave them a regular what-for."

"I reckon I did," he said, sitting up a little straighter.

"I'm sure you did. I wish I could have seen it."

" 'Tis not something a lady should witness."

"I don't know why not." She sank back against him further and yawned. "I suppose being a man does have its advantages. If I were as big and strong as you, I'd have given them a good facer myself."

She couldn't see the grin that curled up into his mustache. "Well, you're not," he said. "And I don't want you running off like that again. There's no telling what could have happened to you." He gave her another squeeze. "You could have caught your death."

"It's colder near Scotland. I'm used to it."

"I know."

"Where are you from?"

Hawksby turned the horse back down the High Road. The traffic was nearly as heavy at night as it was in the day, but he barely noticed. "North of here," he said.

From the way he said it, Maggie realized she wasn't going to get any more information. She sighed. "It's no fun being a girl."

Hawksby didn't know why, but at that moment he was sure as the devil glad she was a girl. But now the problem was how to get her back to London without causing a scandal. Drat! With Lady Margaret, he never knew for sure that if she asked him to take a chair, he wouldn't end up sitting on a bee. She was worse than his sister Hortense.

He changed the subject. "You were chasing after Herr Wehrhahn, weren't you?"

"Yes," she said without one bit of embarrassment. "He told me if he ever had the opportunity to go to Edinburgh to meet Dr. MacDougal he would be honored to escort me if I wished to go, but he was gone before I could get word to him."

"Then you aren't in love with him?"

"In love with him? Don't be ridiculous. I want to see Dr. MacDougal."

The only conclusion he could come to was that Lady Margaret had a *tendre* for the scholarly gentleman from Scotland. Hawksby told himself he should be glad to find out she had some womanly feelings after all. For some reason he wanted to talk about something else. "I surmise by now the thieves have been taken into custody by the magistrate."

"Oh, Hawksby. You are everything my brother claimed you to be. I'm sorry I said you weren't doing your duty."

Her apology didn't make him feel any better. He shouldn't have told her about the box. He should have let her suffer a little.

"I really want to go home, Hawksby."

"That is where I'm taking you now."

"I meant Knocktigh."

What he should have done was left her to continue on to the border. Then he'd have been rid of her. Why, then, were his emotions just the opposite? He was sure this Scot was not for her, even though he'd never met him. Even Curly-head's high regard and praises of the man from Edinburgh couldn't persuade Hawksby to think otherwise.

"Have *you* ever thought of getting married, Hawksby?" Maggie asked.

She'd caught him by surprise, as she always did. "No," he growled. "The matter is of little significance to me. The life of a military wife is one of long separations."

Hawksby had thought about it, of course. But he liked his life as it was. He was not one to spend his time doing the pretty—the receptions, the balls, the endless round of soirees and routs. He liked being free of such obligations. When in town he enjoyed riding his horse in the countryside, visiting the men's clubs, the theatre now and then, and now that he had Luci to visit and parade around in front of his friends, he felt quite content.

Maggie looked straight ahead, narrowing her eyes. "Freddie and Daniel seem to rub along well enough, but I don't see that much advantage in it. Do you? Being married that is." She didn't wait for an answer. It was as if she were talking to herself. "I really didn't know my father. He seldom visited us. My mother seemed happy, though. She had the house and her friends and the eight of us. But I think she was lonely sometimes. Then she would ride out on the hills on her chestnut mare and not come home until dawn. Can a person be lonely when they are with lots of people and not lonely when they are alone?"

Having been raised with a brood of lively siblings and then spending a great many of his formative years in the army, it took Hawksby a while to mull that over.

His own parents had been a love match, or so Mama had said. Something had ignited between the two when they met at a country party. A sort of spark. Hawksby had never tried to analyze the phenomenon before. Could that have been what it was like for Lady Margaret and this MacDougal chap?

Hawksby delivered Lady Margaret back to Terrace Palace without having a single member of the *beau monde* discover that one of the Durham Incomparables had committed the unforgivable. At the inn where they stayed overnight, Maggie did as she was told and professed herself to be the young man's sister. Since her portmanteau had disappeared, they bought a clean dress from the innkeeper's wife, who was three sizes larger. Jack had his leg set by a local surgeon and rode in the carriage with Lady Margaret. Clugg and Hawksby took turns at the ribbons. While one drove, the other rode alongside on his horse. By the time they reached London, they all looked as if they'd relived Waterloo.

Maggie told her family Mr. Wright was a hero for trying to save her life, and all the sisters insisted he be made their guest and occupy Mr. Pettigrew's old room in the East Wing until he was well enough to return to his business.

Then, when the household was settled back into a more reasonable routine, Captain Hawksby said he wanted Mrs. Vervaine and all the sisters, except Lady Margaret, to assemble the following day for consultation. "There are issues which must be addressed," he said, and forthwith departed for his quarters, leaving five young ladies to worry over the consequences wrought by their errant sister.

Eleven

Captain Hawksby was back the next day soon after midday, bathed, shaved, and in a uniform which didn't look as though a horse had bedded down in it. He instructed Beetleworth to advise Mrs. Vervaine he was ready for their meeting.

A few minutes later, abovestairs in her chambers, Lady Margaret Durham sat staring out the window onto the rear gardens of Terrace Palace, awaiting her fate. Below on the ground floor in the library sat five of her sisters and Mrs. Vervaine, solemn, their backs rigid, hands clasped in their laps.

Captain Hawksby, looking like an officer addressing troops about to go into battle, stood straight and tall, legs apart, hands behind his back, a scowl upon his face. A slight twitching of his mustache was the only indication of his annoyance. All eyes of those who sat before him were scrutinizing his expression. How in the devil's name could anyone foresee such shenanigans being committed by the angel-faced ladies in front of him? He'd heard the rumors last Season. He'd thought them unbelievable then. He didn't think them unbelievable now.

Hawksby cleared his throat. "Your brother, Lord Chantry, entrusted me with certain duties and obligations before he and his countess departed London. I fear I have badly failed him." He held up his hand when he heard a gasp of protest. "As we all know, someone in this household has

157

broken the rules. A solution must be found that assures us that the story doesn't get spread about among the *ton* and bring down condemnation on you all, and that it never happens again."

Mrs. Vervaine jingled her keys, a sure sign she wanted Hawksby to get to the point.

"Mrs. Vervaine and I have talked the matter over. We believe the only acceptable path is to send a letter to Lord Chantry informing him of the situation and my failure to secure the battle lines. We have called this meeting to see if you agree—or disagree. Do any of you have any objections to that?"

"Well, I think it is outside of enough that you should take the blame for what Maggie did," Mary said indignantly.

Not one to skirt the obvious, Hawksby thought. Had to give Lady Mary credit for that.

"Yes, why should you take the blame?" Babette and Antoinette said in unison, tears forming in their dark eyes. "But we don't want Maggie to be punished, either."

Lady Rebecca's face showed only confusion. "Lord Finch was going to ask Daniel for my hand in marriage as soon as he returned to London. We talked of being wed in October, and I wouldn't like to have a cloud of scandal hanging over our wedding day," she said, her lips trembling.

Hawksby had never been faced with so many teary eyes before. How did Chantry ever stand it? He turned to the only sensible sister. "Lady Ruth, what do you have to say about all this?"

Everyone's attention turned to Ruth, who blushed. "I must confess that I have already written to Freddie about the situation," she said.

Rebecca gasped. "You told her? But how could that be so? Captain Hawksby has only just brought Maggie home. Even by special messenger it takes a letter at least a week to go up and back to Yorkshire."

"I know, but 'tis true nonetheless. Perhaps I know Maggie better than most. If she is determined to do something she will do it, no matter the consequences. Remember that Freddie almost gave up her chance to marry our brother Daniel when her grandfather, Gilbert MacNaught, the Earl of Gloaminlaw, told her she had been chosen as the next laird of Clan MacNaught and must live in Scotland. I feel Maggie must make her own decision of whether she wants to stay in London or go to Knocktigh. Keeping her here is only going to make her more determined than ever to find a way to return. The pull for her is stronger perhaps than for the rest of us. We cannot judge her or criticize her for that. So I wrote Freddie two weeks ago, but that was before Maggie had run away."

"Two weeks ago," said Mary. "Why, you should have heard by now!"

"I have a letter in my room from Freddie which came yesterday. I didn't say anything about it, because at that time we didn't know what had happened to Maggie—or what the meeting was to be about this morning. Freddie only said Daniel would write to Captain Hawksby. Perhaps the missive is already at your quarters, Captain. Freddie said Daniel refused to tell her what he wrote to you."

Hawksby shook his head. "No, no letter has come yet. I shall advise Clugg to keep an eye out for it."

Ruth's face turned a brighter red. "I told Freddie I was afraid if Daniel didn't permit her to go that Maggie's pig-headedness might drive her to do something foolish."

"Well, she certainly did that now, didn't she?" barked Hawksby. "Going in a cabriolet that has JACK WRIGHT DOES IT RIGHT written across the boot is about as rattle-brained as anyone can get." Hawksby could have sworn he heard several giggles.

"Since I have nothing holding me in London anymore," Ruth said, looking down at her hands, "I proposed to Freddie that she ask Daniel to give his permission for me to accompany Maggie in one of the large coaches. I said we could take Flora Doone with us—she would dearly love to see her mother again—and a driver and footman. And I could accompany Maggie back to Knocktigh. If Daniel agrees, we wouldn't have to tell him of Maggie's indiscretions, would we?"

"And what if Lord Chantry doesn't agree?" Hawksby asked.

Mrs. Vervaine once again jingled her keys and everyone fell silent. The little wisp of a woman stood up from where she sat on a straight-backed chair—which made her no taller than when she was sitting, but everyone knew when the housekeeper stuck her pointy little nose in the air, they'd better listen.

"I would suggest, Captain Hawksby, that we wait a few days. We should then have heard from his lordship and we can proceed from there. And now, ladies," she said, addressing the sisters, "have you forgotten this is the day you are entertaining at home?"

With all the turmoil, they had done just that and forgotten their social obligations.

"Then," said Hawksby, "I suggest that under the circumstances it would be best that we proceed as if all is normal and that Lady Margaret join her sisters in their activities—until we hear from Lord Chantry."

The Durham sisters' stream of visitors that afternoon successfully filled the drawing room at Terrace Palace to its limits. Ruth confided to Mrs. Hefflewicker that she was hoping to accompany Lady Margaret to Northumberland for a visit to Knocktigh, their late mother's home, and the place where they had been raised. "But we don't know if our brother, Lord Chantry, would approve of our going alone."

"Oh, my dear," said Mrs. Hefflewicker. "What a coincidence you should mention it. I was wishing to find a friend to accompany me north. I'm sure Lord Chantry would approve if you were to bring your coach along with mine. How wonderful it would be if we could go in a caravan. Mr. Hefflewicker already returned to our home in Durham with our traveling coach, and I am having to use one of the Lisbones'. My sister and her husband, the earl, have gone off on holiday to the Continent. I was going to stop off at Thessalonia's cottage on the sea east of York. It is a little off the way, but it would be a nice holiday for you, too, to have a layover."

Maggie listened eagerly. "I'm sure Daniel will approve of that, aren't you, Ruthie?"

"It is still a long way from the Border," Ruth said.

"But Mr. Hefflewicker is to come down to Seaside Cottage to fetch me there and carry me back. We could escort your party as far as Durham. It is not so far past that up to the Cheviot Hills, is it? Surely with your servants you will be able to make the remainder of the journey on your own."

"Oh, Mrs. Hefflewicker," Ruth said, "that would much more likely gain our brother's approval. Thank you for your kind offer. I'm sure that Daniel will be perfectly satisfied as to our safety if we were to go with you. I shall write him a letter tonight. Surely he will approve of such an arrangement."

"I shall start packing right away," Maggie said.

Ruth patted her hand. "Don't be too eager, dear. Daniel still may say no."

"I don't care," Maggie said. "I'm going to get ready."

Mrs. Hefflewicker nodded her approval. "You are perfectly right, Lady Margaret. Anticipation that things will work out is halfway there."

Ruth laughed. "Then I shall pack, too. That should make it doubly certain we shall go."

Hawksby had lunch, tended to some banking matters, then returned to quarters to spruce up. He'd sent a note to Luci telling her he'd been called out of town on a military assignment, but now he was back and he'd like to see her tomorrow night.

The meeting with the Durham sisters had run smoother than he had hoped. He did need to have his hair cut, he thought, as he ran his fingers through his hair, but as he was about to pick up his comb, he spied the little porcelain pug dog upon his chest of drawers. It made his brain do a complete twist.

What he needed was a visit to his little buttercup, not a night at one of the men's clubs playing cards and drinking. He'd go round and surprise her when she returned home from the theatre this very evening. He could see her eyes and hear her laughter when she realized she didn't have to spend another night alone in an empty town house. Then he'd give her his gift. After what he'd been through in the last couple of days, he wanted to be with a woman whose only thought was to please him, not someone who told him he wasn't very good at guarding young ladies and punched him in the stomach with her elbow.

Half an hour later, his horse stabled at the mews near Covent Gardens, Hawksby approached the familiar row of town houses, whistling. The fog swirled about his feet and rose in a merry dance about his head. He waited round the corner. A familiar carriage emerged from the mist, just as he knew it would, and approached the town house, then stopped. In anticipation of her surprise and delight, Hawksby smoothed the corners of his mustache with a flourish of his gloved hand and waited for Luci to emerge from her carriage. But it was not his little buttercup who stepped down. It was a gentleman.

Basilbone! The jackanapes. Hawksby almost said it out loud. He would have recognized the sharp nose and high cheekbones anywhere. The rogue, the bounder, the snake in Weston clothing, turned and held out his hand. Luci, his little buttercup, leaped into Basilbone's arms, laughing. Still entwined in their embrace, they made their way up the steps and entered the house together.

Hawksby's hand gripped his sword. Betrayed! Bitten! Bilked! They all spelled Basilbone. "By Jove! I shall call him out," sneered Hawksby. Then the picture of Luci . . . Miss Divine, came to mind. She was the one who had jumped into Basilbone's arms. She was as much to blame as Sharp Nose was, and he certainly couldn't call a woman out, now could he? He put his sword back in its scabbard and made a quick about-face. His evening was ruined, his trust broken. Hawksby did not feel like facing his cohorts at one of the men's clubs, so he returned to his quarters, the little pug dog pressing heavily inside his coat against his heart.

The next day, Hawksby sent Miss Divine her congé, a little silver locket with a jewel that looked like a tiny pink eye in the middle of it. He found it in a jewelry shop in Bond Street and had it sent round to her town house. Let Lord Basilbone see how far he could get in a card game after he'd pawned that. Hawksby had no doubts at all about where all his blunt had been going in the last several weeks. He'd been supporting both of them. He'd been bamboozled, and he wasn't proud of it.

Now what was he to do with the pug dog? Its disapproving,

squished little face was a painful reminder to stay clear of women. He pulled out a drawer and stuffed it under a pile of shirts.

A week later Hawksby received a letter from Lord Chantry asking a favor. Would he escort Ladies Ruth and Margaret to their home in Northumberland? If so, his lordship would be indebted and promised to grant him any boon he might ask. Chantry and his countess would meet them at Knocktigh, for they wished to check on how the staff was faring and see to implementing plans which they had decided to follow to make the holding profitable. Then Hawksby could return to London whenever he wished. They would take over from there.

His wife, Chantry said, had finally persuaded him his youngest sister was fully capable of such a madcap caper as running away if she were not allowed to return to Knocktigh. *I feel you are the only one whom I can trust to keep Lady Margaret from doing anything so foolish.*

Chantry then noted that he'd written to Mrs. Vervaine also. *Only if you agree to give escort to the little caravan is she to permit my sisters to embark for the Border.*

Hawksby groaned. Chantry would probably have him drawn and quartered if he knew the truth of the matter. Was there anyone, God or man, who was capable of reining in Lady Margaret? No, he could think of no one who would be so daft as to try. No! No! No! There was no way he would agree to being watchdog to such a hoyden for over three hundred miles. He would go for a ride and forget the matter entirely.

"Clugg," he bellowed, "I am going to the mews to collect my horse. You need not expect me until you see me."

It didn't take too long for Hawksby to be out into the

countryside. London was not all that large a territory when a person was on horseback galloping along, jumping fences, cutting across fields, not bothering to take note of where he was going. However, sense finally prevailed, and Hawksby slowed down. He might not care that much for his own neck, but he did care for his horse.

After sitting atop a hill overlooking the northeastern side of the City, he let his mount choose its own pace to wander back into Town. He preferred to skirt the theatre district and Covent Garden area and continued to travel westward along the river front. He passed Terrace Palace on the Strand and wondered about it occupants, but did not stop.

Then somehow or another his mount passed through the iron gate of the old Farley Mansion. He turned away from the water steps and continued along the familiar footpath, tied his horse to a tree, and before clearing a spot to sit on the crumbling wall, picked up a stick from the ground. Once settled, he threw the stick out into the current and watched it bobble along until it was sucked under a barge.

"It's not the same as when there is someone to tell things to . . . like Lady Margaret," he said out loud, looking down at the spot next to him as if expecting to find her there. "She certainly can skip pebbles across the water better than most boys."

Right now he didn't want to face any of his cronies at the clubs. They probably already knew Miss Divine had been playing him for a fool. But he reckoned he could tell Lady Margaret. She'd probably laugh, but he wouldn't mind, because she'd think it a joke. Someone who liked bugs didn't care what people said. She didn't like London any better than he did, either.

As Hawksby pictured the look of horror on Miss Divine's face when the *omocestus viridulus* jumped out of her reticule in the park, he felt a chuckle fighting to get out from somewhere deep down in his middle. But he subdued it and leaped upon his horse. Twenty minutes later, he was entering his quarters.

"Clugg," he called out. "There is nothing for me here. I reckon I might as well see the ladies safely to Northumberland. Then I shall request that I cut short my leave and be assigned to join Wellington in France. I have seen quite all that I want to see of London. Yes, I am soundly persuaded that my calling is in the service of my country after all."

The little caravan departed from London a few days later. There were three coaches, with the Durham ladies and Mrs. Hefflewicker trading places off and on so one could lie down and sleep if she felt the need. Besides Hawksby and Clugg, there were Flora Doone and Mrs. Hefflewicker's maid, drivers, footmen, and a groom from each household to help with the horses. Two saddle horses were tied behind for Clugg and Hawksby to carry them back to London from Knocktigh when their mission was over.

At York they exited the Great Northern Road and headed east. The trip hadn't taken them a full three days to reach Cliffside Cottage—not a cottage at all, but a magnificent manor house set above the sea.

"When a woman is traveling to meet her lover, the time cannot go swiftly enough," sang Mrs. Hefflewicker as she bundled herself out of the carriage. "Mr. Hefflewicker should be here in a couple of days."

Maggie looked at Ruth and grinned. All they had heard the whole length of the journey were the wonders and accomplishments of her fine husband. Mrs. Hefflewicker only hoped each of the girls would find happiness with a man she loved.

Flora had made friends with Mrs. Hefflewicker's maid,

and Clugg rubbed along well with the other servants. With each advancing mile to the north, Maggie's disposition became cheerier and even Ruth smiled more. Everyone found it difficult to be around someone so overflowing with goodness as Mrs. Hefflewicker and not be cheery. Only Captain Hawksby seemed more withdrawn with each passing day.

"Well, here we are," said Mrs. Hefflewicker as the butler opened the door and they all stepped into the vestibule of Cliffside Cottage. "Mealtime is not too far away, so I suggest we all retire to our rooms to refresh ourselves and then meet in the drawing room for a drink before going to dinner."

It was as hard to be in the dismals around Mrs. Hefflewicker as it was to be sad around a magpie, and they had seen three of *them* together in a field that morning.

"Isn't it supposed to be a good omen to see three magpies at one time, Ruthie?" Maggie asked.

"Yes, I believe it is," Ruth said.

"Well, I wonder who shall be lucky, since we all saw them."

"Oh, my! Oh, my! Oh, my!" exclaimed Mrs. Hefflewicker an hour later as she came into the drawing room from the balcony overlooking the sea. "Don't we all look lovely. And that includes you, Captain Hawksby."

Hawksby bowed from the other side of the room.

Maggie and Ruth were the last to assemble, and they both apologized for their tardiness.

"There is no need, my dears. I came down early because I wanted to show you all what I found in my room when I arrived," Mrs. Hefflewicker said, motioning to someone to follow her in from the balcony. "My Mr. Hefflewicker, two days early because he could not wait to see me."

In came a roly-poly man, his cutaway coat nearly dragging

on the floor behind him, his lavender brocaded vest not quite covering his belly in front, and a grin so wide it nearly split his pumpkin face in half.

"I reckon then that you are the lucky ones," Maggie said, as the squire bent over her hand.

"Why, what do you mean, my dear?" asked Mrs. Hefflewicker.

"Ruth and I were talking about the three magpies we saw in the field this morning, and we were wondering who would be touched by good fortune."

"Well, I don't see why we cannot all be. With two such handsome men to escort us to dinner, what more could we ask?"

She'd no sooner said that than a servant appeared in the doorway and announced that dinner would be served in twenty minutes in the dining room.

"Oh, posh and bother," exclaimed Mrs. Hefflewicker. "I left my shawl out on the balcony. Would you fetch it for me, Ruth, dear?"

"I will." Maggie started to race for the door, but a strong hand gripped her arm and held her back.

"Lady Ruth is nearer, I believe," hissed Hawksby.

"She is not," said Maggie, trying to retrieve her arm from Captain Hawksby's grip. But that was like trying to wrestle a daffodil away from her brother's great Scots Grey stallion, Precious, who loved to carry a posy between his teeth.

Hawksby tugged her to the other side of the room. "Now she is nearer, I believe," he said, putting his face down to Maggie's level, so no one else would hear. "Do you wish to have someone measure the distance?"

With a little sidestep and a backward thrust, she punched him in the stomach, releasing her arm in the process.

"You are daft, Hawksby. Do you know that?" Maggie

whispered back, rubbing her elbow.

Unaware of the little drama, Ruth continued on out the tall casement doors. A refreshing sea breeze and the smell of saltwater greeted her, but the shawl was not on the railing. Thinking it had been blown off onto the rocks below, she ran to the edge of the balcony and peered over.

"Could I be what you are looking for, Lady Ruth?" The voice came from behind her, near the stairs which led down the cliffs to the beach. She didn't need to turn around to see the speaker. Her hands flew up to cover her mouth and she let out a sob.

"Why are you crying, my dearest?" He came up behind her and turned her to face him.

"Oh, Spencer," she said. "Spencer."

He laughed and kissed her.

Ruth gazed up at her beloved's face. "But how do you come to be here? I didn't even know we were coming until a week ago."

"I'm afraid Mrs. Hefflewicker is an incurable romantic, my darling. She persuaded my aunt we were meant to be together."

"Was Captain Hawksby in on this charade also?"

"No. He was just about as surprised as you when Mr. Hefflewicker brought him out on the balcony a few minutes ago."

Ruth chuckled. "Then that is why he nearly twisted Maggie's arm off trying to stop her from coming out here. Oh, dear, Mrs. Hefflewicker is probably wondering where her shawl is. I must find it and take it to her."

Spencer traced her face with his fingers. "I don't think they expect us any too soon," he said. "Besides, didn't you notice she already had a blue shawl around her shoulders? I heard her husband remark about how pretty it became her."

Ruth placed her head against his chest. "What a ninnyhammer I must seem," she said, laughing. "Now tell me how you got here and why you left London."

"When I knew I couldn't have you, I had to leave. My aunt suggested I come up here. She thought the sea air and sunshine would remedy whatever was ailing me. Her sister, Mrs. Hefflewicker, persuaded her that the only balm for what ails me was you."

"Oh, Spencer, what are we to do?"

"I have had time to think it through, and I have decided, my darling, that I must face your brother and find out just why he objects to me."

"I am taking Maggie back to Knocktigh."

"I know, and as soon as you all return to London, I shall come to Town and confront him. But now I believe our hostess has been overly generous in allowing us this time to ourselves. We will have a couple of days together before we must part again. Let us make the most of them. Now take my hand and let us go in to dinner."

When Maggie had gotten over her inquisition of Ruth about the sudden appearance of Sir Spencer, she turned and took the arm Hawksby offered her to lead her into dinner.

"You knew, didn't you?" she said accusingly.

"Only just minutes before you, Lady Margaret. It was as much a surprise to me as to you and your sister."

Maggie took time to give that some thought, but not much. He'd known, and that was why Hawksby had nearly carried her across the floor. He was thinking of his friend Sir Spencer and Ruth. She had only been thinking of herself. "Hawksby," she said in a hoarse whisper. He had to bend his head down to hear her. "I'm sorry I hit you in the bread basket with my elbow."

Hawksby couldn't help himself. He let out a whoop. So

unusual was it for the captain to show such emotion that all eyes turned his way. He collected himself quickly enough and marched into the dining room with Lady Margaret on his arm, his hand covering hers.

Ruth noticed and smiled.

Twelve

The porcelain pug dog made a very fine parting gift. When they were prepared to leave the seaside three days later, Captain Hawksby presented it to Mrs. Hefflewicker. She was delighted and exclaimed in her usual enthusiastic way that she would treasure it as a memento of a perfect weekend.

Why Clugg had packed it in with his belongings in his trunk, Hawksby didn't know, but there it was, its beady little eyes staring out at him from under his shirts, reminding him of what a fool he'd been, reminding him that he was dull as dust, reminding him of a certain golden-haired actress whom he wished he'd never met.

He was glad he'd found someone of Mrs. Hefflewicker's kind nature who would give the little beastie a loving home. He certainly couldn't give it to Lady Margaret. She'd already stated that she didn't particularly take to pug dogs. Besides, the sight of the little porcelain figurine might bring back memories for her, too.

He recalled the day when they had stood before the window of the novelty shop in Bond Street. Could Lady Margaret have thought he was going to buy the reticule for her? Whatever could have given her that ridiculous idea? He hadn't meant to hurt her, silly chit. And did it matter to him if she did hold some feelings for him? Hawksby shook himself. He'd been hoodwinked by Miss Divine. He wasn't going to get caught in that sort of snare again.

By the time they were ready to depart from Seaside Cottage, Sir Spencer had confided to Hawksby that he couldn't bear to be parted from his sweetheart again and, when he heard that Lord Chantry was planning on meeting his sisters at Knocktigh, he challenged Hawksby to try to stop him from joining his caravan north.

"I shan't put off facing up to Chantry any longer, Hawksby," Sir Spencer said. "I shall beard the lion in his den and ask him why the deuce I cannot marry his sister."

Hawksby didn't try to stop him from coming. In truth, he looked forward to having his friend's companionship. Consequently, Sir Spencer's carriage was added to the caravan, and the coaches set out.

They proceeded north along the coast and picked up the road west of Scarsborough, which hugged the north Yorkshire moors, a pleasant upland carpeted with purple heather and cleft by picturesque glens. On through Pickering to Thirsk, with its view of the Hambletons, then westward until they once again gained access to the Great North Road. Flora Doone, being the only female servant, rode with Lady Margaret or Lady Ruth. And since the Lisbone coachmen and one of their grooms had returned to London with the Lisbone equipage, Hawksby and Clugg rotated duties driving Sir Spencer's carriage.

The innkeepers along the turnpike were more than solicitous to have the patronage of such a large party, which included two daughters of an earl, escorted by a fierce-looking army officer who demanded the best of accommodations. But for the most part the Great North Road took them through a vast, flat, farmed landscape, quite ordinary, and devoid of the beauty they had experienced the last few days. Lady Ruth remarked on this when they stopped to refresh themselves at a wayside inn.

"I say, Hawksby," Sir Spencer said. "Didn't I hear you mention you were from this vicinity? Something about the Tees River . . . or was it the Tyne?"

"And we do have to stay overnight somewhere, Captain Hawksby," Ruth added. "Spencer spoke as though you were familiar with the Pennines. How far is your family home from here?"

Hawksby hesitated. "Well, off in that direction."

"How near?" Maggie asked, her interest perking up.

"Have you heard of Barnard Castle?" he asked hoping she had not.

"Yes, I have. Of course, I've never been there."

Good, he thought. She wouldn't know one way or another. "The Hawksby holdings are farther north. Difficult to get to."

"Are your parents still living there?" Ruth asked.

"They are."

"My goodness, Hawksby," Ruth said. "Of course you must stop to see them."

"There, you see. The perfect solution," Maggie put in.

Hawksby glared at her.

"You needn't look at me like that, Hawksby. We can stop over on our way to Knocktigh. I'm sure you wanted to see your parents but were too shy to say so."

Hawksby doubted that. "That is neither here nor there. 'Tis too far off the path. My duty is to deliver you and Lady Ruth to Knocktigh."

"Listen, old chap," Spencer threw in, "If they don't have the room to accommodate us, just say so. We wouldn't want to overwhelm your parents with four guests and eight servants."

Hawksby sat up stiffly. "There are plenty of rooms, I assure you, Spencer." For a whole army, he said to himself.

They could put Prinny's entire entourage in the tower alone.

How strange he shouldn't want to see his family, Maggie thought. "Well, I know my brother wouldn't expect you to forego the pleasure of paying them a visit."

Ruth agreed. "I hear the country is much more picturesque toward the Pennines. Surely there are secondary roads which we can use to get back to the turnpike."

The others all voted to give it a go.

Hawksby saw that their minds were set, so there was nothing he could do but comply. When they stopped that night at an inn near Darlington, he hired a posting boy, one of the small older men who haunted the inns looking for jobs. For a good fee, Hawksby sent him ahead to his parents' home, carrying a letter informing them he would be paying them a visit with three guests—two ladies and a gentleman—and their eight servants. The party planned to leave the Great North Road sometime the next day and would probably arrive late in the afternoon.

Before dawn, Hawksby climbed onto the box of Sir Spencer's small carriage and maneuvered his horses ahead of the others. "Follow me," he ordered, raising his arm and motioning them onward. Second in line came the Durham traveling coach and four, with the driver, the groom, and two liveried footmen. Inside sat the Ladies Ruth and Margaret, Flora Doone, and Sir Spencer. The smaller Durham vehicle, driven by the second coachman and leading the rider horses, carried Clugg and the valet.

They left the High Road an hour later and headed westward toward the ridge of hills running up Yorkshire into Durham. Soon they were traveling through great reserves of wild and beautiful scenery—stone-walled expanses of rough pasture or long moorland grass, the famous Dales and glorious valleys, all blanketed with sheep. Hawksby had spent much of his life among the wooly creatures. The great fair at Barnard Castle had been one of the highlights of his younger years.

They stopped at a small village inn for lunch and to give the horses a rest. Hawksby was willing to wait while the ladies refreshed themselves, but he was not ready for Lady Margaret's request on her return.

"Please, may I ride up on the box with you, Hawksby? It is not as if any hoity-toity gabblemongers are likely to be lurking about this part of the countryside just waiting to catch a juicy tidbit of gossip. And I can see so much more up there than from inside the coach."

Of course, Lady Margaret had already climbed halfway up without any help from a footman, so there wasn't much Hawksby could do to keep her off. She was going to have her way whether he said anything or not. Stubborn child. Hawksby held out his hand for her to grasp as she pulled herself the rest of the way up and settled down on the seat. But deep down, he was pleased. This was his part of England, and he wondered what she thought of it.

He didn't have to wait long to find out. She literally bounced upon the seat pointing out this and that—the trees, a grouse shooting into the air, a flower, the lambs gamboling about the pastures. "Why, this is beautiful, Hawksby," she exclaimed as they climbed onto the spreading hilltop moors and then down into the glorious valleys.

Hawksby didn't say anything, but inside he was smiling. Then he thought ahead to the consequences of this foolhardy side trip and his spirits plummeted. Eventually the narrow rutted path led them to the top of a wide grassy moor. The vista held their attention as they looked at the valley below.

"Oh, look, Hawksby," Maggie said. "The road divides up ahead."

"I know," he grumbled, his brow furrowing. He reined in his horses and raised his hand to signal the other coaches behind him to stop.

She saw three wooden signs aimed in different directions, but she couldn't make out the words this far away. The left pointed across a meadow and into a stand of trees. The right lane disappeared round a rocky hill. The middle road headed down into a valley where only the tops of trees were visible from where they sat. "Which way are we going?"

"Whatever-which-way."

Maggie gave him a withering look. "Hawksby, I want a civil answer."

He ignored her and waved one of the footmen forward. Then, leaning down, he spoke in a hoarse whisper to the servant, saying something which Maggie couldn't make out, while gesturing this way and that after pointing to each carriage. The footman ran back and spoke to the other two drivers.

The larger coach started forward, circled them, then took the lane to the left. "Where did you tell the footman his coach is to go?"

"Round-about-and-back-again," Hawksby said.

"Well, that isn't very helpful," she snapped, watching his color deepen.

The next carriage circled them and took off to the right. "Where does that road go?"

"Here-and-there," Hawksby barked, hunching down even further so his shoulders would hide his ears. He knew they were turning red.

Maggie would have told him what she thought of his jokes, but Hawksby slapped the reins so hard and the horses sprang ahead with such force that she had to grab hold of the seat to keep from being pitched off onto the ground. "Hawksby, you are becoming quite aggravating," she shouted over the rumble of the wheels. "Where are we going?"

"I told you. Whatever-which-way," he shouted. "Read the signs." Hawksby snapped the reins again, the horses laid their ears back, the wheels spun, and over the hill they flew as if they had wings.

Maggie held tight and twisted her head around as they whizzed past the intersection. *Whatever-which-way. Round-about-and-back-again. Here-and-there.* Names. They were the names of the roads.

He could see from the corner of his eye that her chin was out to there and she was staring at him, trying to drill holes through him, he reckoned. She was very pretty when she found herself confused and didn't know what to say. Hawksby gave himself a shake. He had no right to be thinking such thoughts. His brows came swooping down. At least he wouldn't let her see his eyes. His damned Bixworth eyes. They gave away everything.

Hawksby cracked the whip and snapped the ribbons. He didn't look at her again for quite some time. "It's a family tradition," he yelled. "One of my great-great-grandmothers said she was bored coming home the same way every time they left the estate. So to humor her, my great-great-grandfather had three roads opened to the house. That way she never had to come home the same way twice in a row."

"Then this is your family's land?" She sounded impressed.

"From here on," he said, not relaxing a bit. He knew the hard part was still ahead.

"And so the other carriages . . ."

"Will each go a different route but end up at the same destination."

Hawksby watched her eyes grow rounder. He knew from the beginning it was a mistake to bring Lady Margaret here. He pulled back on the ribbons to slow the horses. "My brothers and I used to race our ponies to see which one could get home first."

They had now entered a forest of ash and oak which was home to many woodland and water creatures. The road followed the river-stream for a while. She was very quiet. He didn't know if she saw the little brown dipper bobbing about on the rocks. He was certain she saw the dragonflies flitting about over the water. Lady Margaret wouldn't miss that. A trout snapped at a dragonfly, but it got away.

"And did you win?" she asked.

She so surprised him that he forgot and looked at her. "Sometimes I did," he said. "We didn't let our sister race."

"That wasn't fair, Hawksby." She turned to look at him, thinking of the races she and her sisters took on the wild donkeys of the Cheviot Hills. "Just because she was a girl?"

Hawksby quickly turned his attention back to the horses. "No, because she always won."

Maggie's eyes brightened. "Will I get to meet this sister of yours?"

"More than likely. Hortense and her husband, Sir Henry, live with their four children in what is supposed to be the dower house. None of my grandmothers would ever stay there, even though it adjoins the park at the back of the main house and they share the gardens."

"How many brothers do you have?"

"Three. You will probably meet them, too."

"They aren't married?"

"Yes. They all have wives."

"Then why aren't you married, Hawksby? Oh, that's right," she said. "You said it was a difficult life for a woman to be married to an officer. So what about your brothers?"

"My eldest brother, William, moved back into the house right after he married Isobelle, and has lived there ever since. They have five children. Hortense was the second born. Albert was the second son and is married to Roberta. They live in the Roman villa part of the house and have a child on the way, I hear."

Maggie wanted to ask about the Roman villa, but didn't know quite how to put it.

"I was the third son. Then came Durwood, who married Sarah about a year ago. I have not met her as yet. I suppose they live in the house, too."

Maggie wanted to ask him why he hadn't been home in over a year. In fact, Maggie had several questions to ask, but at that moment their coach emerged from the wooded glen to a view of the strangest-looking edifice she had ever seen. It looked as if children's building blocks had been piled here and there at random with no particular style in mind. A whimsical tower of gray stones anchored one side. A Georgian-style entrance spread over a large section facing the carriage path. A part which looked like an old castle with half a moat was attached to another of the wings constructed of mortar and brick. Looking like a fireworks display that had exploded, the building ran in all directions, one piece joined hel-ter-skelter to another so there were no true corners, only angles. The rooftops were as diverse in nature and style as the lower half, chimneys jutting out like soldiers making a mad charge over the tiles.

"What . . . what is it called?" Maggie asked.

"There-It-Is."

She gave him an exasperated look. "I know that, Hawksby. I wanted to know what the name of your . . . your home is."

Hawksby reined in the horses and hunted for words to

explain. "From way back at the beginning of time after our ancestor Ceremonious Hawksby bought the last Earl of Wigging's old manor house as a wedding present for his bride and he was bringing her from the church, the new Mrs. Hawksby had been trying her husband's patience beyond measure by asking repeatedly when her new home would appear. So when they finally burst from the woods as we just did, he said the first thing that came to his weary, befuddled mind. 'There-It-Is!' And that is what it has been called ever since."

Maggie clapped her hands in glee. "Why, I think that's a perfect name."

"You do?" Hawksby said. This made Hawksby very happy. If Lady Margaret thought it a good name, then he supposed it was. But there was still the matter of his family to consider. That was not going to be a circumstance too easily dismissed. He cleared his throat.

"Lady Margaret, before any of my family descends upon us, I believe I must warn you you might find the general run of Hawksbys a bit . . . different. No, I must be honest with you and say *peculiar.*"

Maggie's mouth dropped open and she forgot to shut it.

Catastrophe. Hawksby could feel it. The other two coaches had now appeared at opposite sides of the field and were coming up to the common roundabout in front of There-It-Is. He sprang his horses, hoping to arrive at the steps first.

The front double doors had been flung open, and a crowd of people spilled out onto the wide flagstone porch to greet them—old and young, servants and masters, all talking at once. Even though he couldn't hear them, Hawksby could tell because their mouths were opening and closing nonstop. On the front line a large woman adorned from top to toe in bright red smiled and waved a banner above her turbaned head. She was seated in a wheelchair.

A boy hurried forward to hold the horses, and a footman ran round the carriage to help Lady Margaret down from her perch. Hawksby leaped to the ground and took the steps two at a time before either of the other coaches had come to a halt.

"Mama," he said, as she pulled him down and gave him a big kiss on the cheek.

There followed a flurry of movement and instructions and introductions as all the guests were brought up and forward to meet their hosts. In back of Mrs. Hawksby stood her husband, the Honorable Mr. Clement Hawksby, beaming proudly, and the other three Hawksby men with their wives. Except for one who was clean shaven and was introduced as Sir Henry, all the gentlemen were dark-eyed, dark-haired, and adorned by an array of the most spectacular mustaches Maggie had ever seen, the senior Hawksby's being the grandest.

Servants were called forward and told to show the guests to their rooms. They all began to shuffle in, except Hawksby, who seemed to be searching for someone. "Where is Hortense, Mama?"

Mrs. Hawksby smiled broadly and patted his cheek. "She has taken the little ones off to play on the green behind the house so your homecoming would not be such a hullabaloo, Bixie dear. We didn't want your friends to be overwhelmed. I shall send a maid to call her if you like."

"Don't bother," Hawksby said. He knew his ears were burning red. "I shall fetch her myself. I don't mind."

Maggie raised her eyebrows at the exchange. Curiosity and temptation were too much for her. "I'll come with you, Hawksby," she said, as she caught up with him.

"You need not," he said gruffly, glancing back at the stubborn chit only to see the collective family interest . . . and amusement . . . on every damned face. Nothing had changed. Nor would it ever, he was afraid. He straightened up and continued on his march. "Come along then," he barked, hoping she couldn't keep up. But, as he knew she would, she did.

As they zigzagged round and about the strange edifice they came to one side which opened onto a wide, sloping lawn studded with strangely shaped bushes—imaginary creatures. Topiary, Maggie thought, for she'd seen many in London, but none like these. Children and puppies and lambs and a maid or two ran helter-skelter, chasing each other, hitting balls with sticks, hitting each other with sticks, hiding among the topiary zoo, jumping out and yelling, "Boo!"

Standing above them before a low stone wall on the other side of the garden, overlooking the lawn, was a tall angular woman dressed in a pleasant afternoon dress and wearing a poke bonnet. She seemed to have her back to the wall. From the angle of her head, it looked as though she was more interested in something in the sky than the children below.

Then her voice rang out with a strong warning. "Behave yourself, Jonathon! Don't splash water on your nurse, Willie! Sarabelle, if you hit your brother one more time, I shall take your pony away from you."

As Hawksby and Maggie came nearer, the woman seemed to turn her back to them. When she did, she cried out, "Bixie!"

Only then did Maggie realize the woman was not running toward them backward, but that her bonnet was turned round. She pulled it off to reveal very pleasant features beneath her brown hair as she threw herself into her brother's arms. "And who is this?" she said, revealing a pair of beautiful brown eyes as she cocked her head toward Maggie.

Hawksby introduced them. "Lady Margaret, may I present my sister Lady Hortense?"

"Oh, the hat," Hortense said, dangling the bonnet by its ribbons. She looked directly at Hawksby. "I've embarrassed you, haven't I, dear? Your ears are the most becoming shade of scarlet."

The heat was beginning to creep down his neck now. His sister would never change. Whatever nonsense came into her mind could always be counted on to come right back out her mouth. "The explanation can wait until later, Hortense. I have just arrived with several guests, and Mama requests that you leave the children with their nurses and come to the house to meet everyone. I am certain Lady Margaret isn't interested in hearing why you are wearing your bonnet on backward."

"I shall be along shortly, as soon as I tell the nurses to take the children up to the nursery and strangle them," Lady Hortense replied, winking at Maggie. "Watch his ears," she said. "They always give him away."

Hawksby took Maggie's elbow with a strong hand, and she found herself being rushed back to the house. She tugged loose. "Out with it now. What is the story behind the backward bonnet?"

Hawksby kept his gaze straight ahead. "You will insist on knowing, won't you?"

She nodded, not daring to say anything. She knew she would laugh, and Hawksby didn't seem to be in a mood for a joke.

Hawksby brooded a bit. He hated it when a female was silent. It only made a man feel he was being forced to talk. "It's Mama's doing."

"And?"

Hawksby sucked in a deep breath and blew it out again.

"Mama raised us to believe that God gave mothers eyes in the back of their heads, because, she said, he couldn't be watching us all the time to make sure we were being good. For years we believed her. She always seemed to know when we were bad and what it was we had done naughty. We didn't find out until years later that she had her own tricks, like punching holes in the back of her bonnet. She evidently has taught Hortense her devious methods."

Maggie couldn't hold it any longer and let out a whoop. "I like your sister," she said, wiping the tears from her eyes.

Hawksby looked at her in surprise. "You do?"

"I think we shall get along exceedingly well, Hortense and I. That is a trick that I shall want to remember if I have bairns of my own. Wouldn't you?" Maggie caught herself. Captain Hawksby wouldn't really care. He'd already said he wasn't going to get married, and it made her feel quite sad just to think it. He would make a splendid father. Stalwart and true. And he wasn't all that bad looking, either, if only he would smile a bit. "What else did your mother do to keep you all in check?"

"Well, she tried to tell us how futile it was for us to be naughty. And just because she was out of sight didn't mean we could get away with anything."

"Did you?" Maggie asked.

"Not often, but we tried," Hawksby said. He'd never told this story to anyone. He didn't know why he was telling it to a redheaded termagant now, except she seemed as bad as his sister.

"Mama loved chocolates and we would do everything we could think of to snitch a sweet when she wasn't looking. So one day she put out a box and said we could have all we wanted, because she did not want to raise a bunch of thieves and thatchgallows."

"I cannot think your mother would give up so easily," Maggie said.

"Well, no. And if we'd thought hard enough about it, neither would we. But we were greedy buggers and thought we had won. What we didn't know was that she'd poked holes in the bottoms of the confections and replaced the creme centers with soap. We'd swallowed several before we realized something was wrong. We all suffered for our greediness. After that we always thought twice before we snitched anything that was not ours."

"So it worked?"

"I would say that all the Hawksby men have grown up to be basically honest. I wouldn't want to speculate about the womenfolk. It is amazing how sturdy their stomachs are."

"Oh, Hawksby," Maggie said, "I don't think your family is peculiar at all."

"You don't?" He forgot and looked straight at her.

"Not at all," she said, losing herself for a moment in his cerulean blue eyes. For a moment Maggie felt as if she'd floated right up off the ground, and her imagination began to race in a totally new direction.

"Well, that is because you have only been here an hour," Hawksby said, bringing down his brows to hide his own confused thoughts. "Wait until you have been here an entire day before you make such a foolhardy judgment."

Thirteen

It definitely did not take an entire day, as Hawksby had predicted, for Maggie to discern if her judgments were sound. Not at all! It didn't take more than halfway through the dinner hour to find out what sensible people the Hawksbys were. She conceded that they might see the world a bit differently than other folk—say the *beau monde* in London or perhaps the Eskimos in Alaska—but that certainly did not make them peculiar. Hawksby was very mistaken about his family.

Mrs. Clara Bixworth Hawksby sat at one end of the long table in her wheelchair. She had changed into a startling blue gown shot through with silver threads which twinkled like stars in the candlelight, and on her head she wore a turban of similar hue adorned with a large pin in the shape of a half-moon. Maggie was curious about the accident which had left her crippled, but as yet had not felt at ease enough to ask anyone about the circumstances. Hawksby seemed especially wont to avoid the subject.

Their host, the Honourable Clement Hawskby, sat at the opposite end. Maggie had found him to be a jolly fellow of especially good nature, rotund from top to bottom. He had scant hair on top and twinkling brown eyes, and was rather absentminded, but he seemed tolerant of his wife's exuberant fancies. Now that his sons had reached their majority and had taken over the working of the estate, he could talk all he wanted of fishing, he said, for he considered himself a top angler.

He sported a colossal mustache, the ends of which curled up in amazing defiance of gravity. His sons seemed determined to compete, if not by largess then by design. All except Hawksby. His mustache was trimmed and neat, but Maggie judged that to be a product of military practicality.

Also at the head of the table sat a young lad dressed in a neatly mended brown jacket and starched shirt, his sandy hair slicked back and his nose shiny from the scrubbing his mother had given him. Mr. Clement Hawksby stood and placed his hand gently upon the boy's shoulder. Then, speaking in a booming voice better suited for an auction block than a formal dining room, he announced, "I would like to welcome our guests tonight. You have arrived just in time for a very auspicious occasion. This is Billy Buster, and it is his tenth birthday. Billy works in the stables and has been put in charge of combs and brushes—a very responsible job and worthy of mention. When anybody at There-It-Is arrives at such a singular and momentous moment in his life—for he will never be ten again—we always invite that person to the manor to receive our salutations and congratulations. He comes without his mama or papa or siblings, because he is now old enough to represent his family and take on the responsibilities of the adult world.

"Billy will also receive a slate and chalk and will begin to spend an hour a day in the classroom with the schoolmaster who comes to teach my grandchildren. Mama and I agreed we don't want workers who cannot read or write, for if they are cheated by jackanapes who come to do business with us, then we are likely to be cheated also." Mr. Hawksby patted Billy once more and sat down. "Now let the celebration begin," he said jovially.

Three of the older grandchildren—Jonathon, Harry, and Clemmy—met the ten-year-or-older criteria and were also present at the table. Even so, if it hadn't been for the presence of Billy Buster, the stablemaster's son who was trying his best to act like a little gentleman, Maggie was certain the boys would have been full of mischief, if their antics on the lawn that afternoon were any indication of their usual nature.

Lady Hortense did not wear anything backward to dinner. In fact, Maggie thought she looked quite lovely as she entered the dining room on the arm of Sir Henry. He was the only blond amongst the adults, a slightly built, dignified Englishman of impeccable tailoring who took care of the administration of the family holdings. Through his man of business, who had offices in York and London, he had expanded the Hawksby fortunes from wool and agriculture to part ownership of a merchant ship at Liverpool.

Dinner started with pudding. A small cake, with blueberries stuck into the frosting spelling out the letter B, was placed in front of each diner as well.

Maggie glanced first across the table at Ruth, who was looking incredulously at the rich sweets in front of her, then down the table at Hawksby. He was staring at a spot on the tablecloth and would not raise his head. She exchanged looks across the table once more with Ruth, who raised her eyebrows and tried her best not to laugh.

Mrs. Hawksby saw Ruth's and Maggie's expressions. "Oh, my goodness gracious!" she exclaimed. "No one told you, did they? Here at There-It-Is, we go from finish to start. It is quite disappointing, don't you agree, to come to the end of a big feast only to find you don't have room for another bite and have to forego the best part of the meal?"

Everyone at the table agreed, of course, and made short work of the pudding and cake.

Being the eldest son, William had taken over the overall administration of the estate and his wife, Isobelle, the supervision of the manor house and the household servants.

Albert acted in the capacity of steward, as his talents lent themselves to figures and calculations. Albert's wife, Roberta, could not contain her eagerness for everyone to see their month-old daughter on the morrow.

Durwood presented himself as an inventor. He was the one, he said, who had come up with the design for Mama's wheelchair, which she could propel by herself when a servant was not handy. He tended to the maintenance of farm and household appliances and equipment. His admiration of his older brother Bixworth, as well as his opinion of Lady Margaret, rose considerably when he found both had visited the Royal Institution in London and had observed firsthand the many inventions and experiments of Count Rumford. He quizzed his brother unmercifully for his opinions or suggestions on the practicality of changes he proposed for updating the antiquated kitchens of There-It-Is.

By now the dinner had progressed to a more familiar order of removes, all succulent, delicious, and filling. The conversation and quizzing of fellow family members did not stop, however.

Maggie could not understand why Hawksby didn't join in, but sat staring at his plate, talking only when he was spoken to. He looked so lonely.

Ruth had been seated on Sir Spencer's right, where she could hand him utensils or whisper directions while a footman stood on his left to serve him exclusively. Maggie suspected Hawksby had put a bee in Isobelle's bonnet to have arrangements made for Sir Spencer's ease. She watched the interaction between the two lovers with a longing she didn't understand.

Yes, Hawksby had proved himself a man of sober compassion—so why could he not enjoy the gaiety as well? That thought caused her to glance at Hawksby only to find he was also watching her. She blushed and looked down quickly. When she raised her head again, he was saying something to Roberta, who was seated next to him. Maggie wondered if she had just imagined he had been studying her.

But for all the precautions that had been taken for Sir Spencer's comfort, strangeness of customs cause accidents to happen. At the same time as Ruth was handing him mutton on a fork from his right, the footman reached over to remove the plate from his left and Sir Spencer decided to talk with his hands as well as his lips. Hands collided. The meat flew off the fork and attached itself to his lapel. Ruth's hand flew to her mouth, a plate crashed to the floor, and Sir Spencer sat with a look of confusion on his face.

Everyone at the table jerked to attention, wondering what had happened.

"Papa!" Mrs. Hawksby scolded from her end of the table, calling attention to her husband. "Look at you." Everybody did. "You are talking so much that you have spilled who-knows-what on your shirt front. How many times have I told you and the children not to eat and talk at the same time?"

Mr. Hawksby's gaze met his wife's with a knowing look. "Whoops!" he guffawed, slapping his hand to his chest. Sure enough, when he pulled it away, everyone saw a big dab of goo decorated the lace of his shirtfront. With much ado and a great deal of chortling, he peered down over his mustache to inspect the damage. "By ginger! You are right, Mama. There it is," he said, pointing to the offending glob. "But I could not have done such a thing. No. Talking cannot bring about such a disaster. Gnomes!" he said in the direction of his grandsons. "It has to be gnomes. I have warned my neighbors that is what comes of cutting down all the trees in the forests. The little people have nowhere else to live, so they invade our houses with their mischievous ways. We must do something about them."

The children went into gales of laughter. In response to their grandpapa's antics they began to punch each other, until their mothers shushed and their fathers frowned. Billy laughed, too, but he remembered his mother's admonition to watch his manners.

Mr. Hawksby nodded and winked at him. "Oh, I have seen them stalking about in the shadows of late, not having enough to do, I reckon, but make trouble for the lot of us. They wreak havoc with my shirt drawers, and my man says my socks always have one of a pair missing."

While all eyes were turned to their host, Ruth quickly took her napkin and cleaned Spencer's coat and whispered something in his ear. He threw back his head and laughed. Oh, indeed, he was the handsomest man at the table.

Maggie giggled and covered her mouth with her hand to stifle her laughter just as her gaze met Hawksby's across the table. His large blue eyes were unguarded for a moment until he saw her looking at him. He quickly lowered his brows. He was wearing an odd expression. Was he seeking to discover her response to his parents' tomfoolery?

Hawksby damned himself for staring. Lady Margaret was proving to be a damned good soldier, no two ways about it. Game to the end, sitting there acting as though his family was as normal as the next. When she'd turned and smiled at him his heart had flopped, completely and entirely. Jumped and bounced and knocked against his rib cage. He was certain everybody at the table would have heard it or seen it pounding to get out if they hadn't been so wrapped up in

Papa's crazy tarradiddle.

He wanted some structure, some sanity in his life. And what did he get? Silliness. Quirks and twaddle and absurdity.

He'd promised himself he would never make a commitment to a woman. Not a commitment for life. Hand tied. Shackled. Collared. Let his siblings do that. He would be content with his life as it was before he came back to England. Besides, Lady Margaret was already in love with a Scotsman named MacDougal.

"Look at him," his brother William said to Maggie. "Do you see what I mean? Bixworth is the funniest of all. How he can maintain that sober mien is outside of enough. We always break down before he does."

"Hear! Hear!" cried Hortense, raising her glass. "A toast to Bixie."

Hawksby didn't understand them at all. His ears burned, and he tried to tell himself they meant well. He made an effort to smile. Thank God he'd told Mama that they could stay only two full days.

A toss of a coin determined Maggie would be the one to put her dress back on and go downstairs to the library to find some books. Both she and Ruth had volunteered so the other would not have to be inconvenienced. Maggie reckoned a call of heads or tails was the easiest solution to the problem.

It had been a long and busy day with much to think over. A book of poetry or one that touted some dull subject such as *How to Stack Hay* should lull their minds into sweet slumber.

Maggie turned and raised her hair so her sister could finish buttoning up the back of her dress. "Ruthie, do you know the reason why Mrs. Hawksby is confined to a wheelchair? I thought Sir Spencer might know, since he is such a good friend of Hawksby's."

"Spencer said he wondered about that, too. He is hoping the captain will confide in him someday. He thinks for some reason Captain Hawksby feels himself responsible for the tragedy."

Maggie whirled around. "How can that be?"

"That is all I know, dear. But even if Spencer does learn the reason, I wouldn't expect him to betray a confidence."

"No, of course not," Maggie said, still curious to find out.

Picking up the candlestick, she walked quietly into the corridor. The stairs and hallways were so well lit by the tapers in the sconces along the walls that her own candle wasn't needed. She blew it out.

The elder Hawksbys had their apartment on the ground floor so Mama could maneuver her wheelchair in and out of the main rooms without contending with stairs. After a filling dinner, everyone had agreed to retire early. Maggie was quite surprised, then, to hear the voices of Hawksby and his father coming from the book room. Hawksby's back was to the doorway, quite blocking her from entering. She looked with admiration at the expanse of his shoulders while she waited for him to finish whatever he was saying so she could announce herself. She could not believe he would hurt his mother.

"Don't tell me Mama still has Herbert," Hawksby spouted.

"I'm afraid she does, son, and it has been a great trial for us all. Your Mama insists if I put him out, he will get caught and eaten. I don't even have the use of my own tub anymore because he spends most of his time in it now. Even that is too small. He keeps leaping out."

"But, Papa, she found him three years ago. He fit into a little glass bowl then."

"Your Mama has become quite fond of Herbert," Mr.

Hawksby said. "He comes when he hears her voice. We tried putting him in the summer pool with the water fountain, but he ate all the goldfish. She cannot go in search of food herself and the servants are beginning to complain about having to catch insects for him to eat. He has a voracious appetite. Can't just feed him bread. 'Twould take half our wheat harvest."

Maggie could stand it no longer. "Who is Herbert?" she asked.

Hawksby jumped as if an explosive had gone off under him.

Mr. Hawksby peered around his son. "Oh, my dear Lady Margaret. I didn't see you behind Bixworth. My son really is quite large, isn't he? Don't know how Mama and I hatched a chick so tall. Do you think he may wear lifts in his shoes?"

"Papa, we were discussing Herbert, not my size."

"Oh, yes . . . Herbert," Mr. Hawksby said, giving Maggie a wink. "Herbert is a brown trout, my dear. Mama found him on the bank of the stream when he was yet barely bigger than a dragonfly. That was after the accident, you see, and Mama became very upset when she saw any creature in trouble."

Maggie saw Hawksby wince and wondered at it.

But Mr. Hawksby seemed not to notice. "So we humored her and let her bring him home. We thought when Herbert grew bigger she would let us put him back in the river, but she has become so fond of him that she won't let him go. I can tell you it is a demmed nuisance. It isn't so bad in the summer months, because I can take a dip in the stream, but it's more than enough when winter comes round and I don't have a tub to bathe in unless I share it with a brown trout. Tried it once, but he bit my toes," Mr. Hawksby said, a twinkle in his eye.

Shock registered on Hawksby's face. "Papa, you didn't!"

Mr. Hawksby, his mirth silently shaking his body, bent

over and slapped his knee. Maggie wrapped her arms around her stomach to keep the laughter from bubbling out.

Hawksby looked back and forth between the two of them, blinked several times, then shook his head. "You're quizzing me, aren't you, Papa?"

Maggie had to save Hawksby. "Well, I must have you show me Herbert tomorrow, Hawksby. Now I shall have to say good night, for it is late and I believe we are to be interviewed by all your nieces and nephews early in the morning. Good night, sir," she said to Mr. Hawksby, and ran back to her room. She didn't bother getting books. She had too much to tell Ruth.

The following morning, the younger children who hadn't been at the dinner the night before were brought down to their Grandmama's sitting room to meet their Uncle Bixworth and his guests. Three little boys, three little girls, and the latest, little Clara. Ruth immediately took the baby and would not surrender her until the nurse declared it time to go back to the nursery.

Hawksby was seated when he had his nieces presented to him, two fairy princesses about three or four years old and a mushroom named Pipsy. He looked so helpless Maggie wanted to laugh.

The first climbed up upon his knee and took possession of his right arm. The second, not to be outdone, climbed the other leg, only to get stuck halfway up. He had to grasp her by an embarrassing part of her anatomy to help her finish the task. She claimed her spot and began to try to pull off the cords and buttons decorating his uniform.

Pipsy, seeing all stations were occupied and she couldn't sit on his lap, claimed a boot, settled down, and entwined her arms around his leg, ready for her ride.

Thus saddled, bridled, and securely anchored to the spot, Hawksby met his nephews.

After the three boys he'd met the night before had come in to pay their respects, the remaining three advanced to stand at Hawksby's knees. They stood transfixed, awed by the ominous wings which perched above their Uncle Bixworth's eyes. They possibly would have remained there all day if someone had not overheard Maggie mention her insect collection in her bedroom above. This put a whole new complex upon the situation and they all—including the older ones—insisted on seeing them.

Maggie obliged wholeheartedly and had all the boxes, including the lovely carved one, brought down. They were then opened and displayed upon a breakfront alongside one wall, low enough to be seen by most, but out of the reach of the small fry.

"Oh, I say," said Jonathon. "This is smashing."

They were an immediate success with young and old alike. Mrs. Hawksby in particular thought the collection quite remarkable and told her so. "You are a very brave young lady, Lady Margaret."

"Thank you, Mrs. Hawksby. And please, call me Maggie. All my friends do."

Hawksby was clearly relieved when the interviews were concluded, for he planned on using the afternoon to show his three guests about the estate.

"I won't go until I meet Herbert," Maggie said. "Your husband told me about him last night," she explained to Mrs. Hawksby.

Maggie was taken into the next room and introduced to the brown trout. He was still in Mr. Hawksby's tub under a blanket, which was stretched across the top to keep him from jumping out. They peeled a corner back for her to see him.

Herbert had a brownish back graded into yellowish on the sides, with black spots. There he waited for a servant to catch him in a bucket to carry him down for his daily swim in the garden pond.

Hawksby clicked his heels, gave a little cough, and finally cleared his throat to get their attention. "I am taking the landau, Mama. I told Cook last night to have a picnic nuncheon packed in a hamper. We shall be back before suppertime."

Mama gave Herbert a scrap of bread and pulled the blanket back over the opening before she turned. "If you are going to be hiking about the moors or scrambling over rocks in the stream, why don't you wear some of your country clothes, Bixie dear? Your wardrobe is still as you left it in your bedchamber. Just as good as new."

"I prefer my uniform, Mama. My regimentals give me a feeling of having some purpose in my life," Hawksby said.

"Oh, yes. I forgot. He always was the one who had to have a purpose in life," Mama said in an aside to Maggie. "I never could understand what he meant by that."

At that moment a maid came in to inform them that the driver was out front with the carriage. "Lady Ruth said she and Sir Spencer are ready whenever you are."

Maggie looked over at the collection.

Mrs. Hawksby gave her arm a pat. "No need to bother with the boxes, my dear. They can be carried to your room when you return. Thank you for bringing them down. Now run up and fetch whatever you need for your outing. I want to talk to my son for a few minutes before you leave."

Hawksby seemed very quiet at the beginning of their ride, almost as if he were asking questions of himself and couldn't quite get the answers. But he was informative, showing great knowledge of the area. He told them where they were and what they were seeing as they passed over the Hawksby lands. They ate their picnic on the topmost section of moorland overlooking the hills and valleys in the distance. Everywhere they saw sheep, looking like popcorn scattered over the hills.

"There is one more place I wish to show you, Lady Margaret," Hawksby said as he told the driver where to turn. "I have saved it for last." He looked as if he were a small boy with a secret.

They rode into a wooded area and down a shaded lane. Ruth and Spencer were lost in their own little world, so it didn't matter to them that Hawksby said he was afraid Spencer would not be able to come down to the river. Not that it was too steep, but they could enjoy it just as much staying on the bank. Besides, Hawksby rather wanted to show his little corner of the woods to Lady Margaret alone.

Ruth spread out a rug and said she and Spencer would be quite content to sit on the bank where they could hear the waterfall cascading over the rocks and into the river below.

Hawksby led Maggie down to the little glen where the water was calmer and a little pond had formed. A curlew flew into the air, a widgeon broke cover, and a ring ouzel bobbled about the rocks. Wildflowers abounded and a willow dipped heavily over the water.

"Why, this is beautiful, Hawksby," Maggie said just as a fish jumped from the water and caught a moth before it splashed back in and swam away. Butterflies, wildflowers, moss and dippers and a sandpiper. A mallard scooted among the liverworts and mosses. Jewels of every color.

"I wanted to see if it was still as I left it," he said. "This is a part of the river that flows in and out of my father's land. The angling is excellent. I never told Papa about this place. I wanted to keep it to myself." They watched the water fall from the cliff above to plunge into a pool below, continuing to splash and whirl round rocks until it swung off into all sorts of habitats and niches for bird and beast alike.

"You amaze me, Hawksby. Do you know that?"

"Do I really, Lady Margaret? In what way?"

"That you should know the names of so much of the wildlife—and sheep. You must know everything there is to know about sheep."

"Well, I suppose it is because I was raised with them. I cannot say I know everything, but I went to lots of sheep auctions in the market towns when I was young. Couldn't help but pick up their breeds and uses and habits. I never applied it to any practical use, though. In the army, the cavalry isn't permitted to ride sheep."

"No, I suppose not," Maggie said, looking at him in a new light. "Do you know you made a joke, Hawksby?"

That stopped him. "Why, I do believe I did, Lady Margaret."

"Perhaps it is truly a magical place, Hawksby. Thank you for showing it to me."

Hawksby pondered this new talent which he had begun to display since Lady Margaret had come into his life. "Yes, perhaps it is something special."

"I do believe I'm beginning to see the wheels whirling in your head, Hawksby. I have been thinking all afternoon that you looked as if you were keeping something to yourself."

Hawksby ran his gloved hand over his mustache. "You know, it is quite amazing you should say that to me. You see, my mother just told me something equally surprising only a few hours ago. Mama has always had a soft place in her heart for animals. Years ago she had an orphan lamb, and she gave me the responsibility of feeding it. I wasn't especially fond of the little noisy beast, because it followed me around all the time. When it disappeared one day I was actually happy. Mama wanted me to go hunt for it, but it was late and I was hungry. I refused to go."

Maggie sat waiting, but patience wasn't one of her best attributes. "And what happened?"

"Mama went out instead."

"I mean, what happened to the lamb?"

"The lamb had tumbled into a crevice in the rocks. Mama heard it bleating. When she tried to rescue it, she fell and broke her back."

"And you felt it was your fault." It was a statement of fact.

"Yes, but she told me this afternoon her own stubbornness made her fall. Papa had forbidden her to go out in the dark, and that is why she went—not because I'd said I wouldn't go. She told me she would never have forgiven herself if anything had happened to me, and she should not have asked me in the first place."

"So it wasn't your fault."

"She said Papa felt he was the cause, because he should have known never to order her not to do anything, especially when it came to being kind to animals."

"And is that why he won't make her give up Herbert?"

"I suppose it is. Papa never says *no* to her anymore."

"I'm glad she told you, Hawksby. My sister Ruth says we can always learn from our experiences, but it seems that some things come with a high price." She gave a sigh. "I reckon we shouldn't make demands on the ones we love. It makes people do very foolish things sometimes."

"Like running away, getting robbed, and being left in a field in the dark?"

She punched him in the arm, but not very hard.

He took her hand in his.

She withdrew it.

What was he thinking of? He shouldn't be taking such liberties, alone as they were. It had to be this place. He'd never told anyone about Mama's accident before, either. He must remind himself, too, that he was taking Lady Margaret home to her true love, Dr. MacDougal. "I think it is time we returned to the carriage, Lady Margaret. Will you to take my hand? I don't want you to slip and fall."

Put that way, Maggie placed her hand in his. The sensation was very pleasurable, but she warned herself to remember that Hawksby planned on returning to active service as soon as he had done his duty and seen her safely to Knocktigh.

Fourteen

Mama was at the front entry waiting to hear all about their day.

"It was a glorious ride," Maggie said, handing Ruth her bonnet to carry upstairs. "I shall be up in a minute after I've seen to my boxes."

"They are right where you left them, dear," Mrs. Hawksby called out. "You go on in. I shall wait here for Bixie."

Hawksby took the steps two at a time. By Jove! It had been an enjoyable afternoon. He felt lighter of heart for some reason, and kissed his mother on the cheek. "The lands are looking well, Mama."

He would have said more if there had not been a cry of anguish from the direction of his Mama's sitting room.

"My goodness! Whatever can the matter be?" said Mrs. Hawksby, turning the wheels of her chair to chase after her son.

Hawksby ran into the room to find Lady Margaret pointing to one of her boxes. He peered in, fearing what he would see—or not see. "Mama! Where are Lady Margaret's insects?"

"I fed them to Herbert," Mrs. Hawksby said.

Hawksby watched Mama's eyes growing into those large blue mirrors he knew were reflections of his own.

"I didn't think you would mind, dear," Mrs. Hawksby said, looking anxiously at Maggie. "We have ever so many insects down by the river and in the pastures and in the flower gardens, but I'm not able to go fetch any. The servants have become more and more reluctant to collect them for Herbert, but I'm sure Bixie will be happy to show you any number of places where you can replace the ones I used. Why, every flower and every blade of grass seems to have some sort of bug crawling or buzzing about it."

"Mama, do you know what you have done?" shouted Hawksby.

Maggie couldn't stand to see the kind lady's eyes fill with tears. She thought of the lost lamb.

Mrs. Hawksby began to wring her hands. "Oh, dear. Did I do something wrong?"

"No, no. It's all right, Mrs. Hawksby. Truly it is," Maggie said, her gaze falling on the bare wooden blocks which only that morning had exhibited her *omocestus viridulus* and *chorthippus parallelus*. "Please give it no nevermind. I'm sure Hawksby will show me just the right places to find more." She turned so they wouldn't see her lips quiver.

"There, you see," Mrs. Hawksby said to her son, as she wiped a tear from her cheek. "She isn't making a big fuss about it at all."

Maggie insisted that they check on Herbert. With all the tarradiddles that the Hawksby family had told so far, she couldn't believe Mrs. Hawksby had thrown her year's work into a tub bath. But there they were, floating about: Bits and pieces of legs, a thorax, and a wing of *Ephemera danica,* the little British mayfly, decorated the surface of the water.

"Oh, my!" Mrs. Hawksby said. "He spit the bugs out. I don't suppose you could put them together again. No, I suppose you couldn't," she finished, sighing. Herbert stuck his head out into the air as soon as he heard Mama's voice.

"Mama, entomologists sometimes use chemicals to preserve their specimens. I'm certain they are quite repugnant even to a fish." Hawksby knew he should not have come home. Things were worse than they had ever been. Lady Margaret would have to believe what he'd told her about his family. There-It-Is was another name for Bedlam. Now he had two females on the verge of tears, and he didn't know how to handle the situation. "I'm sorry, Mama," Hawksby said. "I didn't mean to shout at you."

"What's this? What's this?" said Mr. Hawksby, coming into the room at that moment. "Who is shouting at whom? Why do you have tears in your eyes, Mama?"

"Papa . . . sir." Hawksby cleared his throat. "You have miles of streams and dozens of ponds in which to fish. I don't see why you cannot give up one small section for Mama's peace of mind."

"Oh, I see. This is about Herbert, isn't it?" He could tell by the looks on the three faces about him that he'd hit the target right on the mark. Mr. Hawksby pursed his lips. "Suppose I could. Right, oh! I'll do it. Give him his own little pit and put up a sign declaring the area HANDS OFF! GO BACK! We'll give the fellow a regular send off. How about that, Mama?" he said, with a big grin in the direction of his wife.

Mrs. Hawksby clapped her hands. "Oh, Papa! What a splendid husband you are. You will make the signs big, won't you?"

Hawksby slapped his forehead with the heel of his hand.

"That won't do any good, Mama. Fish can't read and they don't stay put in one place. Do you think Herbert will turn round and go back when he sees the signs?"

"Oh, dear," said Mrs. Hawksby as the tears welled up in her eyes again. "What shall I do?"

Maggie closed the lid of the intricately carved wooden box

and clicked the latch. Hawksby had called her an entomologist. That was the first time he'd admitted she was something other than just a silly girl who chased bugs. Maggie stood a few feet away chewing on her lower lip trying to concentrate. Her collection was gone. There was nothing she could do about that now, she thought sadly.

"There is a magical pond at the base of the waterfall which the river forms as it rushes to the sea," she said, with sudden inspiration. She didn't tell them it was where she and their third son had stood and talked and he'd told her the innermost fears he'd had as a little boy. She looked at Hawksby hopefully. "Can't some sort of fencing be constructed across the places where the stream enters that pond which we visited today? Then the water can continue to run its course but keep Herbert in that area—a large aquarium of sorts."

Hawksby looked at Lady Margaret with admiration, then back to his mother. "By Jove! There you are, Mama."

"Right, oh!" agreed Mr. Hawksby. "I'll have Withers see to it at once. By jingo! You can give him the directions of where to go, son. We'll give Herbert his own little home safe and sound where you can go visit him, Mama." Then he turned back to Hawksby. "You've got a bright little gel there, Bixworth. Better hang onto her."

They planned a picnic and ponding party for Herbert the next afternoon. Withers had the men working all night to gather the materials. As soon as the sun rose, they carried the fencing down to the river and started pounding it into a semicircle to close off the pond—a regular little picket fence, slats half inch apart and twelve inches out of the water.

The entire family and many of the servants attended the festivities. The caravan of carriages and wagons, pony carts, and a donkey or two strung out along the road for half a mile on their way from There-It-Is to the Magical Place. Mama's carriage that held her wheelchair came, too. Herbert was the only one who had to come in a bucket with a lid, but he was going to be set free, so he could not have complained of his few minutes of discomfort over his manner of transportation.

Cook had prepared an excellent repast, and many of the cottagers and workers brought victuals from their own kitchens. Billy Buster was there with his family. His father drove one of the big farm wagons loaded with food from the manor house. They wouldn't have missed the party for anything.

They carried Mama down to the river. She cried when they placed Herbert in the water, then watched him anxiously as he swam around the perimeter of the slatted picket fence. He pushed his head into the spaces, but they were too narrow for him to escape.

"You can come down to see him as often as you wish, Mama," said Mr. Hawksby. "You can bring him scraps. See, we have put signs up all along the enclosure that say that it is out-of-bounds for fishing."

Mama tried to be brave, but she was still dabbing her eyes when they wheeled her back to the carriage to take her home.

Maggie thought Hawksby quite splendid in his blue uniform, directing the movement of evacuation, making certain all the carriages and horses moved out in orderly fashion. She placed her hand on Hawksby's arm, stopping him for a moment. "Could we stay here just a bit longer?" she asked. "It is such a lovely place—the loveliest, I think, of all you have shown me."

"Why, of course, Lady Margaret," Hawksby said, a bit surprised, but pleased nonetheless, that she should want to stay a while at his favorite place. "I shall tell them we will follow along in a moment in one of the pony carts."

The clickety-clickety-clack of the horses' hooves and the voices of the revelers became fainter. Maggie went back down the path and found a grassy place to sit overlooking the pond.

Hawksby walked beside the rocky stream throwing sticks in the water while Lady Margaret sat silently staring into nowhere land. He wondered if he'd ever be able to make up for what Mama had done.

"I still have my sketches," Maggie said, startling him into thinking that she must be reading his mind.

He turned to look at her.

"I still have my sketches and notebooks about the insects to show to Dr. MacDougal. Don't blame your mother. She meant well."

"Buggers!" he grumbled, picking up a stone and throwing it into the pond. The splash was very rewarding. She may have made light of it, but he knew how important her insect collection was to her. Her whole year's work wasted. He picked up a bigger rock and pitched it high. It came down with a louder, more spectacular splash. "Hah!" he said. This time he dug until he loosened what amounted to a small boulder and hoisted it over his head. He heaved it as far as he could. The splash—an explosion of waves ballooning out in all directions—was quite the thing and very rewarding . . . until she yelled.

"Hawksby! You startled Herbert. He's trying to jump the fence. Now he's almost over the barrier. Do something!" A flash of the setting sun reflected off Herbert's scales as he arced and twisted into the air.

Hawksby did the only thing left to him. He jumped into the stream after the ungrateful rascal. His boots slipped on the mossy rocks, smashing a section of the fence as he did so. He grabbed. "Spawn of the devil, come back here!"

Herbert went *zoop* up into the air once more.

Hawksby stumbled to his knees, regained his balance, and dived. He slapped at the escaping renegade, knocking him up into the air again, missing him on the way down. Both splashed into the water. Hawksby rolled over, taking down the remainder of the barrier.

"Don't hurt him," Maggie cried, slipping and sliding her way down the bank. She came to a stop in a soggy spot at the edge of the pond.

"Hurt him?" Hawksby bellowed as his face hit the water. He came up sputtering. "I'll kill the turncoat and serve him up for dinner." Hawksby made one last attempt to capture Herbert. No use. The brown trout gave a wag of his tail, fluttered his fins, and sped away up the river.

Hawksby heard a gasp and turned to see Lady Margaret on the bank near the willow, her face buried in her hands, her shoulders bent and shaking.

"Hell and damn!" he grumbled, pulling himself up from where he sat. He flapped his arms and pulled a patch of spaghnum moss from his hair. His boots were full of water. There wasn't a dry spot on him. "Now you're crying, too. I suppose I shall be labeled a vulgar brute. I suppose you will announce to the world that Captain Hawksby has no heart— an absolute monster who is not to be tolerated."

Maggie raised her tear-streaked face a wee bit to peek at him, her hand over her mouth.

Hawksby stopped his diatribe. Lady Margaret wasn't crying. Worse, she was laughing. She didn't fool him a bit. He could tell by her eyes. He'd made a jackass of himself. His uniform was ruined—or nearly so—full of weeds and muck and something wriggling up his arm. He shook his sleeve furiously, whacked it on the side of his jacket, and flapped some more. Out popped a silvery, wiggly sliver that flipped into the air, arced just like its big brother had, hit the water, flapped its tail at Captain Hawksby, and swam away. "Begone, ye prehistoric beast!" he bellowed.

Maggie let out a choking sound and bent over coughing.

Hawksby lowered his brows to shield his thoughts, but it did no good. He felt the laugh coming from somewhere deep down inside himself and he couldn't stop it. The corners of his lips twitched upward. Damn!

"Enough!" he bellowed, removing his water-soaked gloves and slapping them against his thigh to remove some of the water. He couldn't help but cast another quick glance Lady Margaret's way. He didn't know if she'd caught the chuckle or not. Damned nuisance if she did. She'd think he had a weak spot, and that would never do if he was going to maintain any sort of control over her capricious behavior on their way north.

Lady Margaret seemed to have a penchant for disarray. Her bonnet had slipped to one side, and her red curls cascaded over one eye and down over her shoulders. Dirt smudged her left chcek and the sides of her frock where she had wiped her hands. She looked adorable. Too adorable for her own good. Worse yet, dangerously adorable for *his* own good. Hawksby growled, a pithy expletive poised on the tip of his tongue.

"You aren't supposed to say *damn*," she warned.

Hawksby checked himself. He wondered what else she'd heard him say. "No, I suppose not," he said, sloshing up over the bank of the stream. "I beg your pardon, milady. But the circumstances seemed to warrant something stronger than *Oh, my goodness.*"

"I don't know why you insist on calling me Lady Margaret. I'm Maggie to your mother and father. Everyone close to me calls me Maggie."

Exactly so, my saucy one, he thought. *Exactly why I mustn't.*

210

You are going to your sweetheart in Scotland, and I will be leaving for other climes. At that moment, he knew he loved her.

They trudged up the bank to the pony cart. Fortunately for Maggie and Hawksby, There-It-Is had so many sections and doors and hidden entrances that they were able to enter their rooms without their disheveled appearance being noticed except by Ruth and Clugg, but they wouldn't tell anybody.

What to say about Herbert to Mama was another matter. On their ride back to the manor house, they decided to leave their fate to chance. "Cry even," they both said.

They took Mama down to the stream early the next day before they left for Northumberland. She insisted. Neither Hawksby or Maggie knew what they would tell her when they arrived and she saw the shambles that had been made of the fence.

But there was Herbert, flipping his tail, sticking his head out of the water, waiting for his handout. It was indeed a Magical Place.

Papa persuaded Mama to leave the barrier down. The fish was clever enough, he said, to keep away from hooks. Herbert was used to seeing the hand that fed him, so he was sure her brown trout would stay near. Besides, if he was smart enough to spit out a dead insect, he'd be smart enough not to take an artificial fly. At least that was the tarradiddle he told Mama.

The caravan of three coaches left for Northumberland soon after. It took them a day to get back to the Great North Road and another two days to reach Knocktigh. When Maggie glimpsed the peak of the Cheviot to the west as it rose to its nearly 2,700-foot summit, she knew they were no more than a day from Knocktigh.

Maggie told Hawksby that the roads leading into the hills

were few and far between and for him to tell the other drivers to leave the main road at Wooler and head toward Kirknewton, else they would have to travel all the way to Cornhill-on-Tweed at the border and then head back to find Knocktigh.

They drove around and over the steep, smoothly rounded hills, dissected by deep wooded glens, almost deserted except for a few shepherds' cottages. Off in the distance atop a knoll, Maggie thought she saw two horses silhouetted against the light. But before she could blink her eyes, the illusion evaporated and only the empty hilltop remained. Then there it was, her beloved Knocktigh set high upon its hill, facing the downward slope of the landscape, which spread like honey into the broad expanses of low land. Beyond that lay the tiny ribbon of silver which was the River Tweed. They arrived in the evening in time to watch the sun setting.

"We're home," she said excitedly. "Oh, look, Ruth, the carriageway has been resurfaced and there are flowers and shrubbery everywhere." It did indeed look quite different than when they all had departed for London to attend their first Season the year before.

At the front door a new, much younger houseman, in sharp dress and manner and going by the name of Makeshift, had replaced the beloved elderly butler Dinn-Dinn. Makeshift was his nephew. Dinn-Dinn had been handsomely pensioned off and gone to live with a niece in Cornhill-on-Tweed.

The earl and countess had arrived two days before and were there to receive them. As soon as all were out of the carriages and accounted for, the coachmen were instructed to drive the equipage and baggage to the rear courtyard.

Mrs. Doone was overjoyed to see her daughter, and Flora was dismissed immediately to go help her mother in the kitchen if she wished. Which, of course, was what she had wanted to do all along, and she was off with a hop, skip, and a jump.

Dinner was enjoyable and proceeded without incident. No mention or questions were asked about the presence of Sir Spencer, for which Maggie and Ruth were grateful. The earl and countess kept the conversation light and full of tales of their journeys.

The only low point for Hawksby was when one of the servants informed Lady Margaret that Dr. MacDougal had come several times into the Cheviots to continue his studies. When he was in the vicinity, the distinguished scholar always stopped at the manor house and asked after her. This bit of news brought an expression of delight to Lady Margaret's countenance. But then what did he expect? Wasn't that why Lady Margaret wanted to return to Knocktigh? However, on Hawksby's part, it only renewed his wish to box the fellow's ears.

Chantry touched lightly on the management problems he had encountered at his Yorkshire property. With the death of the old steward and the absence of its lord and master, misconduct ensued at the estate. But Chantry had finally persuaded the steward's youngest son to leave his position as bank clerk in York to take over for his father. He had some schooling and came with unexceptionable references. "Now if we can find someone of equal competence for Knocktigh, we can return to London content."

Maggie had been watching her sister Freddie trying to catch Daniel's attention with some sort of signal.

Daniel held up his goblet. "I see, gentlemen, that it is the time when we usually allow the ladies to withdraw to gossip about us while we have our port and cigars and talk about business matters. But I am going to break with custom this evening, if I may."

Daniel ignored his wife as she shook a spoon at him. "I'm afraid I have been warned I am not to discuss anything pertaining to the affairs of Knocktigh without the presence of my wife, since this property was willed to her by her mother. Subsequently, it would seem we men will not be able to find anything of interest to talk about without the ladies. So if I may make a suggestion, my dear," Daniel said, fixing his gaze upon Freddie, "I believe everyone is in need of a good night's sleep. If no one has any objections, I think we should permit our guests to retire."

The way he said it, Maggie felt the suggestion was directed at Freddie, and it was more than a suggestion. It was a command. No one really disagreed, though, for it had been a long and tiring day. Besides, Maggie had much to do on the morrow.

Hawksby, true to his nature, rose early the next morning. A fast ride over the hills alone sounded more bracing than breakfast, especially after what he'd been put through the last few weeks.

Last night Lord Chantry had thanked him for a job well done. He didn't know when Spencer planned to speak to the earl about himself and Lady Ruth, but Hawksby wanted his friend to know he was there to lend him his support. As soon as Spencer had his say, then he and Clugg could be off to London.

Hawksby had been assigned a room on the second floor at the rear of the house overlooking the back courtyard. He insisted Sir Spencer be placed near him in case his friend needed assistance. He emphasized to Chantry the friendship part.

Now shaved and fully dressed in his cleaned and dried regimentals, he was in the process of telling Clugg to see to having his horse saddled, when they were interrupted in their discourse by the most earsplitting whistle he'd ever heard. "What is that noise?" he said, rushing to the window and throwing up the sash to look out. "By Jove, Clugg, it is Lady Margaret! She is standing by the stables with her fingers in her mouth, making that terrible sound. And there is a giant out in the stableyard waving and shouting like a madman. Do you suppose someone has escaped from a mental institution? She must be terrified. I shall shout to try to distract him."

But just as Hawksby leaned over the sill and opened his mouth to cry out, he heard a great thundering and rumbling, which could only foretell a great storm coming their way. Yet the morning sky was clear and there wasn't a single cloud to be seen. Around the corner of the stables raced a dozen wild donkeys, flipping their heads, braying and hee-hawing. At the same time, Lady Ruth and Flora Doone came tearing out of the tack room, long leather thongs trailing behind them in the air.

Hawksby tore through the corridor, headed for the servants stairs at the rear of the house.

"Devil take it, Clugg, I must stop them! Silly women."

"*We*, sir. I am coming too. I don't fancy having that pretty little maid break her neck any more than you do the ladies."

"So that is the way the wind blows, is it, Clugg? Then let us be gone. We must stop them before they do themselves harm."

They reached the ground floor and burst out into the courtyard just in time to see deft fingers quickly knot the leather strips around three of the donkeys' noses.

Each girl grasped a fistful of mane and swung herself onto her donkey's back. Lady Margaret raised her arm in the air and shouted, "Are ye bridled?"

"Aye!" the others answered.

"Are ye ready for the calf?"

"Aye! Aye! Aye!"

Maggie lowered her arm, pointing forward. "Then aff an' away!" The wild thing under her stretched out its neck and shot off across the hills, the others close behind.

The huge man Hawksby had seen from the window stood now with his fist beating the air, shouting after them. "*Buadhaich!* Conquer!"

Hawksby had heard that call before, during the war. It was an old Scots battle cry. The monstrous man stood with his cap of snow-white hair spilling down the sides of his face, curling around his chin, to continue over his jacket and down over his waist. For all Hawksby knew, he could be an over-sized king of those gnomes his father talked about so much.

The giant turned and gave the astounded Hawksby and his batman a wide grin. "I be Loof MacLiesh, gents. Welcum t' ye noo. What can auld Loof do fir ye?"

Fifteen

Hawksby came in from his morning ride to find Lady Ruth and Lady Margaret already at the breakfast table eating their porridge as calmly as you please, not as if he and Clugg had hunted all over for them, afraid they would find all three somewhere in a canyon with their necks broken. He was not at all in a mood to be conciliatory.

"Lady Margaret," he said, bending over so he could speak in her ear. "I will not have you riding about the countryside on wild beasts. Do you know what concerns your very unladylike departure from the stableyard caused this morning? I cannot speak for Lady Ruth or Flora Doone, but I reckon it was your influence which brought about such harum-scarum behavior in those young ladies. I do not know if Lord and Lady Chantry are aware of what transpired, but after this you will deport yourself with more decorum, or I shall have to ask Lord Chantry to take steps."

With that, he went to the sideboard and began to fill a platter with victuals from the vast array Mrs. Doone had spread out for them. When he had finished, he took his plate and sat with the earl and countess at the other end of the table.

Freddie rapped her husband's knuckles with her fork when he started to laugh. Ruth whispered something in Spencer's ear. Maggie just shrugged and went on eating. She knew all in the room had heard every word Captain Hawksby had said. He didn't whisper very well.

Although he didn't approach the subject of her riding again, Hawksby kept shooting warning looks at Maggie. Otherwise he ignored her and joined in the general conversation on sheep raising and other possibilities of income for Knocktigh, which Freddie and Daniel had been discussing.

Daniel told Hawksby of what he'd observed of farms as they traveled north, and Hawksby offered information of what his brothers were doing on their land in the Dales.

"My brothers raise cheviots for their medium-weight fleece and Leicesters, which have a longer wool," Hawksby said. "At Knocktigh you might want to add the Scottish black-face. They seem to do well up here in the north and produce a coarse wool that makes fine carpets. That would diversify your market."

Freddie was contributing as much if not more to the conversation, because after all Knocktigh was hers. But Maggie listened with only half an ear. Her attention was taken more with Ruth and Sir Spencer, who were noticeably silent and uneasy at their end of the table.

Finally, Sir Spencer spoke. "Lord Chantry, I would appreciate it if I might have a word with you."

Silence fell upon the room. Daniel frowned, but stopped talking about sheep. "Perhaps one of the smaller rooms off the entrance hall would give us more privacy," he said, motioning to Sir Spencer's man, who always stood near to assist him when needed.

Whether the earl wished it or not, everyone at the table rose as one body and followed. The servants found one excuse or another to come into the hallway. Ruth took Spencer's arm and refused to let go. Hawksby stepped forward and placed his hand firmly on his friend's shoulder. Of course Maggie had no intention of leaving her favorite sister to face their brother's wrath alone.

Flora and Clugg had informed the staff previously of the romantical tangle, and they and others now formed a cloudy mass of faces out in the vestibule.

The earl's own man, Tilbury, got wind of the situation and the sad plight of the lovers from Sir Spencer's valet. Being a faithful reader of Gothic novels, he was not going to be kept out of the drama, either. No siree. He descended from the balcony where he'd been listening in on the conversations below. Tilbury was no worm. What good was a gentleman's gentleman if he did not stick his nose into everything that concerned his master?

Daniel entered the small room, which he'd been using as an office. He walked round the desk, which was the only piece of large furniture in the room, and turned to discover half the household was either in the room or crowded outside.

"I thought this was to be a private interview," he protested. "Not a parade." No one left. He sighed. Ruth and Spencer stood in front of him. "All right, out with it. What is it you wish to ask me?"

Sir Spencer patted Ruth's hand. "Chantry, I want to marry Ruth. For some reason you seem reluctant to accept my suit. I want to know why."

"Quite simply because I don't think you would make a good husband."

Their was a collective gasp.

"It is not what you think," the earl said, shaking his head. "Years ago, I observed your behavior toward your own sisters. You teased them until they cried. I cannot allow my sister, for whom I care a great deal, to be married to a man who would so cruelly treat a lady."

Freddie moved around to the other side of the desk and put her hand on her husband's arm. "Daniel, all children tease their brothers and sisters. You never were brought up with siblings, dearest. They can be a trial, I agree, but that doesn't mean they are cruel or they don't love each other."

"Especially sisters," said Sir Spencer.

"Lord, don't I know that," barked Hawksby.

Spencer laughed. "So, you see, my lord, your premise for the dimissal of my suit has no validity."

"None whatsoever," agreed Ruth.

The earl looked from one face to the other. "By the chastisement I am getting, I suppose I will have to admit I was wrong," Chantry said. "I am sorry, Spooney."

"*Spooney?*" They all shouted in unison.

"Why, yes," Daniel said, the hint of a grin breaking his austere countenance. "We called him Spooney at school. He was fat and obnoxious, a most atrocious little braggart. The only reason I went home with him for Christmas was because it was better than spending a long lonely holiday with a houseful of servants. His sisters were pretty little things, and I thought his treatment of them abysmal."

Everybody looked at the well-looking man standing before them, perfect in every feature. When the laughter had died down, Sir Spencer, who was chuckling harder than anyone, declared, "Then I take it my suit has been accepted."

"It has," said Lord Chantry, coming forward to take the handsome man's hand. "And I daresay with all the witnesses present I shall not be allowed to go back on my word."

By Jove! This was a happy day for Sir Spencer. Hawksby was glad for his friend. Now that he stood in the good graces of the earl and his happiness for the future with his lovely Lady Ruth seemed imminent, Hawksby told himself that he was now free to return to London. He duly informed them he and Clugg would be departing in two days' time.

★ ★ ★ ★ ★

Maggie was more disconcerted by Hawksby's announcement than she ever imagined she would be. Two days. That was all the time she had to see him before he went away, probably forever.

"Freddie," Maggie said, "have you visited Granny Eizel yet?"

"Yes, dear. I saw her the first night I was back."

Maggie had never seen Granny Eizel. None of the sisters had, except Freddie. Granny had been their mother's nurse when Gillian married Freddie's father, the Honourable Frederick Hendry, and had come as a young bride to Knocktigh. The ancient blind woman had lived for years at the end of a long corridor in a dark room under the eaves of the ancient manor house. She allowed only old Agnes and Freddie to visit her.

"Did Granny say anything about me?" Maggie asked. "Anything about what is to happen to me, or what I should do?"

Freddie reached over and patted her youngest sister's hand. "No, dear, she didn't. She said you would find your guidance from another source. You will be given a sign."

"Oh?" said Maggie, waiting expectantly.

"Granny Eizel says all will be revealed in time."

Maggie felt disappointed, but didn't say so. "Do you think Daniel will allow me to stay at Knocktigh?"

"That we will have to see. We shall be here a while longer. First we must find a steward to manage the property."

"How long do you think that will take?"

"Daniel has been making enquiries in Cornhill-on-Tweed and the villages south of here. He has interviewed a couple of promising candidates. If the men have wives who could chaperone you, he may permit you to stay. You will just have to be patient."

"Or if I were married?"

Freddie raised her eyebrows. "Well, of course, if you were married." Then she laughed. "Do you have someone in mind?"

Maggie snorted. "Don't be silly. Of course I don't. I was just wondering."

One more day. That was all that was left to him. Hawksby waited for his horse to be saddled and brought to him in the stableyard.

"She's gone off again? By herself? I told her I forbade it!" Hawksby roared, then stopped himself when he saw the amusement on Loof MacLiesh's face. Of course, Hawksby no longer had any influence on Lady Margaret's activities. If she insisted on going off into the wilds alone, that was her brother's responsibility. He'd still found himself keeping an eye on her, though. It had become a habit, he reckoned. Never could tell what trouble she'd get herself into. Crazy chit. He thought he'd voiced his disapproval well enough yesterday after she'd ridden off with Lady Ruth and Flora.

Hawksby thought he'd take one more ride round the hills before he went back to London. After seeing the vast expanses of the Yorkshire Dales and now the silent whisperings of the Cheviots, he began to question what there was for him back in the southern part of England. But then, what did he have here? None of it belonged to him, and he certainly didn't have the blunt to purchase land.

He had been riding for half an hour when he saw Lady Margaret in one of the deep rifts which split the rounded hills in half. Little copses which streams had cut through the rocks, surrounded by trees and flowers. What in tarnation was she doing down there? The vixen hadn't ridden a donkey after all, but was on foot and stood at the entrance of a cave.

She had a lamb wrapped around her shoulders. Probably found it lost among the rocks and rescued it as Mama had tried to do. But Mama had fallen and broken her back.

Hawksby cringed to think of what could have happened if Lady Margaret had an accident out here this morning all alone. They were at least three miles from Knocktigh. It could be days before someone found her.

He watched her from above, debating whether or not to make her go back with him. A wreath of flowers crowned her head. She appeared to be talking to someone, and he thought it must be the lamb. But his mother talked to a trout named Herbert, so what was so bad about talking to a lamb?

Then he saw the horse, a beautiful little chestnut mare. It had to be the pony born and bred for the mountains of central Europe, which Lady Chantry had said the former earl brought back from the Austrian Tyrol for their mother.

He'd heard the stableman MacLiesh say that there was a filly sired by Lord Chantry's Scots Grey, but aside from a few sightings, no one could get near mare or foal. Hawksby reined in his mount and waited.

The mare hesitated for a moment, pawed the ground and shook her head. Lady Margaret placed the lamb on the grass and held out her hand. The mare came forward, sniffed her palm, and finally nuzzled her shoulder, then her cheek. Hawksby had heard that Lady Margaret and her twin looked just like their mother, the former Countess of Chantry.

They stood for a moment, horse and girl, as one, when out of the cave behind them came a dark-coated foal. Not hesitantly, but boldly. The lamb and colt pranced and danced about each other on their stiff spindly legs, touching noses, tossing and turning like children around a Maypole.

If Hawksby had dared, he would have laughed. Nothing shy about the ladies from Knocktigh.

Then a neighing sounded from the opposite side of the hollow. The earl's great Scots Grey stood near the rise, a flower dangling from his lips, calling. Lord Chantry said he was a rogue. The mare and foal took off up the steep slope. Lady Margaret picked up the lamb and began her ascent.

Hawksby, not wanting to be found spying, turned his horse and rode down on the other side of the hill.

He had ridden no more than half a mile when he encountered an apparition. It appeared in the form of a strange little man in a kilt, with a round little belly and thin knobby-kneed legs, hopping and skipping along among the grasses, swishing this way and that, with a net at the end of a long pole. His face was nearly obscured by bristlebrush, mutton-chops, and smoky gray hair pulled back with a leather thong. He was singing at the top of his lungs:

> *"Nieve-nievie nick-nack,*
> *Whit haun wull ye tak?*
> *Tak the richt, tak the wrang,*
> *I'll beguile ye gin I can."*

Whing-whang went the net. Then, reaching into its depths, the jipperty-jabberty little fellow pulled out a grasshopper and stuffed it into the canvas bag he had slung over his shoulder.

Hawksby began to think this part of the country was peopled by an overpopulation of gnomes and giants. The funny little gent ran right into the legs of his horse and would have been trampled if Hawksby hadn't turned his mount. He leaped off and put the fellow back on his feet.

"Didn't see ye," the old man said, chuckling and peering up through myopic gray eyes. "Don't expect t' see soldiers riding about among the heather. We're not being invaded, are we?"

Hawksby picked up the net and handed it to him. "All my fault, I assure you, sir. Just a friendly reconnaissance."

After feeling his own arms and legs and looking behind himself to see if his backside was still there, the stranger held out his hand. "I get to singing bairns' nursery rhymes and forget to watch where I'm going. Name's MacDougal."

The man didn't even come up to Hawksby's chin. "Mac . . . MacDougal?"

"Well, I think it is," the man said, placing a finger on his chin. "After a jolt like that, one can never be sure what one remembers."

"Hawksby. Captain Bixworth Hawksby at your service, sir." The understanding of what he'd just heard was still sinking in. "Not Dr. MacDougal of Edinburgh?"

"Don't know where you've heard of me, but yir right, young man."

"I am a guest at Knocktigh," said Hawksby.

"Ah, that is it, is it? Aye! Recall now. Someone mentioned yir name in her letter."

"Someone did?"

"Thought I said so a moment ago. You say the family is at home?"

"Lord and Lady Chantry and two of their sisters," said Hawksby, watching for Dr. MacDougal's reaction. "Lady Ruth and Lady Margaret."

"Well, noo, then I must stop and pay my respects this evening." He cocked his head to one side. "Are the young ladies attached?"

"Lady Ruth has just become engaged to Sir Spencer Packard of Hampshire."

"And Maggie?"

Hawksby didn't like the way MacDougal was so loose and free with Lady Margaret's nickname. "Lady Margaret is not yet affianced, as far as I know," he said.

"Well, noo. Is that a fact?"

"And what are your intentions, Dr. MacDougal?"

"My intentions?" he asked, his little eyes blinking merrily. "If I didn't have a good wife back in Edinburgh who has put up with me for over forty-two years, eight children, and sixteen grandchildren, I'd have intentions. I can only say I don't know what's wrong with you Englishmen. No Scotsman would allow such a bonny lass as Lady Margaret to get away."

Hawksby stared right through Dr. MacDougal. "By Jove!"

"I must be going if I'm to catch my quota today," said the professor. "There is a nursery rhyme that might be worth repeating, young man:

> *"Happy is the wooing*
> *That's not long a-doing."*

And off he went, skipping and jumping and swishing his net before Hawksby could say good-bye.

"I say!" said Hawksby, swinging up into his saddle.

Hawksby wasted no time finding Lady Margaret. After all, he was on horseback and she was walking—and carrying a lamb on her shoulders besides. "Lady Margaret," he called, the minute he saw her. Reining in his horse, he leaped to the ground.

Maggie caught her breath at the sight of him. How very splendid he looked in his blue regimentals. She had hoped in some way they would be able to say good-bye when they were not surrounded by family and friends.

"There," she said, setting the lamb on the ground and

giving it a shove. "There is your mother down there crying for you. Now go and stay out of trouble."

"Lady Marg . . ."

She turned so quickly that they collided before he could finish her name. It seemed the most natural thing in the world for her to throw her arms around his neck. Maggie pressed her finger to his lips and suddenly felt an unaccustomed shyness come over her as she saw the expression on his face. But she gathered her wits quickly and stepped back. "I think we are friends well enough, Hawksby, for you to call me by my nickname."

"Well, yes . . . that is, you may be right . . . Maggie. Now, where was I?" Tarnation! She did have the most disconcerting way of distracting a person.

He was going away tomorrow, probably never to see her again. She turned away toward the heather-covered hills. It was easier that way. She had already memorized his face.

Hawksby cleared his throat. "Once before . . . perhaps twice before, I sought your advice on a matter. A hypothetical matter, of course." He didn't have to worry about Maggie's understanding long words like *hypothetical*.

She forgot she wasn't going to look at him. "You did? What was it about?"

"Well, perhaps we had better skip that part. I would like to set forth a question to you as if you were a woman . . . no, let me put that another way."

"Hawksby, you are being not only obtuse but just plain stuck in the glue pot."

He took a deep breath and tried again. "Lady Margaret . . . Maggie. If you, as a woman of great intelligence and forthright character, were to be approached by a man who, let's say, was not exactly handsome or debonaire or even the first stare of fashion and he proposed that you marry him, what qualities or manner of address would make you say yes?" He put up his hand before she could say anything. "Now, I know you have said that you—as Lady Margaret Durham—do not plan to tie the knot, but remember, we are talking hypothetically here."

Hawksby was doing it very badly. Always did. Probably never would get the knack of it. It seemed to be a flaw he could not amend. She did look fetching in her country dress, her hair shining like copper in the sunshine, flowers entwined in it . . . like a bouquet! There was that word again. He let out a whoop. It seemed he was doing a lot more laughing of late. She *was* his bouquet. He was so enamored he forgot to hide his eyes from her.

Maggie gasped. "My goodness, Hawksby." Something in the way his gaze had grown liquid made her hand unconsciously come up and cover her heart. Her action mirrored what she saw in his eyes, and the most pleasant sensations ran through her. Was she reading his thoughts or was she seeing her own?

She managed to pull her attention away from his eyes, but then found herself concentrating on his lips instead. "I think she would like him to have a strong determination and be brave . . . yes, brave enough to kiss her and declare he loved her and definitely not stand about spouting silly platitudes when the little wheels in his head are saying something else."

Lady Margaret's suggestions had worked well enough before and Hawksby saw no reason they shouldn't do so now. He kissed her, rather tentatively at first. Then, holding her at arm's length, he roared with great conviction, "By Jove! You are right again."

Without further ado, he pulled her to him a second time and kissed her well, and a third time far better yet. "Excess does impress, my darling Maggie, but I do believe now that I am getting the hang of it, there is a limit to what even a brave man can endure."

All of a sudden Maggie was finding breathing to be quite difficult. "What do you recommend?" she said, hoping he would try it a fourth time.

"I do believe the next step is marriage," he said with a huskiness Maggie had not heard in his voice before. "But for now, I suggest we go back to the house and I shall speak to your brother."

Her eyes misted over. "But you are leaving tomorrow, Hawksby. I will not do as my mother did with my father and go months and months without seeing you."

"Well, I just may have an idea by then," he said, turning round so she couldn't see his frown.

"I will not leave Knocktigh, Hawksby."

He led her toward his horse. "Trust me," he said, squeezing her hand. He took hold of the bridle and began to walk with her. "Just say you will cry even for now."

"Cry even," Maggie answered.

As they walked back to Knocktigh, Hawksby decided the first thing he must do was speak to Chantry. Then he would seek out Lady Chantry and ask for her advice on a way he might best persuade her stubborn sister to follow him wherever he was sent.

Sixteen

That evening they had a guest. Maggie was overjoyed to see Dr. MacDougal. He was very sorry to hear of the loss of her collection, but he said he would like to take her sketches and notes back with him to Edinburgh. Yes, he had been delighted to meet Herr Wehrhahn from Germany, who was full of praise for the meticulous work she had done in London. High praise, Dr. MacDougal said, from someone of his elevated status in the scientific world.

Hawksby didn't get a chance to speak to the earl until after everyone else had left to seek their beds. Maggie watched them go into the little room which Daniel used as his office.

The next morning at breakfast, she couldn't tell anything from her brother's expression of what had transpired, but she didn't see any signs that Hawksby was leaving, either.

Dr. MacDougal was his cheery self and said he had another day or two in the field before he planned to depart. He asked Maggie to accompany him. Of course, she said she would be very pleased.

She threw a glance toward Hawksby, but the last she saw of him, he was marching once again into the study, this time with Daniel *and* Freddie. She glared at them all, but it did no good. She didn't know why she was not included in such an important decision in her life.

It wasn't until she returned that afternoon with Dr. MacDougal that Daniel called her into the study. He was standing behind his desk. Freddie was there. Hawksby too, looking rather pleased with himself. Smug was perhaps a better word.

Maggie couldn't help but exclaim, "Hawksby! You are still here."

Daniel laughed. "It has taken my lady wife, your sister, to come up with the solution to your problem. She has offered Captain Hawksby the position of steward here at Knocktigh. He has impressed us all with his knowledge of sheep husbandry, and I told him if he accepts, he shall have your hand in marriage."

"Oh, Hawksby," cried Maggie, flinging herself into his arms. "You would give up your commission to marry me?"

"I would," he said, not knowing what else to do but hug her back.

"Then I can stay here at Knocktigh," she said.

Freddie came over and put her arm around Maggie. "Not until you are married, dear. Captain Hawksby will remain and start working to make Knocktigh a profitable holding. When it is doing well, he will come to London and you shall be married. Ruth and Rebecca were planning a double wedding. You and Captain Hawksby shall make it three. Just think—it will be the most spectacular social event of October."

"But now your brother and I must return to London. The Season is almost over, and we have left your sisters long enough."

"I don't want to go back," Maggie said. "And I don't want a big wedding. I'd just as soon have it at the Tower Menagerie."

Daniel faced his sister. "Margaret," he said quite forcefully. "Did you ever think others may also have reasons for returning to Town beyond your own wishes?" He looked at

Freddie. She blushed.

"Oh, Freddie!" Maggie exclaimed. "Do you mean . . . ?"

Freddie laughed. "Yes, and your brother is quite certain I am so fragile that he must get me back to London even though it is quite a full six months away yet."

Then Maggie looked over at Hawksby. He was looking miserable. She reckoned he was sorry he'd ever agreed to such a ridiculous scheme, and she was more than sure he was sorry he'd asked her to marry him. He had promised to give up his career in the army to stay at Knocktigh and she would be in London. "Oh, what shall we do, Hawksby?"

Before Hawksby could answer, a jolly voice sang out from the hallway.

"I, Wullie Wastle,
Stand here on ma Castle:
An' a' the dogs o' your toon,
Will never drive Wullie Wastle doon!"

Dr. MacDougal stuck his head round the door frame. "I hope you don't mind my interrupting, my dears. But the door was ajar and yir voices do travel in this old pile. Has something to do with the echo effect, I expect. Haven't studied that phenomena to any great extent, since my expertise is insects."

The professor reduced everyone to silence. He stepped in. "Couldn't help but hear you talking about the children's dilemma, and thought I'd give my own suggestion for a solution—for what it's worth. After all, I have seen eight bairns go through the pains of courting and matrimony."

"Then you have my sympathy, professor. Do come in," Daniel said. "You of all people will understand what I have been put through this last year after I found I had eight young

232

ladies to present to Society at one time."

"That I doo," he said. "Now to my understanding, our young couple here would just as soon have porridge as partridge."

Hawksby and Maggie nodded alike.

"Then the solution is plain as a pikestaff. I return to Scotland tomorrow. Ye kin all cum wi' me across the border to Coldstream and the bairns kin pledge their troth to me there. Scottish Law says only two people need be present, but if all at Knocktigh cum who want to, there will be so many witnesses even the king himself cannot undo it."

"No!" said Daniel, rising from his chair. "I will not permit it. No sister of mine will be married under such a barbaric law."

"And what is wrong with Scottish Law?" Freddie asked, shaking her finger in his face. "Don't you forget that my grandfather is the Earl of Gloaminlaw, the MacNaught."

Daniel sat down again. "You are right," he said, feigning defeat.

Maggie, on the other hand, had no doubts. She looked at Hawksby, her eyes alight. "Well?" she said.

"I will," he said, with an assurance in his tone which she'd not heard before.

Early the next day all the staff, family members, and guests of Knocktigh piled into every available carriage and wagon and drove out of the hills to Cornhill-on-Tweed at the border. Maggie and Captain Hawksby said their vows on the north side of the five-arched bridge separating England from Scotland. Mrs. Doone had packed several hampers of food and wine and they ate on the grass alongside the River Tweed. When the others returned to Knocktigh, they left the smallest one-horse carriage for Hawksby and Maggie, who stayed the night at a hotel in Coldstream.

The men were more concerned for Maggie than were the women. "For heavens sakes, Daniel. Will you quit fretting? Did you have anything to worry about on our wedding night?" Freddie asked.

"Of course not," he exclaimed. "I was there."

"Well, so was I," said Freddie giving him a punch in the arm. "If you have anyone to be concerned about, I say for you to think of Captain Hawksby's welfare, not Maggie's."

"I suppose you are right, as always, my sweet. Now it is my son I must be concerned about."

"Or daughter."

"Heaven help me," Daniel said. "I hope to have at least one other male on my side in the future."

Hawksby stood for a moment looking about the small room they had been given at the James Hotel. It was a well-run though old establishment in the center of town, the only accommodation they could find on such short notice. He wished he could have offered her more.

As she unpinned her hair and let it fall down around her shoulders, Maggie watched this man who was now her husband. "Hawksby, I hope you aren't going to be hypothetical on our wedding night." She turned so he could unbutton her dress.

"I hadn't planned on it." He swung her back round and looked at her with an intensity which set her blood afire. "Are you willing to take my advice on that subject?" he asked, curling up one corner of his mustache with his free hand. Then, seeing the expression on her face, he broke out in a grin. "Do you want to know what I propose?" he said, wrapping both arms around her again.

She kissed him. "Is that a good start?" She kissed him again, but this time instead of breaking away, he picked her

234

up and carried her to the bed, where he placed her gently down on the comforter. "Do you know something, Hawksby?"

"What now, my love?"

"Your ears aren't turning red. That must mean you aren't embarrassed anymore."

"I have no idea what you are talking about. But shall we try another kiss to see if your theory is correct?"

Her eyes twinkled with delight. "You know, Hawksby, you are beginning to have quite a sense of humor. I shall have to tell Hortense when I see her."

"Don't you dare," he growled. "Some things are meant to be kept secret, my sweet. Starting tonight, I expect you to obey me on that."

"Are there any other matters in which you wish me to obey?"

"You probably wouldn't anyway, so we will leave it at that. Right now I'm working on a devilish strategy," said Hawksby, running his finger down the side of her neck.

Maggie's eyes widened. "By Jove, Hawksby! That feels great!"

Hawksby threw back his head and laughed. "Do you know, my love, you are even beginning to sound like me. Now put your arms around my neck and kiss me."

Epilogue

Knocktigh prospered under the direction of Captain Hawksby. Clugg agreed to remain as his valet, which was satisfactory for all, because Flora Doone had decided to stay there, too. Clugg, being the efficient servant he was, had taken the liberty of packing a trunkful of Hawksby's country clothes before they left There-It-Is. How many soakings could his master's regimentals take before they disintegrated altogether?

In October, Hawksby and Maggie traveled to London for the double wedding of Maggie's sisters, Rebecca and Ruth, to Lord Finch and Sir Spencer. Hawksby sold out his commission and they returned to Knocktigh as quickly as possible.

Four months later, Lord and Lady Chantry welcomed a daughter whom they named Gillian. The earl sighed and said he reckoned he was so used to females he wouldn't know what to do with a son if he had one—but it would be nice to have an ally now and then. Freddie said she would work on it.